THE SCROLL

Book One

Passage to the
House of Power

— a prophetic parable —

BY JIM SAMRA

ISBN: 978-1-7354567-0-6

Interior Layout: James Armstrong, UpWrite Publishing

Cover Design and Illustrations: Emily Franklund

First Edition

For George, Grace, Abigail and James,

May you trust in the Lord with all your heart and not lean on your own understanding. In all your ways acknowledge God, and He will lead you along straight paths.

Let the prophet who has a dream tell the dream . . .

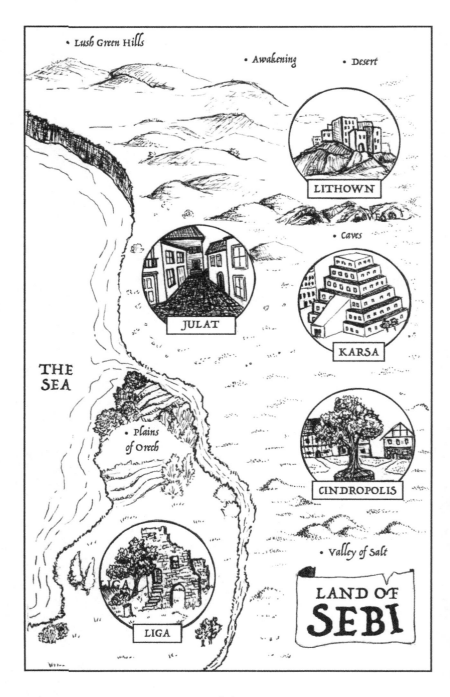

PROLOGUE

"The time has come," announced the king to the assembled council. "It is time to summon the messenger. Is his iron scepter ready?"

"Yes, my lord," replied the blacksmith, standing to his feet. "His name is forged deep within the handle just as you requested."

"Who will go and bring him to me?"

The king turned his attention to his captains seated before him, but no one answered his request. They glanced nervously at each other.

Finally, a voice spoke. "He can't come here. This one you have chosen cannot wield the scepter. He doesn't deserve this assignment, nor a place among those seated here. He was neither born in Sebi nor does he belong with its people."

Murmurs mingled with low whispers of shock as the defiant words hung in the air.

"Will you try to stop him, Mot?" asked the king.

"If for no other reason than to show you he's unworthy. Let him be tested. If he completes the pilgrimage, all here will know you've chosen well. If he turns back, then let him wander, and let another take his place."

"Very well," said the king.

"And remember your own declaration," Mot insisted. "He must not come empty-handed."

"So be it."

Mot arose from his seat. A handful of captains stood and followed him out. Silently they trailed him back to his chambers.

"The messenger must not complete the pilgrimage," ordered Mot. "Take him captive. Make him suffer. Cause him to stumble. Block his way. Distract him. Keep him wandering from place to place. The journey is long, and the road is dangerous. He must not reach the temple. Divert him to the great city instead."

Mot pulled back a heavy, charcoal-gray velvet curtain to reveal a stone chest. He slid back its engraved lid and drew forth two forged iron boxes. A salty-sweet smell filled the chambers.

"Take these," Mot commanded. "Make sure he finds them. And make sure they find him."

"But won't the king try to protect him, providing him with encouragement and strength along the way?" asked one of the captains.

"The king can't protect him from himself, and one can't be helped by what they can't see. Pride in all its forms is your best weapon; employ it well."

PART 1: AWAKENING

CHAPTER 1

"Get up. It's time to start for home," a gentle voice whispered in my ear.

But I'm already home.

Again, I heard the gentle voice. "Don't be afraid. I've heard your crying. Now take my hand, and I'll give you the strength to get up."

I tried to open my eyes, but my eyelids were incredibly heavy. *This is the strangest dream. I just need to keep sleeping.*

"You're not asleep," the voice insisted.

I'm not?

"No. You're dead."

Dead? What? But how did I die…

"You died the same way everyone dies," said the voice. "You were born into death. But I've mastered death and earned the right to wake you. Now get up."

And then I heard the voice speak a name, a beautiful name, which echoed in my soul and in my heart as it washed over me. The name came at me like a sound from the real world breaking into my dream and shaking me awake. The name was so familiar, yet so strange.

Only one explanation made any sense to me: *That must be my name. I'm being told to get up.*

So, I got up.

·

CHAPTER 2

Where am I?
I found myself lying on a huge slab of rock. Wherever I was, it was unfamiliar terrain. Everything was brown, like a desert, but without sand. There were rises and valleys all around, but less like mounds of dirt and more like the jagged edges, jutting points, and deep crevices of the same enormous rock. The whole place felt hard.

And dark. It wasn't nighttime, but it was hazy and hard to see, like it was the first light of morning. The sky was cold and gray, a heavy canvas through which light came but did not shine.

Just then the notion of thirst kidnapped my thoughts, and I became agonizingly thirsty. In that moment, quenching my thirst became an all-consuming passion, like an itch demanding to be scratched. My eyes moved frantically from the distant horizon to search the ground around me. I fell to my knees, groping wildly for something to drink.

In the dim light, an object caught my attention. In contrast to its surroundings, the object shone bright and strong, though it didn't glow. It was a goblet, and I knew it contained what I so desperately wanted. Snatching it up, I heedlessly drank whatever was inside, my thirst eroding all caution and common sense.

The liquid tasted vaguely like water but was richer, cleaner, fuller, and more alive. Its thickness made it feel like a mighty river rolling down my throat, but at the same time it tasted pure and light. I drank and drank and drank. Despite my thirst having been quenched. the moment the liquid first hit my lips, I couldn't—and didn't—want to stop drinking. It felt as if life itself was rehydrating my withered body, and I felt fully and completely satisfied.

Finally lifting the goblet from my lips, I realized I had drunk far more liquid than it could have possibly contained. When I set it down so I could get my bearings, it instantly vanished.

Was that even real?

I looked around for some sign of what to do or where to go next, but the hazy darkness and rocky landscape prevented me from seeing very far in any direction. My eyes strained for some visual clue in the distance when something fluttered past my foot. Startled, I stooped down to find at my feet a tiny male bird. He had a gray-brown body with a darker, slightly more colorful head and a pointed beak. He also bore strange white markings, something like letters, but not in any script or language I had seen before.

His eyes were fiery red and enchantingly beautiful. I couldn't help but stare. He made no effort to resist, nor did he look away.

I put my hand down next to him, and he fearlessly and eagerly climbed on. As I stood, he ran up my arm to my shoulder and perched next to my right ear.

Although he was small, having him on my shoulder made me feel powerful, a master of beasts. Feeling confident, I climbed off the slab and took my first steps away from the rock. No sooner had I taken a single step than he began to chirp in my ear. He had a surprisingly loud voice for such a small bird.

As I continued walking, his chirping grew louder. Trying to block the noise out, I concentrated on where I was going.

In front of me was a rocky ridge that I decided to climb. When I reached the top, a large misty valley opened below. As I started to descend, the bird chirped louder still. But in the midst of all that chirping, I heard another sound coming from the valley. It, too, sounded like a bird, but it had a more melodic and sweeter sound than the chirping in my ear.

Attracted by this enticing call, I continued my descent. Suddenly the bird on my shoulder jumped off and started hopping back up the hill.

Is he leaving me? Doesn't he like the melodic sound?

Confused, I turned and began to follow him out of the valley. Then I heard the beautiful melody again from the valley floor below.

I'll just go check out what's making that beautiful sound. Then I'll come back up this way and see if this bird will still be here.

I turned to go back down into the valley and descended a few more steps when suddenly the bird was back on my shoulder. I felt a sharp pain as he dug his talons into my skin.

"Ow!"

I instinctively swung my hand to swat him off my shoulder, but at that exact moment the seductive call transformed into a terrifying roar.

Run!

I dashed up the incline and along the ridgetop as fast as I could, running and running, not knowing or caring where I was going. After what seemed like miles, my legs refused to move anymore, and the pain from my feet overpowered my terror. I stopped running and sat down, exhausted.

Despite the flurry of physical activity, the bird was still on my shoulder, silent yet appearing rather pleased with himself.

Catching my breath, I stood and began walking, putting more distance between me and the valley of terror.

"So much for being a beast master," I said. "Maybe I'm just a master of birds. Or, more likely, the master of one very small bird with a strong talon pinch. That counts for something, right?"

I looked at him, and he looked back at me.

"Go get me some food," I said on a whim. He didn't move, but it didn't matter because in that moment I realized I wasn't hungry.

That's good, because I have no idea where I'd get food.

"You need a name," I offered. But no name came to mind, so I kept walking.

I reached the top of another ridge that opened into another hazy, foggy valley below. Knowing better than to make the same mistake twice, I turned to walk along the ridge to the left. The bird started chirping again.

Does he not want me to go this way?

I reversed direction on the ridge, but the bird kept chirping.

This is silly.

I kept walking.

The chirping grew louder.

I ignored it.

Finally, the bird hopped off my shoulder and slowly descended into the valley. So down the ridge I went, following him into the valley. As soon as I did, he flew back onto my shoulder, and so we descended together.

CHAPTER 3

R eaching the bottom of the valley, the bird led me down a well-worn path that twisted and turned back and forth as we advanced. Although I had trouble seeing where we were going, I simply followed the path in front of me.

After walking what felt like a mile, I arrived at the entrance to a cave. The opening was no more than four feet tall and maybe three feet wide. Etched above the cave were characters similar to the markings on the bird.

Is this his home?

Ducking down, I entered the cave. It was pitch-black, but as soon as we got inside, the bird began to glow brightly, illuminating the interior. The rock walls were the same gray-brown color as the bird. They were barren, flat, and uniform, too uniform to be natural—someone or something had carved the cave. There was a doorway off to the right.

The bird hopped through the doorway into a smaller room that had two stone slabs hewn out of the wall.

Clothes—a shirt, pants, and sandals—were laid on one of the stone slabs. Embarrassed, I realized then that I was naked. Hastily, I dressed myself. The clothing was of woven linen, though whether it came from flax, cotton, or something else, I couldn't tell. The shirt and pants were simple, loose fitting, and comfortable. Comfortable leather-like sandals welcomed my feet as if I'd been wearing them for years. Like everything else, they were dirty brown. The bird looked pleased. Fluttering over to the stone slab on the opposite side of the chamber, the light from his little body illuminated an opened scroll. The scroll was like vellum, with words composed of characters similar to those engraved above the door and on the bird.

What am I supposed to do with this? Does he think I can read it?

I stared at the bird, and he stared back. I turned to leave. He chirped. I picked up the scroll. He stared. I rolled it up and put it in my pocket. He kept staring.

"Um . . . thank you?"

The bird fluttered past me, back into the entryway, and out of the cave. I followed. He moved quickly, flying ahead of me and leading me down the same path we traveled before, but in the opposite direction from which we had come. I had to hustle to catch up.

"Slow down," I called. My stamina was flagging, but the bird kept flying forward. On we went, scaling a long incline as we headed out of the valley, which only increased my exhaustion. Soon he was farther and farther ahead, disappearing into the dim sky.

"Come back," I pleaded. "I don't know where I'm going." My voice dissolved into the sky above me. "I'm scared to be alone." But he was gone.

As I emerged from the hazy valley, the horizon opened in front of me. Straight ahead, on the highest hill in the area, was a fortified city with a flock of birds circling above it.

PART 2: LITHOWN

CHAPTER 4

The path led toward a set of iron gates, the entrance to the city. The city was a fortress, built on a mountain plateau. It looked as if someone had sawn the peak off the mount and the city had emerged in its place. The whole city looked to be made of stone—the walls, watchtowers, houses, everything.

As I apprehensively approached the city gates, I saw two guards.

"Greetings, young one," the guard on the left said to me. I turned to face her.

She didn't look like a guard. She didn't have any weapons or armor that I could see. She was wearing clothes like mine, except hers were white. When she greeted me, she bowed slightly. Her voice sounded welcoming and kind.

"Hello," I replied.

"Welcome to Lithown. My name is Hudati. What's your name?"

I stared blankly at her while my mind raced. *What's my name? I should know my name. I've been asked my name thousands of times, haven't I?*

But when I tried to answer, nothing came out.

What was the name the voice had used? That name was in my soul, but it was beyond the reach of my mind.

"I'm not sure," I sheepishly confessed.

Hudati's demeanor changed. "You don't remember your name? Where are you from?"

"I don't know that either. I'm really confused. You're the first person I've seen. Can you help me?" I asked hopefully.

"I'm not supposed to answer any questions. You need to see the Elder in charge of the city. Come with me."

The massive iron gates had a smaller inset door that allowed people to enter. Hudati led me through this door into a bustling city.

She walked swiftly along a stone path toward the left. After some distance, the path turned right, and we began to encircle the inner city. I kept my eyes on her as we walked, struggling to keep up while all around me the city was buzzing with activity. People were buying and selling, sitting and talking, walking and carrying on business. No one acknowledged my presence, but Hudati said hello to a few people as she weaved her way through the crowd.

Arriving at a small, unassuming wooden door, Hudati knocked, and a short, heavyset woman opened it. Hudati addressed her as Dolia, quietly speaking a few words to her. Dolia ushered me down a long hallway to a quiet, torch-lit room in the back.

"Come in," said a friendly male voice.

"Another special case," Dolia said. "He just arrived. Didn't know his name, so Hudati brought him straight to you."

"Good, good," he said eagerly. "Take a seat."

The man across from me slouched in a chair behind a round, wooden table. In front of him was a thin book. He was much older than I was—perhaps fifty—with sandy brown hair, mysterious eyes, and a muscular build, though he was not very tall. He wore a robe with strange writing that looked official. Though his voice was friendly, his body language was unwelcoming.

"Tell me your story," he inquired.

"Well, there's not much to tell. I don't know where I am or how I got here. I remember waking up this morning on a rock slab outside the city." I was going to keep going when he interrupted.

"Did someone wake you up?"

"There was a voice, but when I woke up no one was there."

"You heard a voice, but no one was there?"

"Well, there was a bird—"

"A what?" He interrupted me before I could say anything more. He sounded agitated.

"A bird," I repeated.

"There aren't any birds around here," he declared.

His response puzzled me. "What about the birds flying above the city?"

"What are you talking about? There are no birds flying above the city."

"Yes, there are. I'm sure if we go outside we'll see them."

Curiosity appeared to weaken his confidence, so he stood up, and we went back outside. He looked up. I looked up, and I thought I saw a bird flying in the dark haze overhead.

"See, there's nothing up there," he gloated.

I looked again. If there had been something, it was gone. My confusion must have shown, because he chuckled as we walked back inside.

"What a strange idea," he said.

Embarrassed, I followed him back to his office.

"That's okay," he said as he slouched back into his chair. "Let's go back to talking about how you woke up. Tell me what things were like before you woke up."

"I don't remember anything from before, but after I woke up, I remember a golden goblet near me."

"A what?"

"A goblet . . . a cup of some sort. It was filled with liquid, and I drank it."

At first, he didn't respond. He only stared.

"A goblet? What did it look—" He stopped. Again, more silence.

Then, with a new edge to his voice, he said, "Son, I don't think you're telling me the truth. Who put you up to this?"

"No one," I said, taken aback. "I did find a goblet and drank. A bird kept me from going into one valley and led me to another. There was a cave, and in the cave I found these clothes and a scroll. Look, I have the scroll right here. See for yourself."

"Give that to me," he demanded.

Naively, I handed him the scroll. He turned it over, looking for a place to unroll it but not finding one. He tried to pull it apart, but it wouldn't open. The more he tugged and pulled, the more it resisted opening.

"Where did you get this? It won't open." As he spoke, he shook the scroll at me with his right hand.

"It opens. Give it to me." I snatched the scroll back from him. In my hands it unrolled easily to reveal the strange writing inside— in the same script that was on his clothing. I proudly held it up for him to see.

Wild-eyed, he stared intently at the scroll and me. I couldn't tell if he was angry or surprised, but he was certainly no longer slouching. Forcefully, he came across the table and snatched at the scroll. I pulled it back and in one motion tried to get up and run. But he was fast. I stumbled backward when his hand locked onto my arm.

Intense pain shot through my body.

"Stop. Let go! You're hurting me."

His vice-grip on my arm squeezed tighter, and the pain became unbearable. I dropped the scroll and fought to pry his hand off my arm, but to no avail. He squeezed tighter still, as if to crush my bones. I dropped to my knees.

"You're coming with me!" Picking the scroll off the ground, he threw it back on his desk and dragged me toward the door. I thought nothing of the scroll, only of the desire to free myself, but I couldn't escape his grip. He strode purposefully out the door, down the corridor, and into the street with me flailing behind him.

Soon we reached a large open area surrounded by an iron fence. He threw me to the ground like a child's toy, ripped open the gate, and dragged me in by my arm. With a final merciless yank on my arm, he threw me forward. I landed awkwardly on my back, at the feet of a large man. I heard my tormentor's voice addressing the large man, saying, "Put him to work and train him well. This one is a troublemaker."

"Yes, Elder. What's his name?"

There was a pause.

"Rom," he said with a sly smile. Then he left.

CHAPTER 5

*R*om? Is my name Rom? I still couldn't remember what my name
was, but Rom, though it felt close, wasn't quite right. I did at
least know that.

My thoughts were interrupted by the large man reaching down
and helping me to my feet. Bowing slightly, he said, "Rom, it's nice
to meet you. My name is Josef. I'm one of the Guardians here. Welcome to the Quarry. This is where we mine and shape the building
blocks of the city: men, women, and rocks." He smiled broadly.

Josef led me down a flight of about thirty stairs chiseled into
the side of the hill. It felt like we were descending into a prison.
Sheer rock walls hemmed in the large, open space on every side.
The flight of stairs was the only way in or out.

At the bottom were groups of young men and women congre-
gating together. They looked like teenagers, and since I couldn't remember how old I was, I assumed I was the same age. Each group
was accompanied by an older man or woman.

"We are almost done for the day, but you can at least meet
the boys in your group," Josef said as he led me over to one of the
groups.

"This is Rom." Josef said to the stern-faced leader among them.
"He just arrived today."

The next thing I knew, the boys went around introducing
themselves. None looked very happy to be there.

"Rabah," said the boy standing nearest me.

"Esah."

"Domi."

"Minal."

"Hazar."

When they were done, I wondered if Rom sounded as foreign to them as their names sounded to me. Nothing felt familiar.

"Okay, boys," the leader said. "Have a nice night. See you tomorrow bright and early."

The group began to disperse, but I stood frozen in my spot, not knowing where I was supposed to go. The tiny glimpse of normalcy that came from exchanging names was slipping away. I felt as if I was sinking into the ground, fading into nothing. No one invited me to come with them. I felt absolutely alone and abandoned. Mindlessly, I ascended the stairway back to the iron gate. There stood Josef.

"Is the Elder coming back to get you?" he asked.

"Who?"

"The man who brought you here. Aren't you staying with him?"

"What? No."

"Where do you live?"

"Just out there a little bit," I lied, my mind racing to invent some way to get out of that place.

"I can't let you go unless the Elder comes back to get you."

"Oh, he told me to meet him out in the street after I was done today." But it was no use. Josef wasn't buying it. The iron gate was locked. Josef showed me a small, empty cave back down on the Quarry floor where I could sleep.

The cave was to the right of the stairway, back a small distance from the central area. It had no door, but inside was a simple, woven reed mat with a lumpy pillow inside a scratchy, coarse-textured pillow case. I laid down on the mat.

I spent my first night in near total darkness. I hadn't been hungry or thirsty since drinking from the goblet. I thought I might not need sleep either, but I was exhausted, so I closed my eyes.

* * *

The next morning as I awoke, the previous day's events came cascading back.

Why did that bird lead me to this city? And where did he go? He led me to the cave, the clothes, and the scroll, but now the scroll is gone—that jerk stole it—and I'm stuck in this place. Maybe I wasn't supposed to come here at all.

I emerged from my cave out into the open space of the Quarry. Rabah was already there, waiting for others to arrive. Reluctantly he struck up a conversation with me, but it quickly became awkward because I couldn't answer any of his questions. For a while he pushed through the awkwardness by telling me a little about what went on in the Quarry—he'd been coming to the Quarry for about two years. But once Esah and Domi arrived, he hurriedly deserted me to hang out with them. Minal and Hazar made no effort to welcome me into their private conversation when they arrived, either. I was simply there, hanging around the edges of both groups of friends.

The morning began, not with breakfast, but with very specific instructions on how to chisel that day's blocks of stone. I still wasn't hungry, but it seemed odd to me that no one else mentioned eating. It appeared as if food was unnecessary in this strange place. So, I lazily pushed the idea of eating out of my mind while trying to listen to the instructions.

My group leader—I learned his name was Plute—corrected me a few times throughout the morning for not following the procedures closely enough. My job consisted of dropping iron wedges and splints into a line of holes drilled into the rock. Then I was to proceed down the line of wedges, hitting each one with a small iron hammer until the rock split. If I didn't align the splints correctly or hit the wedges evenly as I progressed down the line, problems arose. The work was tiring and monotonous, but the worst of it was feeling lonely as I watched everyone else engage with each other and completely ignore me. We worked on stone blocks cleaved from the wall opposite the entrance to the Quarry, as if we were tunneling further away from freedom into a prison in the center of the mountain. The working wall was about two hundred yards long and rose maybe fifty feet in the air. It was far rougher than the other three walls, though it was still unscalable. The other three walls looked like they had been mined by previous generations of youths. Many groups worked on higher ledges and scaffolding on the rough wall, but I was assigned to work on the floor with Esah, Domi, Rabah, Minal, and Hazar.

The constant pinging of hammers on chisels and wedges droned on like hail raining down on a metal roof.

After what seemed like hours and hours, work stopped for a drink. I wasn't thirsty, but I craved more of that amazing liquid that I drank from the goblet. I eagerly grabbed a wooden cup and swallowed the liquid in three gulps.

"Pttew!"

The water was not sweet, rich, or thick. It was bitter and brackish, so I spit it out.

"What are you doing?" roared Plute from across the way.

Feeling cross, I replied, "This water tastes horrible. I'm not drinking it." Everyone gaped at me.

"Drink it," Plute demanded.

"No," I said defiantly. *Enough's enough.* The abusive treatment, the loneliness, and the sheer confusion had conspired to foment a spirit of revolt in me.

As Plute strode angrily toward me, his appearance began to change. Whatever strange things I experienced up to that point, this surpassed them all. Plute's face and forehead began to harden until his face became metallic. Even his eyes became like cast bronze. The muscles in his neck began to bulge and stiffen into iron bars. As the transformation washed down his body, his shoulders and chest hardened. His loose-fitting clothes tightened as stone replaced flesh. His hands came to look as if they had been roughly hewn from the land itself. The transformation spread down his legs and into his feet until he was living, breathing stone, bronze-faced and iron-necked.

My jaw dropped. I wanted to scream, "Are you seeing this?" but no words came. Defiance gave way to terrified regret at the thought that I might have picked a fight with a monster.

The enraged mass of living stone and metal advanced toward me, his footsteps thundering like the first rumblings of an avalanche. Everyone else shrank back.

When he came within a few feet, his right hand shot out and smashed dead center into my chest. I folded in two, flying backward and sprawling to the ground. The wind was knocked out of me. I gasped for breath as Plute towered over me. Grabbing me by the arms, he lifted me straight into the air and onto my feet.

"I'll teach you to be disrespectful, you rebellious whelp," he growled. "Do as you're told and don't ask questions." He shoved the wooden cup into my hand.

I struggled to catch my breath so I could take a drink. When my breath came, so did the pain. But I managed to get the water into my mouth. It was nasty, but I drank it down.

"That's better," he said, his voice softening slightly.

Turning to everyone else, Plute continued, "The rest of you know better than to be so insolent, don't you? We will beat the arrogant rebellion out of this one soon enough. Like cracks in a rock, the smallest flaw can spread if not dealt with immediately. Just like the Elder always says, 'Tools of iron reshape hearts of stone.' Even so, work is done for today. It's time for swimming." As he spoke, his body melted from stone back to flesh.

Humiliated, hurt, and confused, I looked around, but no one seemed surprised at what had happened. Some wore looks of sympathy; some looked as if I got what I deserved; some weren't paying much attention at all.

Plute and the other adults led the rest of the group toward the left-hand corner of the wall we'd worked on. I hung back.

It's time to get out of here.

I turned and ran back toward the opposite wall, sprinting toward the sole stairway that led to freedom. I hadn't gone far when—wham! I was hammered in the back. Down I went. Standing over me was another bronze-faced, iron-necked, and stone-fisted leader.

"Where are you going? Everyone is going the other way. You must obey the law and stay with the group." With that he picked me up and threw me over his stony shoulder. Both my chest and my back stung with pain.

The enforcer carried me back toward the group. About a hundred and fifty yards down the wall was a swimming pool, carved out of the rock at the corner of the working wall and the left-hand wall of the Quarry. The pool was essentially kitty-corner to the cave where I slept the previous night. Everyone splashed and played around for the longest time. I sat sullen and embittered at the side of the pool until, just like the previous day, everyone left.

Apparently, they all had homes outside the Quarry, though they were required to come to the Quarry each day and work from early morning until late afternoon. Rabah said goodbye to me as he walked up the stairs and out of the Quarry.

Dejected, I went to my cave and laid down on the mat. It was still early, but my body was tired from the grueling manual labor—and the beatings—and I had nothing else to do. While I lay there, one question kept returning over and over again.

Am I trapped here?

CHAPTER 6

The next day went like the last, working alongside Rabah, Domi, Esah, Minal, and Hazar doing the same job as the day before. We each worked separately, cutting blocks of stone intended for use in building projects around the city. Because we worked in close proximity, there was occasional back-and-forth bantering, but long periods of silence dominated most of the morning. As opposed to the first workday when no one said anything to me, Rabah occasionally threw a few spare words my direction, as if he were tossing scraps of bread to a stray dog. In the afternoon, we had more nasty, foul water. During the late afternoon fun, I again refused to participate in the swimming, thinking that perhaps my one-person protest might somehow punish the leaders for their cruelty or maybe start a rebellion of sorts. But by the end of the day I began to regret that decision. Everyone else seemed to be having a great time and my sulking had accomplished nothing except to isolate me. That evening was as boring as the evening before. I tried to fill the time by dreaming of ways to escape what was feeling more and more like a prison.

* * *

My fourth day in the quarry followed the same pattern until midway through the work period. Suddenly out of nowhere, I heard a roar and saw Stone Plute hammer Domi in the face with his rock fist. Domi crumpled underneath the blow and fell to the ground. He lay still. Shockingly, everyone else started back to work, paying no attention to Domi.

29

Are they just going to leave him there?

The memory of my own humiliation and pain compelled me to run over to Domi to see if he was okay.

"Leave him alone," Jaykah, one of the other leaders, barked at me. I ignored him. By the time I reached Domi, Jaykah was angry, forcefully calling out, "Didn't you hear me? Leave him alone!"

Defiant, I picked up the first thing I found and hurled it at him. An audible gasp rose from the onlookers. The stone I threw bounced harmlessly off Jaykah, but my act of rebellion summoned Plute and the other leaders. As they joined the fight, Jaykah swung his stone hand down at my head. I managed to dodge the blow. Desperately, I ran, searching for someone who might help me. But no help came. Plute and another leader closed off my escape, and Jaykah turned to pursue me. I was trapped.

Out of the corner of my eye I saw rocks flying through the air. *Others are joining my fight!* I exulted. *But who?*

I scanned the crowd. My eyes fell first on Esah and Rabah, but they weren't throwing the rocks. Both were frozen in fear. Panning further, I discovered workers from the other groups were throwing the rocks.

The first few rocks fell harmlessly to the ground, but when one struck me squarely in the chest, I knew I was not beginning a rebellion. The rocks were not being thrown at the leaders. They were aimed at me.

I was disappointed for a split second, but then my attention was arrested by something else. Plute, Jaykah, and the other leader had reached me. They fell on me like stone walls. Multiple stone fists from different directions landed on my head at the same time and everything went dark.

* * *

When I awoke, I wasn't in my cave. I was lying on a bed in a warm room. I tried to figure out where I was, but I couldn't. I tried to remember exactly what had happened, but I couldn't. I tried to stand up, but I couldn't. When I tried to move my arms or legs, debilitating pain shot through my whole body. I could turn my neck, but that was it. My head throbbed. I tried to focus on how scared I felt, but my brain was so tired that I drifted back to sleep.

Again I awoke, but this time was startled to find someone else in the room with me.

"How are you feeling?" asked the woman kneeling beside me.

I tried moving again, but I couldn't. "Everything hurts."

"I'm not surprised. From what I hear, the Guardians gave you quite a beating."

"Am I going to be okay?" I didn't even know what that meant, but it seemed like the right thing to ask.

"I can fix your body's wounds if that's what you mean. As for any emotional wounds, I can't say."

"How long have I been here?"

"A few hours. After the Guardians realized how bad they had beaten you, they rushed you here so I could heal you."

"I'm not in the Quarry? I don't have to go back, do I?" I begged.

"You can talk to the Elder about that," she replied, "when he comes back."

Fear gripped my heart. "Why is the Elder coming here?"

She laughed. "The whole city is talking about you. The Elder arrived here not long after you did. Word travels fast in Lithown. You were unconscious, but he left strict orders for me to tell him the moment you woke up."

"Are you going to call him?"

She glanced around quickly and then said, "Actually, I was hoping to ask you a few questions if you don't mind."

I nodded slightly, feeling momentary relief. Anything to delay seeing the Elder again.

"They told me your name is Rom. Is it?"

"Well, that's what they call me here, so I guess so," I mumbled without moving my jaw, which felt broken.

"Where are you from?"

"Not sure. I arrived a few days ago and have been at the Quarry ever since."

"Did anything happen to you on your way here? Did you see anything or experience anything unusual?"

Is she hinting at something? Remember what happened with the Elder...

"Why?" I responded, casting her a cautious look.

"That beating should have killed you. Yet none of your bones were broken, and you didn't lose much blood. Your body is healing remarkably quickly. I am wondering if something happened to you on the way here that might somehow have imbued you with life."

"Nothing all that unusual," I said evasively.

She looked at me with a reassuring smile, leaned over my right shoulder with her hands cupped around her mouth, and began whispering indecipherable words. Her eyes glowed faintly, almost like the bird's eyes. My shoulder began to tingle; heat was surging through it.

"Try moving your shoulder."

It moved easily with no pain. "How did you do that?" I asked as I felt my body relax.

She just smiled. "Are you sure there wasn't anything unusual that happened to you?"

I ignored her question. "What's your name?" I asked.

"Emma," she replied.

"Could you do for the rest of my body what you just did for my shoulder?"

With a wink she said, "I already have." Suddenly her head snapped to attention. "The Elder's coming. Quick, pretend you are

32

asleep."

Shutting my eyes, I heard heavy footfalls enter the room. My pulse quickened. My body stiffened. *Relax, or he is going to notice. Relax! Relax!* But the more I tried to relax, the more I tensed up.

"He's still not awake? What's taking so long? Just wake him up!" the Elder bellowed.

"Have patience," Emma told him. "What do you know about the boy? Anything you can tell me could be useful in determining how to best help him. Did he bring anything with him when he came to Lithown?"

My ears perked up. *Is she trying to help me?*

"Nothing that would help you heal him," he said, cutting off her inquiry. "I have a meeting to attend. When I return, he had better be back at the Quarry, or I'll take him back myself whether he's awake or not."

With that, the Elder left.

"He's gone now, Rom," Emma whispered. "Tell me what you brought with you to Lithown."

Opening my eyes, I moved my neck, left arm, and legs. Everything felt fine.

"A scroll," I confessed. "But the Elder stole it."

"What did it say?"

"I don't know. I couldn't read it. The Elder tried to read it, but it wouldn't open for him."

Emma walked over to a wooden table covered in jars and pottery. Reaching beneath the table, she pulled out a piece of ancient parchment from a secret compartment. She brought it back to me. "Did the writing look like this?"

"I think so."

"If you ever get the scroll back, I know someone who can read it for you, if you'd like."

"Who?"

"When you find it, come see me, and I'll take you to him."

"Did he help you read yours?"

"He did."

"What does yours say?"

"It's a story about what's good and what's not." Her face flushed. "It's about how I'm good and how I'm not. When I read what's on the paper, it's like a voice is speaking to me telling me who I am, where I'm going, and what I'm here for. I mean, there isn't actually an audible voice and the words don't really talk about those things, but for whatever reason I feel known whenever I read them."

"Can I hear what your paper says?"

"If I read you the words, all you would hear is a story about two women who lived a long time ago. It wouldn't make any sense to you. But for me it's a compass, a guide in this confusing world. It means everything to me."

While she spoke, I couldn't take my eyes off her. She seemed to radiate peace from the depths of her soul. My own soul ached to know what was on my scroll. I thought maybe it would help me to figure out what was going on.

Emma suggested we head back to the Quarry before the Elder returned.

I got up from the bed, still in awe of my quick healing. We walked down some stairs to the front of the building, which I realized was her home. The rest of her house was just as warm and welcoming as the room we just left. As opposed to the Quarry or the Elder's house, it was full of handcrafted decorations. We proceeded out the door and onto a road. I had no sense of where we were, but we couldn't have walked more than a quarter mile before arriving back at the Quarry.

Josef was waiting. "Welcome back," he said. "Time to get back to work."

Chills ran down my spine as he said it, as if he was talking about the Guardians getting back to work on me, breaking me in.

"May I have a word with you, Josef?" Emma asked. Her voice lost its sweetness.

"Go on in," Josef said to me, his eyes fixed on Emma. I looked at her, and she nodded in approval before returning Josef's stare. With trepidation, I muttered a quick word of thanks, crossed the threshold, and reentered the Quarry.

CHAPTER 7

"Are you okay?" Domi whispered to me as we worked the next day. "Man, I'm so sorry for what they did to you. I don't know what to say. Nobody has ever stuck up for me like that before."

Esah dropped his gaze, avoiding eye contact with me and Domi.

"That was really brave," Rabah said. "But it didn't accomplish anything, except to get you almost killed. Even if we'd all worked together, it wouldn't have made a difference." He glanced over at Plute to make sure he wasn't watching. "Now the Guardians are just going to hate you more. They beat you so badly because they want to dissuade others from rebelling."

"Maybe it was a dumb idea, but at least he did something," Esah said, still staring at the ground. "At least he didn't ignore his friends."

Rabah blushed.

The metal pings of our hammers on metal wedges filled the ensuing silence. Plute shot a glare our direction.

After his gaze left, Rabah shifted the conversation's focus.

"So where did they take you?"

"To Emma the Healer's house."

"What was she like?" Esah asked earnestly. "I've never seen any-one beaten that badly before. Did she whisper the healing words?"

"What do you mean, 'healing words?'" Domi interrupted. "You don't know anything about healing words, so quit pretending you do. If you did, maybe you could heal your face." Domi laughed at his own joke.

"Doesn't matter if he could heal himself. One look at you and he would be messed up again," Rabah countered with a wink.

Domi and Rabah smiled broadly in return.

"Hey, how'd you guys end up working in the Quarry in the first place?" I interjected.

"What do you mean?" Rabah said. "Everyone our age in Lithown has to work in the Quarry. Didn't they come and enlist you?"

"Enlist? No. I showed up at Lithown and was brought to the Elder, who stole my scroll and imprisoned me here."

"Where are you from?" Rabah asked inquisitively.

"What do you mean the Elder stole your scroll?" Domi asked with a hint of anger in his voice.

"Is that why you stay at night?" Esah probed.

The three different questions came at the same time, so my answer included my own thoughts and questions about what had happened to me.

"I had this scroll with ancient writing on it, but when I showed it to the Elder, he got mad and took it from me. But the crazy thing is that Emma the Healer seemed to know about my scroll. She kept trying to get me to tell her about it. She even showed me a piece of parchment that she said was like my scroll. She said someone helped her to read it and that they'd help me read mine if I could get it back. Whatever was on her parchment gave her life purpose and told her about the journey that she's on. Have you ever heard of anything like that?"

"Did her scroll teach her the healing words?" Esah asked eagerly. "Maybe if we got yours back, I could read it and learn to heal others."

Just then Plute interrupted our conversation with an announcement. Calling us all together, he told us that we were taking a trip into the city to transport the stones we'd cut to work sites where they'd be used to build new houses. As a reward for the work we'd been doing, we'd also be allowed to go into the market and select a treat.

A ripple of excitement flowed through the group. Even though the others left the Quarry each evening, going to the market during the day was apparently a big deal. For me it was the opportunity for a taste of freedom.

We began to line up at the stairs in preparation for the excursion.

"Rom, where do you think you're going?" Plute inquired loudly. "You don't think that we'd allow a troublemaker like you to go out into the city, do you? What would people think?"

Everyone stared at me. I tried my best to look defiant, yet I couldn't suppress the feelings of humiliation.

"Get out of line and go sit over there." He motioned toward the cave where I slept.

Seething, I stepped out of line and walked off in exile.

What do I care whether they let me go? Anyone happy about going on this trip is just too stupid to know this whole city is a prison.

Everyone left, and the iron gates slammed shut.

I wandered around the Quarry. I tried swimming in the pool, but it wasn't much fun by myself. Mostly I sat and brooded. I found myself thirsty for the brackish water and drank it freely. It didn't exactly taste good yet, but it was growing on me.

Why is there water and no food? I wondered.

Though there was no food in the Quarry, I hadn't felt hungry. I hadn't felt thirsty, either, until I started drinking the brackish water. I hadn't needed it when Plute first made me drink it, but I'd come to need it since then. The liquid in the goblet had quenched my thirst, but the brackish water seemed to create thirst. It never satisfied.

As I continued to contrast the two liquids, I realized the goblet's liquid felt soft and alive, as if it was a fountain flowing into my mouth. The brackish water, however, felt hard and dead, like I was drinking the stones all around me.

Unable to unravel the mystery of the liquids, I turned my attention to the people I'd met. Domi, Rabah, and Esah felt like friends, like I could trust them. Emma was something special, with an aura about her that reminded me of something warm and soft. The Elder, Plute, Jayka, and the other Guardians were brutes, and I despised them. As I thought about them, I imagined scenario after scenario in which I beat them down and humiliated them in front of everyone. In my mind I was a great hero, rescuing the people I liked in the Quarry from the stone-warriors. I playacted my triumphs, punching the air with wild haymakers and pretending that I was landing devastating drop-kicks to their faces after I revealed their folly while everyone watched. The cheers of the imaginary crowd grew louder with each dreamed-up scenario.

It turned out that daydreams fueled by bitter anger and selfish ambition ate up more time than reflectively pondering the truths of the journey of life. Once my mind was consumed with scenarios of revenge, the time flew by. I thought the group might return at the end of the day, but they didn't. I lay down to sleep still consumed with thoughts of getting back at my enemies.

* * *

The next morning, I discovered that everyone planned to leave again, without me, to deliver stone blocks around the city. As I dejectedly headed back toward my cave, I heard Plute say, "Esah, you're staying too."

"What?! Can't I just leave and go home?" Esah asked.

"Not until the end of the day. Josef will let you out at the regular time. Rom, of course, has nowhere to go, so he'll be staying here," the Guardian gloated.

An embarrassed Esah got out of line and joined me. As the rest of the group left, Plute walked over to us, his fists transforming to stone. Slamming his fist into my chest, he grabbed me and held me up against the wall. He did the same to Esah.

"If you would just learn to follow the law, we wouldn't have these problems," he growled.

Releasing us, we both dropped to our knees. Plute departed.

"What a jerk," Esah gasped.

"Yeah. What law did you break?"

"Who knows? There must be a law against having fun. Domi and I were laughing too loudly near one of the shop merchants. The merchant reported me to Plute, saying that I needed to 'act my age.' He said I was evidence that the Guardians were abandoning the traditions of the Elders when it came to acceptable behavior. You'd think the shop merchants would be scared of the Guardians, but I think the reverse is true. The Guardians care about what people in the city think of them, so Plute must have decided to punish me."

I simply nodded.

"So, what do you do when everyone is gone?" he asked.

"Nothing. It's really boring."

"Have you figured out how to get your scroll back?"

"If I could find a way out of here, I'd break into the Elder's office and reclaim my scroll."

"Break into the Elder's office? Do you know what they'd do to you?"

"Well, no. But what's the worst thing they could do? Throw me back in here? I'm already trapped. What difference would it make?"

"Getting thrown back in here is not the worst thing. You got beaten to a pulp when you tried to help Domi. No one was ever beaten like that before. We thought the Guardians killed you."

"But I survived. Don't you see? If they wanted to kill me, they would have. They either can't or won't."

The more I spoke, the more resolve I felt and the more I could sense my confidence emboldening Esah.

"Whatever is on that scroll has to be valuable information. Why would Emma hint that I could get it back if it was impossible? Why would she offer to have someone read it if whatever is on it is useless? Maybe it's the secret to her healing powers. Wouldn't you like to find out?"

That caught Esah's attention. Sensing my opening, I pounced. "Do you know where the Elder's office is? If we find it, we can figure out some way to get in."

"I don't know, but I'm sure Timela does."

"Timela?"

"You know, that girl who's always hanging out with Ina? Brown hair, weird laugh? Timela has some connection to the Elder. Rabah told me. I think Rabah and Timela are friends, though Rabah tries to keep that hidden. I think they spend time together outside the Quarry."

The idea that things were going on outside the Quarry that I didn't know about and couldn't participate in further drove my desire to escape.

"Would Rabah help us?"

Esah shrugged. "I know that Domi would. He'd be up for anything to stick it to Plute and the Elder. He and Rabah go way back. If Domi is in, I think Rabah would be too, except his friendship with Timela might complicate things. She's one of good ones in here, not a troublemaker like us."

We spent the rest of the day talking, making fun of Plute and the others, and trying to plan my escape. When everyone returned, Stone Jaykah was carrying Domi over his large shoulder, his brass face frozen in harshness. He threw Domi to the ground near us and grumbled, "He'll be staying with you two tomorrow."

"What happened to you?" Esah whispered.

"Minal offered me his treat from the market if I'd ask Jaykah why Guardians didn't actually guard anything. In front of everyone."

"You didn't!" I laughed. "What did he say?"

"He said he guarded the good kids from troublemakers like me. And then I got a free ride back to the Quarry on his shoulder."

It was almost time for my friends to leave. Esah gave Domi a helping shoulder out of the Quarry, waving back at me as he left. I began meandering toward my cave for the night when I heard the loud, distinctive laugh that I assumed belonged to Timela. She was talking to two other girls as they headed toward the exit. Brimming over with resolve to get my scroll, I hustled over and caught up to them.

"Hi," I said casually, trying not to appear too eager. "I'm Rom."

The other two girls stared in disbelief, but Timela looked straight at me. It was the first time I saw her up close. She was about my height, with curly brown hair. She was half-smirking, half-smiling at me, and her eyes twinkled. She reached out her hand, grabbed mine, and said, "Yes, we know quite well who you are." Her voice was throaty. "It's too bad you didn't come today. It was great fun. We even got to have a meal at the end of it all."

Her comments caught me completely off guard. I had no idea anyone missed me. All I could manage in reply was, "Well, it's not like I chose to stay here."

"Yes, you did," she said. The words sounded accusatory, but she finished with a wink and a playful squeeze of my hand.

Suddenly I felt disoriented, dizzy even, and couldn't remember what I was there to ask her. Then she was gone. The other girls must have left as well, but I didn't notice. My palms were sweating. I went back to my cave confused.

CHAPTER 8

The next morning Domi, Esah, and I gathered again before everyone else left to work in the city. While we stood together, Timela walked up behind me.

"Staying here again?"

I was surprised at how excited I was to hear her voice—and that she came to talk to me. Domi and Esah appeared stunned that Timela, with her sterling reputation, would talk to a troublemaker.

"Like I said, it's not my choice. I'd rather go," I replied, though it wasn't entirely true. I did want to get out of the Quarry and see more of the city, but the excitement of staying back to plan my escape with Domi and Esah was stronger.

"Well, if you stopped acting so stupid, I'm sure they would let you go," she said with a playful tone and a twinkle in her eye.

"You think so? What exactly have I done this morning? Or what did I do yesterday?" I tried to respond playfully, but what came out was tinted with anger.

"Well, if you promise to behave, perhaps I might be able to help."

As she talked, Plute walked over to us. When he noticed Timela standing with our group, he looked at her with a mixture of confusion and alarm. Perhaps he was trying to determine whether Timela was willingly engaging in this conversation or if I was somehow seeking to corrupt her with my rebellion.

"Timela, it's time to go."

"What if Rom promises to behave? Do you think he could come with us today?"

By this time, a small crowd formed around us. Any situation that involved me, Timela, and Plute together was ripe with potential. As Plute processed Timela's request, he became terribly uncomfortable, and his muscular body flinched under the stress. I couldn't tell if he was fighting to keep from transforming, but I was enjoying his misery.

After a few moments of awkward silence, Plute responded slowly and deliberately, "Rom is not one of us, Timela. You will soon be like us, but he never will. He's a troublemaker. You're here to be trained, but he's here so we can keep him from causing trouble in the rest of the city. You'll take your place here in this city, but Rom is destined for the Valley of Salt . . . or worse. To take him along with us would be a waste of time."

Getting hit with his stone fist probably would've hurt less. Timela's face registered shock, as if Plute's blunt harshness was a side of him she hadn't seen before. I didn't bother to look at anyone else.

"Let's go," Plute ordered. The small group around us broke up and began to follow him toward the exit. An I-told-you-so expression was all I could manage to offer to Timela before she left. *What do I care if they don't want me?* But, unfortunately, I did care.

I turned back to Domi and Esah. "What in the world is the Valley of Salt?"

Domi answered, "Lithown can't run without salt. We use it for lots of stuff, especially as part of the mixture to fuel the lights in the city. But there's no salt in Lithown. However, in the Valley of Salt, there is another city called Cindropolis. I've heard it's huge. Salt runners from Lithown go to Cindropolis and return with salt. It's a dangerous job and many salt runners never come back. I don't know what happens to them, but sometimes people aren't surprised when salt runners don't return. Some people believe there's a hideous beast near the Valley of Salt and that salt runners get attacked and eaten. But no one ever talks about it."

"I heard what sounded like a hideous beast in a valley when I first arrived," I said. "At first there was this beautiful voice, and it almost lured me into the valley, and then—uh—the beautiful voice turned into a horrific roar." I decided not to mention the role the bird's talons played in revealing to me the true nature of the sound.

Esah laughed. "Sounds like Mot to me."

"Mot? Who's Mot?"

"Nobody knows," said Domi. "It's just a name that the Elder mentioned one time. Every time Esah hears about the disappearance of a salt runner or something else mysterious, he calls it Mot. Just forget about it."

"Salt runners have a strange position in Lithown," Domi continued. "They're very important, though, because without them there would be no salt. But they're despised by the people. No one talks about how Lithown gets salt. They just pretend it shows up."

"I once knew someone who was a salt runner," offered Esah. "He could make himself essentially invisible. It was the coolest thing."

"What did Plute mean when he said that Timela would soon be like the Guardians?" I said.

Esah and Domi told me that many of the young men and women in the Quarry hoped to become endowed with the same powers of transformation as the Guardians. Neither one of them had any idea how it happened, but once it did, that person was allowed to leave the Quarry and take a position in the city. For most people it was a question of *if* they would transform, but for Timela it was more a question of *when*. Everyone assumed she would be the first in the group, given how highly the Guardians esteemed her.

"What did Timela say when you talked to her?" Domi asked.

I filled him in on the plan to see if she could help us get the scroll from the Elder's office.

"Are you sure we can trust her?" Esah wondered.

"Yeah," Domi agreed. "She's pretty tight with the Guardians. What if she turns us in?"

"She's our only good option," I countered. "I know we can trust her." And then, my heart beating faster, I added, "But just to be sure, maybe I should hang out with her. You know, not just ask her to help, but to get to know her and see if we can trust her."

* * *

The next day everyone stayed in the Quarry to cut more stone blocks. I couldn't get anywhere near Timela during work, but it was much easier during swim time.

Timela seemed to want to steal a minute with me too. Despite the frenzied fun going on all around us, it felt like we were the only two people in the pool. As I swam toward her, nervous excitement welled up within me, and I couldn't wipe the huge grin off my face.

"I told you it wasn't my choice to stay here."

"I'm so sorry for what Plute said to you," Timela replied earnestly.

"It's no worse than how I was treated by the Elder."

"What do you mean?"

"Well, when I first arrived in Lithown, he didn't exactly treat me kindly. He even stole something that belonged to me."

"What?"

"I can't tell you," I said, hoping she would ask again. "For all I know, you're friends with him. Plute's not the first one to call me a troublemaker, you know."

"You *are* a troublemaker," she answered sweetly, "but maybe there's hope for you."

My nervousness suddenly returned.

"So, what did the Elder take from you?"

If Domi and Esah had been there to help me think rationally, I might not have said anything. But I was caught up in the moment.

"A scroll. Someone important gave it to me, and it meant a lot to me." Not exactly the truth, but close enough.

"What did the scroll say?"

"That's the thing. I couldn't read it. I showed it to the Elder because I thought he could help, but he got angry, took the scroll, and dragged me down here. Then he told Josef that I was a trouble-maker, and that's what I've been ever since."

"The Elder wouldn't do something like that," Timela said defensively.

"Oh yeah? Just like Plute would've let me come with you yesterday if I was willing to behave myself?"

She blushed.

I pressed on. "Why don't you ask the Elder about the scroll and see how he responds."

"Maybe I will," she said.

Just then Ina swam over, and our moment was gone. "We're playing a game of Statues," she said, looking only at Timela. "Come join us!"

Timela turned to me. "Come play with us," she offered. "Tell Rabah to come too." Timela gave me a smile, but Ina looked horrified.

The game itself was great fun, though I'm not sure I ever understood exactly what was going on. I just watched Timela and did whatever she did. At some point Esah and Domi joined us. I wondered if this was the first time troublemakers had mixed with good kids.

The afternoon flew by, as did the next several days. I spent a lot of time with Timela—and because of that, Ina—but also Esah, Domi, and Rabah. My friendship with Timela changed things around the Quarry. No Guardian attacked or even threatened me.

It was still strange that everyone else left and I spent the night in the Quarry, but I was having such a fun time during the day that I didn't mind. The work wasn't that bad, and the afternoons were a blast.

I had almost forgotten about the scroll until one day Timela pulled me aside during the water break. "I'm going to see the Elder tonight. I was thinking of asking him about your scroll if you still want me to."

I couldn't tell if I was more excited about the scroll or the fact that Timela wanted to do something for me. In either case, I was too excited to stop and ask why she would have such an opportunity with the Elder.

"Yes, I still want you to ask."

I could barely sleep that night.

CHAPTER 9

He said you were lying."

"What?!"

"He said you were lying. There was no scroll. Hudati brought you to him because you were confused and didn't even know your name." Timela sounded angry.

"Why would I make up a story about a scroll?"

"If you couldn't remember your own name, how could you remember having a scroll? Did you show the scroll to Hudati when you arrived in the city?"

In that moment, I wished I had. Then I remembered Emma. "I told Emma the Healer about it, and she believed me. She said if I get it back, she'll find someone to read it."

This gave Timela pause. "Did you show it to her?"

"How could I show it to her when I didn't have it?"

"Oh, right. But why would the Elder say you were lying?"

"Do you think if he took it, he'd own up to it?" I was growing frustrated.

"Then why did you have me ask him about it?" Timela shot back.

Good point. I should've known he wouldn't tell the truth. But why? What was on the scroll that would cause him to lie?

"Were there scrolls in his office?" I asked.

"Of course. He's the Elder. There are all sorts of scrolls in his office. Why?"

"I'm sure that if I could get into his office, I could find mine."

I had no reason to be sure, but—inexplicably—I felt extremely confident that I'd find it.

"How are you going to get into his office?" Timela asked.

"You tell me where his office is, and I'll find a way to sneak in."

"Do you know the kind of trouble you'd get in if you got caught? If you think the Guardians are tough, they don't even begin to compare to what will happen to you out there if you tried something like this. Besides, do you know what would happen to me if anyone ever found out I helped you?"

She sounded genuinely anxious. I hadn't really thought about what kind of position I was putting her in, even simply asking her to talk to the Elder about the scroll.

But I need the scroll . . . and she needs to know the Elder is a liar. I'm doing this as much for her as I am for me. Or so I rationalized.

"No one will ever know. Please."

She looked at me for a long time. I smiled at her. She rolled her eyes, and a smile forced its way onto her face. She bent down, took some stones, and began to make a map. She sketched the main road that ran in a circle inside the city. The Quarry was on the opposite side of the city from the main gates. The Elder's office was east of the Quarry. Just before arriving at the central market, there would be a series of wooden doors. The first one, the one closest to the market, led to his place.

I pressed her for as much information as I could get. She told me that he was usually gone in the early evenings, helping judge disputes at the entrance gates to the city. That sounded like our opening.

* * *

"That's why I've been spending so much time with Timela," I rationalized to Esah, Domi, and Rabah. "I was trying to get this information out of her."

"Sure," Rabah said, shooting a knowing glance at Esah and

Domi. I ignored their silent innuendo.

"How are we going to get you to the Elder's office?" Esah asked. "The three of us can meet in the market after we're done in the Quarry, but you're stuck here."

"Perhaps your new 'friendship' with Timela might help," Domi said, stressing the word friendship in a teasing way. "She's a superstar in here. Maybe Plute and Josef will be more sympathetic to letting you out for an evening."

"If they wouldn't let Rom come when we delivered stones, even though it was supervised, they'll never allow him to go out in the evening. It doesn't matter how many games of Statues he plays with Timela," Rabah retorted.

He was right, and we all knew it. "This stinks!" I cried out, slamming down my fist. "The only time I've ever gotten out of this miserable place was when I was at Emma's! I'm never getting out of here."

"That's it!" Rabah exclaimed. "What if Emma asked to see you to make sure you're fully healed?"

"Can she do that?" Esah asked. "I've never seen that happen before."

"No one was ever beaten as badly as Rom since I've been here," said Rabah.

"But it's been a long time since the beating," I countered. "Won't the Guardians be suspicious?"

"The only way for them *not* to be suspicious is if you stay in the Quarry, avoid trouble, and find some way to make them like you," said Domi.

"Yeah, I can't wait that long. I have to find out what's on that scroll! If one of you can get a message to Emma, she might be willing to help. I got the sense that she loves helping people. Besides, it was her idea to get the scroll."

"Let's do it," said Esah. "I'll talk to Emma."

"This is crazy," said Rabah. He paused only a moment before adding, "But I'm in!"

"We're going to find that scroll and shove it down the Elder's throat!" Domi gloated. "Not a word of this to anyone—especially not Timela," he added, looking at me. "She's not one of us and never will be, no matter how many times she smiles at you. She's the system. And we're going to stick it to the system!"

* * *

When Esah arrived the next morning, he was smiling, which only meant one thing: Emma was going to help! She would pick me up that evening. I was ecstatic.

As we discreetly finalized our plans during the spare moments of the day, Timela stole glances at us. But every time her eyes asked mine for information, I quickly looked away.

Esah volunteered to search for the scroll with me, while Domi and Rabah wanted to stand guard: Domi near the city gate, Rabah in the market near the Elder's place. We estimated we had an hour or so while the Elder was away. Any longer and Josef would grow suspicious. It wasn't ideal that Emma's house was on the other side of the Quarry from the Elder's, but Domi offered to distract Josef so that when I left with Emma, we could turn right rather than left. Emma would then walk around the city back to her house while the four of us made for the Elder's office.

As the evening approached, my heart pounded, my hands shook, and I couldn't focus. I was confident that retrieving the scroll was the answer to all my problems. I hadn't stopped to consider that it might not be. Nor was I willing to consider that the scroll might not be at the Elder's place. It had to be.

At the end of the workday, Josef found Plute, and the two of them approached me together.

"Emma the Healer has asked for you to come and spend some

time with her this evening. She'd like to ensure you're fully recovered," Josef said blandly. No remorse showed in their eyes.

I feigned surprise.

"You're behaving much better than you did when you first got here," Plute said almost kindly. But his voice hardened again as he added, "Don't do anything to embarrass us or make us regret allowing you out of the Quarry. It won't go well for you. Do exactly what she tells you, and don't cause any problems."

I nodded.

Josef escorted me up the stairs, and I saw Emma outside the Iron Gate. She smiled and threw me a casual wave. She looked eager to help, a faint glow of red radiating in her eyes. I wondered if anyone else noticed.

Josef opened the gate and handed me over to her as others began to exit past her.

"Hi, Rom. You look great. How are you feeling?"

All I could manage to say was, "Thank you."

Perfectly on time, I heard Domi's voice call out over the din of the crowd, "Josef, Josef, I need to ask you a question."

When Josef turned to engage Domi, Emma, and I made our way east as discreetly and quickly as possible. As inconspicuous as we tried to be, my leaving the Quarry was a noteworthy event. Josef might not have realized that we walked in the wrong direction, but I could feel the gossipy eyes of others all around us. I wondered if anyone would remember this incongruity later.

As Rabah, Esah, Emma, and I hurried along, Emma whispered to me, "How are you going to get past Dolia?"

"Who?"

"Dolia. The Elder's assistant."

I stopped dead in my tracks. Esah ran into me from behind. Emma and Rabah circled around us. Domi soon joined our impromptu huddle.

Dolia must be the woman who let me into the Elder's office on my first day. What a fool I am! How could I have forgotten about her?

"Won't she be gone by now?"

"I doubt it," Emma replied. "I think she lives there."

No! I thought. *This is never going to work.*

"I might be able to help," Emma offered. "When we arrive, Esah should go up, knock on the door, and then hide against the wall of the house."

"What are you going to do?"

"You'll see. Healing is not my only power," she said with a wink.

When we arrived at the house, Domi kept going toward the city gates, Rabah stationed himself in the market just past the Elder's door, and Esah trekked up the path toward the wooden door of the Elder's office. Everything was exactly as Timela had drawn for us in her map, but it suddenly dawned on me that Emma would've known how to get here.

I've needlessly dragged Timela into this. Another foolish mistake!

As Esah walked up to the door, Emma motioned silently for me to duck around the corner back onto the main road.

"Keep a look out," she whispered.

Emma signaled Esah. He knocked. I waited. I could see Emma on my right, but not Esah nor the door. Emma focused straight ahead and said something aloud in a language I didn't understand. As soon as she said it, she walked past me and headed back toward her house.

"Good luck," Emma said. "Go quickly. She won't be out for long."

I raced around the corner. There at Esah's feet was Dolia, immobilized. Esah was standing over her. The door was open.

"What happened?" I asked.

"Don't know. I was standing behind the door, and Emma was staring at it. As soon as it opened, she said something. I heard a crash, and Dolia fell forward as if she was dead."

"Quick, let's get her inside."

We managed to drag her into the office and get the door shut without attracting any attention. She was still breathing but unconscious.

"Hurry! It's at the end of the hallway," I said.

We burst into the Elder's room. The same thin book sat prominently on his table. *The Law of Lithown*, it read. Scrolls were stacked on the shelves on every wall. Although they all looked similar, some scrolls were taller and some shorter; some were thicker and some thinner. After we opened a couple, we noticed some had more writing; some less.

"What does yours look like?" Esah asked.

I froze.

"Rom, what does yours look like?" Esah asked louder and with more urgency, as if I hadn't heard the first time.

How can I have been so stupid!

"I—I don't know," I replied.

"What do you mean you don't know?!"

I assumed that mine would be the only one that opened for me. Or, that when I opened mine it would have some distinguishing feature that I'd remember. Or, that I'd just know.

Esah must have thought me a monumental fool, but he tried to rescue the unraveling plan. "Maybe we could just take all of them and try to figure it out later?"

But there were too many to carry through the city without attracting attention. A gigantic pit formed in my stomach. It was as if the walls were closing in. I felt trapped.

I have to get out of here!

I turned and ran out the office door and down the hallway. Esah tackled me from behind.

"Where are you going?" he yelled. But as soon as he saw my

face, his expression changed. Surely my face had grown pale. It felt like all the blood had drained out of it.

"It's okay," he said. "Don't be afraid. We'll figure it out. Maybe we can eliminate some of the scrolls. Did yours have a lot of writing on it or a little?"

That simple question reignited my mind. While Esah helped me up, I worked to suppress tears of frustration.

"It was quite a bit of writing, several feet or so," I choked out.

We hurried back into the office and started sorting through the scrolls. About fifteen of them were easily eliminated because they had too little writing. Another seven had more writing, but still not as much as I remembered on my scroll. That still left eleven and little time.

"Now what?" I said.

We sat there for a moment.

"Didn't you say you carried the scroll in your pants pocket?"

"Yeah. So?"

"Try putting these in your pocket. See if they fit or if any of them feel the same."

"Great idea!"

I stuffed the first one in my pocket. It was too long—way too long, in fact. I tried the second. Also too long.

"Find me the shortest one."

Esah lined them up and grabbed the two shortest. I shoved the first in my pocket. Still too long. So was the second.

"There have to be more scrolls," I said, feeling the panic rise again in my chest. Though it was obvious there weren't any more scrolls, we looked anyway.

Just then, we heard movement in the hallway. Esah and I froze. Rabah burst into the office breathing hard.

"It's the Elder. He's coming back. Domi signaled from across the market. Did you find it?"

I couldn't answer.

"Not yet," said Esah hopefully.

"We have to get this place cleaned up and get out of here!" Rabah yelled.

They hurriedly began to tidy up. I slumped to the ground.

I can't go back, I thought. *Timela will think I've been lying. My friends risked themselves for nothing. And worst of all I'll be trapped in the Quarry until they banish me to the Valley of Salt.*

"Rom, hurry up and help us."

"I'm staying here."

"What?!" Both Esah and Rabah stared at me wide-eyed.

"I don't care what he does to me. I can't go back. He can kill me for all I care." My strength was gone. My hope was gone. Blackness was everywhere, like a crushing weight on my chest. It was over, and the darkness was too much.

"We have to get him out of here," I heard Rabah say to Esah.

Esah and Rabah gripped my arms and worked desperately to drag me out of the room. I closed my eyes and tried to wake up from what felt like a bad dream.

"Rom! Rom!" They shouted. "Get up! Get up!"

Get up . . . Get up? I've heard those words before . . . in the darkness. I felt trapped and without hope then too. But I obeyed and got up and—

Suddenly I saw it. "No!" I shouted.

Esah and Rabah pulled hard at me, yelling, "We have to go!"

"No. Stop! Stop! Let me go!" I was almost hysterical, fighting to get free while they dragged me out. "I'm okay. I'm okay. Look. Look!" I pointed.

They stopped pulling and looked.

"Did you see that?" I shouted.

"What?"

"The bird! Did you see the bird? He was right over there." He was gone by then, but I was sure that something like a bird had fluttered in the back corner of the office.

Esah and Rabah let go. I raced over to the corner, energized by renewed hope. Knocking on the stone, a hollow echo answered back.

"It's in here!"

I pulled frantically at the stone, trying to open it. Esah rushed over to help, but Rabah ran down the hallway toward the door.

"Dolia's stirring," he shouted.

Then, even worse, "He's coming!"

CHAPTER 10

Esah and I wrenched the stone loose. Inside were about ten scrolls. I grabbed two of them. Neither would open.

My scroll will only open for me. These scrolls must belong to other people.

"Rabah, get out!" I yelled. "Esah, you too. Hurry! I'll be right behind you." Rabah left. Esah didn't.

I tried another and another. They wouldn't open. But then my hand grabbed hold of one, and I immediately knew it was mine. Grasping the scroll felt like putting on a well-worn glove. It opened at my touch.

I shoved it into my pocket. Pushing the stone back into place, I heard a tremendous roar. Esah rushed back to me from the door, which he had slammed shut.

"It's the Elder! He's found Dolia. He's in the hallway." Esah panted. Beads of sweat formed on his brow. His eyes were wild with fear.

The roar was followed by huge crashes, like a gigantic hammer rhythmically smashing a rock. Closer and closer it came.

We were trapped.

Frantic, I snatched a torch off the wall and hurled it into the shelves of scrolls. Immediately they burst into flames. Esah's eyes grew as wide as saucers. I grabbed him and yanked him to the ground behind the Elder's desk. No sooner were we down than we heard a wood-splintering smash. Another bone-shaking roar assaulted our ears. It was followed by the sound of iron boots tramping toward the blazing scrolls. On instinct, I grabbed Esah's arm and we raced for the door, running behind the Elder's back as he faced the flames. My head was down, my face turned away from the Elder in a futile attempt to remain anonymous. We barreled through the door just as Dolia tried to enter. We crashed into her, knocking her backward so hard that she flipped, landing face down. Both Esah and I stumbled forward but managed to stay upright. Regaining balance, we sprinted toward the exit and burst onto the front walkway. I slammed the outer door behind us. We continued to sprint down the walkway and into the back entrance of the market.

Turning toward the city gate, we tried to act naturally and blend in with the crowd to avoid detection, but I was breathing heavily and sweat poured off my face. We kept our heads down and blindly hurried through the market.

If people had been paying attention to us, they soon weren't.

"Find them!" demanded the Elder's livid, authoritarian voice. I didn't dare look back as the sound of his voice made clear that he had emerged from his office.

Everyone else halted immediately and looked toward the Elder. I kept walking. Esah grabbed at me, forcing me to stop.

"What are you doing?" I half screamed and half whispered to him.

"Rom, trust me." Esah turned me around to face the same direction as everyone else. He started walking slowly back toward the Elder, partially dragging me along with him.

"What is that?" I sputtered

Standing at the entrance was an iron giant. He must have been at least seven feet tall. He didn't look human. Rather, he was a living, solid iron statue. I also now understood what Timela meant when she said something much worse awaited us out in the city. The iron giant could have easily smashed Plute, Jaykah, or any other Guardian with his massive iron arms.

"That's the Iron Guardian. It's the Elder transformed. He's what everyone in the city fears."

"We have to get out of here," I hissed.

"Rom, he doesn't know it was us," Esah whispered. "If he did, he would have yelled 'stop them,' not 'find them.'"

Brilliant.

We continued back toward the scene of the crime.

"Let's separate," Esah suggested. "If anyone noticed us come out together, they'll search for two people, not one."

Esah drifted away from me at the back of the crowd forming around the Elder.

"What are you waiting for?! Find the insolents who set fire to my office!" The Elder screamed.

The people instantly scattered. Some ran to get water to put out the fire; others tried to figure out who they were searching for; still others tried to gather evidence of anything suspicious.

A man near me spoke up.

"I think I saw them! Did you see the two people who came running into the market? Weren't they headed that way?"

"What two people?"

"They were boys, I think."

"Where were they headed?"

"I saw them go toward the city gate," I volunteered.

"Let's go!"

A group of us broke off from the gathering and moved quickly toward the city gate. As we neared it, we trudged upstream as the action drew everyone else toward the market.

"Did you see two people come running this way?" I asked everyone I could find.

"What did they look like?" one woman asked.

I have no idea where the idea came from, but when I opened my mouth, I heard myself say, "I think they were two salt runners."

"Of course," she said. "No, I haven't seen them."

As I left, she turned to a woman next to her and said, "Two salt runners caused a problem in the market. Did you see them running this way?"

Overhearing the conversation between the women made me realize the power of my idea.

Perfect. That's how I'll get them off my trail.

On my walk back toward the scene of the crime, I stopped as many people as I could and asked, "Have you seen two salt runners escaping from the market? They broke into the Elder's house and set fire to his scrolls." Or I said, "Two salt runners broke into the Elder's house and knocked out Dolia, have you seen them? They took some scrolls and burned the rest."

After sowing my deception, I approached a group gathered by one of the market stalls.

"Did you hear what happened?" I asked.

"It's terrible!" One of the men cried, his voice quivering with anger. "Two salt runners broke into the Elder's house. They attacked Dolia his assistant, knocking her out. Then they defaced his desk, stole some gold, and tried to burn the place down."

"Do they have any idea who they were?" I asked, anxious to see if my plan had worked.

"I heard Kauma was one of them," someone volunteered.

My work was done. It was time to head back. I wanted to go to Emma's house, but I had no idea where it was, so I returned to the Quarry.

Josef wasn't at the gate when I arrived. Fortunately, it was unguarded and unlocked. I slipped in, went down to my cave, and lay down on my mat exhausted. I reached into my pocket, felt my scroll, and fell fast asleep.

* * *

By the time I awoke, the Quarry was already full. No one was working. I wandered out of my cave into the dim morning light. The air crackled with energy. Everyone was talking, debriefing the events of the previous night.

Nothing like it had ever happened in Lithown before. I was genuinely pleased with myself, though I might not have been had I known what was coming. I was anxious to talk to Esah, Rabah, and Domi. Part of me couldn't wait to show the scroll to Timela and prove to her I hadn't been lying. But I was still leery of making her an accomplice. Plus, I didn't want to have to explain to her what happened.

As I walked toward the large group in the center, I saw Plute, Josef, and the other Stone Guardians standing side-by-side. Seeing them transformed yet not attacking someone was unnerving.

I became more nervous when Josef walked over before I could reach the main group. His large stone hands enclosed around my arms like a vice. Tightening his grip, he picked me up and carried me back toward the cave.

"Where were you last night?" he demanded. "It couldn't have taken that long for Emma to check you over."

I summoned all the courage I could to sound as calm as possible.

"Did you not see what was happening last night, Josef? The city was absolute chaos. I went with Emma, but by the time we were done people were everywhere. I even heard rumors that two salt runners did something bad. Is this normal? I thought the people in the city were better behaved. Maybe they should spend some time with you here at the Quarry, being shaped like we are."

I force a grin onto my face. "Then they'd learn what I've been learning: it doesn't pay to cause trouble."

Josef noticeably softened and lowered me to the ground.

"Yes, there are troublemakers everywhere. They would do well with a little discipline."

"Look at the good it's done me," I said. "I appreciate you taking time to teach us the value of following the rules. I'm sure if you were in charge of the whole city, there would be far less trouble."

"Well," Josef continued, "I wouldn't mind getting moved up to guarding the city gate. I have some ideas on how to make this a great city."

I tried hard not to laugh. He's eating this up! I can't wait to tell Esah.

"Josef, I hope they give me a chance to tell them what a great job you've done here. In fact, knowing how committed you are to this assignment, I was surprised you weren't here when I got back last night. The gate was unlocked, so I slipped in and went to my cave."

"Well, yes, I . . . I rushed in to help with crowd control. I thought it was better to leave my post because I might be needed for important work."

"Now that you mention it, I'm not surprised you were quick to serve. The same thought crossed my mind when I saw the chaos. In fact, I probably picked up my love of serving from watching you."

Sensing the danger with Josef had passed, I asked the question eating away at me. "Did they find the salt runners?"

"Not yet. But I think they have a lead on who it might be. I know that salt runners are a shady group, but to set fire to the Elder's house—wow! I can't imagine what they were thinking."

I tried to stay calm. *They don't suspect me!*

Our conversation was interrupted by Stone Jaykah, who told us to return to the group. As we walked back, I overheard Josef tell Plute that my story checked out. I found Esah, Domi, and Rabah just as Plute began to speak.

"As most of you have heard, last night there was an attack on the Elder's house. To the best of our knowledge, two salt runners attacked Dolia, the Elder's assistant, and set fire to the office. Neither the Elder nor Dolia were seriously injured, but there's a tremendous amount of damage. Priceless scrolls were destroyed and plundered. It will take some time to dig through the mess to assess the damage. At this point, all we have are rumors about who was behind this vicious attack, but we'll leave no stone unturned in hunting down the perpetrators. We'll not be discussing these events today while we work."

Yeah, right.

At irregular intervals, Rabah, Esah, Domi, and I managed to share bits of our stories in hushed whispers. I relished telling them about the salt runner rumor. Rabah was afraid, but Domi was almost giddy at the destruction of the Elder's office. I think he would've been disappointed if we'd simply stolen back the scroll.

The leaders remained Stone Guardians for the rest of the day. Plute gave me a beating for talking at one point, but it felt more like a halfhearted attempt to show he meant business. It would've been more effective if he'd hit one of the "good" kids, but that never seemed to occur to them.

Esah was the first one to bring up the obvious questions: Now what? How would we read the scroll? How would we get word to Emma that we had the scroll? Adding to the dilemma, I realized that I had to be the one to visit the scroll reader because my scroll wouldn't open for anyone else.

Having Emma request to see me again wouldn't work, and there was no way Plute would let me out of the Quarry. We wondered if Emma would give the name of the scroll reader to Domi, Esah, or Rabah, but that left the same problem of how to get me and the scroll out of the Quarry.

Only one solution held promise, though I certainly didn't relish the idea: I'd have to get beaten badly enough to get sent back to Emma for another healing. All afternoon I spent time figuring out how to induce a beating that would qualify me to see Emma, all the while working hard to avoid Timela, who kept trying to catch my eye.

As long as I was with people, I knew that she wouldn't mention anything. Fortunately for me, Ina's unceasing labor to keep Timela away from me was finally useful.

As everyone left for the night, I watched Timela depart and then turned toward my cave. Just then, Ina ran over. "Timela wants to talk to you tomorrow," she said. "She thinks you're avoiding her. She'll be here extra early and wants you to meet her out here."

That night I pulled out my scroll and opened it up. The writing was so beautiful. Tracing some of the words with my fingers, I imagined what it might say.

I needed to get to Emma.

CHAPTER 11

The next morning Timela was waiting for me when I emerged from my cave. No one else had arrived yet, except Josef, who was standing guard by the gate as always. It was impossible to avoid having a conversation with her.

"Hi," I said as nonchalantly as possible.

"Were you at the Elder's office when the fire happened?" she demanded.

"Why do you ask?" I said, stalling.

"Why do I ask? Answer the question!" She was almost yelling. "You wanted to know how to get to his office, so I told you, and the next thing I know someone sets fire to it!"

"Didn't you hear? It was two salt runners."

"You haven't answered the question! Were you at the Elder's office when the fire started or weren't you?"

"Listen, Timela. The Elder lied to you. He took my scroll. He was hiding it in his office, just like I told you."

I reached into my pocket to get the scroll to show it to her, but she was staring straight at my face, eyes flashing.

"Did you set his office on fire?"

"Look! I have the scroll right here."

"Did you set his office on fire?"

"He was lying to you, Timela."

"Did you set his office on fire? Answer the question."

"The fire happened while we were there," I said.

"What does that mean? Did you start the fire or not?"

"It was all a blur. Things happened so quickly. We found the scroll he stole from me. He was coming back and then there was a fire."

She glared at me.

"Yes, I started the fire."

Tears formed in her eyes. "I helped you burn down the Elder's house."

I felt horrible.

"You burned down the Elder's house," she said, her tone changing. And then it happened.

As I looked into her eyes, her face hardened. She drew back . . . and slugged me in the face.

* * *

I woke up in Emma's house. She sat next to me whispering healing words as I lay there. I turned toward her and asked, "What happened?"

"It was Timela. She transformed into a Guardian and attacked you. Josef had to pull her off, or she might have killed you. He brought you to me. While everyone expected she'd become a Guardian, she seems awfully young to have morphed already. What did you say to set her off?"

"She knows I set fire to the Elder's house."

Worry crept into Emma's face. "About that," she said. "What happened?"

I told her the story. She was especially interested in the secret vault containing the scrolls. As I recounted finding my scroll, my hand shot down to my pocket. It was still there! I pulled it out and showed it to her.

"I'm surprised I still have it. I thought in her anger Timela would have taken it to spite me."

"She probably would have," Emma guessed. "But in her rage, she didn't stop to think to search for it. Transforming for the first time was probably just as confusing for her as it was for you."

"But a lot less painful for her."

Emma laughed. "Yes, less painful. But also less rewarding, since she didn't get the scroll. May I see it?"

I opened the scroll for her. She admired the ornate writing. "There's a lot written here." She sounded almost jealous.

"You said you'd find someone to read it."

"Yes. I waited until you woke up to see if you had your scroll before I sent for him. But now that Timela knows you set fire to the Elder's house, I think we should go to the scroll reader's house together. We aren't safe here anymore." She spoke candidly, and I could sense anxiety in her voice. I wanted to apologize for involving her in my mess, but I didn't. The words just wouldn't come out.

"When can we go?"

"We should go now, if you're ready. I'll have to make sure the way is clear."

I tried to get up, but the pain was too much. "Emma, you forgot to heal me." I grimaced. "I can't move."

"No, I healed you. But while I can heal your body, I can't heal your mind—at least not this way. The pain is gone, but you need to believe that you're healed, or it'll still immobilize you."

Though I'd experienced her healing power before, it still seemed impossible to recover from such a beating so quickly. The pain felt too real, and the slightest hint of pain, real or imagined, shattered the possibility of healing.

"Focus on the fact that we're on our way to read your scroll."

I did as she said and was able to distract myself enough from the pain to get up. I still felt stiff and sore, but I was determined to keep going, eager to get the answers I longed to find.

"Just remember, Rom, that I have the power to heal your physical wounds, but whatever emotional wounds you've endured from your encounters are still there. The wounds that we can't see or feel are always the most problematic."

* * *

It wouldn't have been wise to walk in plain sight in the city, especially since we were going past the city gate and the Elder's house. So, Emma loaded me onto something that looked like a cross between a cart and a chariot, covered me with a blanket, and pulled me as if I was in a rickshaw. She told me we were going to see a man named Avi. He was well respected in the city, but she didn't mention anything else about him.

As I bumped and bounced over the paved stone roads, I thought of those who came before me in the Quarry. They probably dressed those stones, and I wondered if Avi was one of them. Maybe Emma, too. Perhaps that was why she was willing to help. Though her attitude seemed to go beyond empathy. It felt more like genuine compassion, which made me trust her recommendation of Avi. Her selfless actions gave me a sense of peace, even as I sensed that she struggled to keep her own worries in check.

Avi's house wasn't far from the Elder's place, and the smell of burnt wood and parchment still hung in the air. But as opposed to the night before, it was eerily quiet. I'd expected to hear the heavy footfalls of Guardians or the Elder tramping around, but the silence was more frightening. Not knowing what the Elder was doing made me extra cautious as I climbed out of the rickshaw and walked with Emma to the back door.

She knocked softly. A couple of seconds later, the door opened, and we were face-to-face with a man with a bushy head of tangled black hair. He had a weathered and unshaven face, hairy forearms to match his head, and light brown skin. He was a little less than six feet tall and looked a bit older than Emma or the Elder, maybe in his mid-fifties, which was probably about the same age as Josef. He smelled like mint and leather, and he had a twinkle of humor in his dark brown eyes.

He greeted me with a broad smile and called me by name as he invited me in, which caught me off guard. It was as if he knew I was coming. Motioning for me to follow, he told Emma to wait for me in the back entryway.

He led me into the main room of his house. Strangely, it was lighter inside Avi's house than it was outside. He had the same torches illuminating the walls as the Elder and Emma did, but something was different.

We sat down on cushioned pillows around a low wooden table in the center of the room, and he asked me to share my story. Feeling safe, I divulged everything I could remember from the past several days. The more I shared, the more I wanted to share.

"A bird, huh?" He smiled joyfully. "Did you notice that the bird appeared as soon as you finished drinking from the goblet?"

Is that how it happened?

I wanted to ask him more about it, but he moved on.

"Do you have the scroll?" he asked.

Pulling it from my pocket, I handed it to him. It unrolled easily in his hands.

"Can you read it?" I inquired.

He laughed. "Yes, I can. But I'm not going to." Seeing my confusion, he continued as he handed it back, "It's your story. You should read it."

"But I can't read it," I countered. "I've tried."

"That's what I'm here for," he said. "Look carefully at the scroll and tell me what you see."

As I focused on the handsome script, I slowly scanned the same letters I'd seen before. They were beautiful and shapely, like calligraphy, yet they made no sense to me. While I tried to describe what I saw, Avi put his rough hand on my forehead and whispered in my ear what sounded like "Mayplanasthe." As his voice registered in my mind, the foreign letters began to swim around on the page, reforming and reshaping themselves. They were still blurry and misshapen, but they began to look less strange and more familiar.

I stared intently at them, hoping the power of concentration would enable me to bring meaning out of nonsense. Avi then whispered in my ear: "Ginoskete."

Wait a minute, these aren't strange letters at all! I know that word. It's the word "the." And that looks like the word "king." I think I can actually read this first sentence.

Inside my head, I heard my inner voice begin to read the words . . .

CHAPTER 12

The king of Sebi summoned Akouso, his chief minister, to his private chamber.

"I want you to go and appoint a replacement for Gaon as captain of my royal forces."

"Why, my lord?" replied Akouso. "I have heard reports from the field that he has won a great victory over the desert bandits who harassed our people on the eastern border. And he drove back the sea peoples on the western front. Why do you want him replaced?"

"Akouso, you are looking at external things, not at what's going on inside his heart. Go and take a closer look. Take Haron with you. He will help you to see. Come back and report to me what you find."

Haron, a large hawk flew over to Akouso, landed on his shoulder, spread wide his wings, and carried Akouso off. They journeyed to a plateau near the base of the mountains in the eastern desert, where Gaon and another warrior were walking. The king's forces were assembled in the valley below. "Captain," said the warrior. "I spoke with some of the men, and they praised the way you led us today. I have to agree. It was brilliant military strategy."

Gaon beamed with pride.

"But they are questioning your order to return to the palace. We have come all this way and there are so many towns nearby where bandits are hiding. Should we not pursue them into those towns as well?"

Gaon replied, "I have my orders. The king said we are not to attack any other villages."

"Did he really say that?" questioned the warrior. "Why would the king not want you to destroy all the bandits? Why would he send us out here only to do half the job? Look at how easily we routed them under your leadership. If you were to lead us to destroy all the bandits, imagine the response!"

"I would like it," mused Gaon.

"Maybe the king does not want you to gain too much glory because you might become a threat to him," pressed the warrior. Imagine what your men would say about you if you led them to utterly rout the bandits. Imagine what the people of Sebi would say. They would forget your failings, and you would finally receive the adulation and acclaim to which you are entitled."

"I have labored hard. I don't need a lot of recognition, but I do need some."

"Worthy heroes make their own decisions," nudged the warrior craftily. "They don't sit idly by waiting for permission or guidance from others."

"Yes," said Gaon firmly. "I make my own decisions."

A roar of approval went up from the camp when Gaon announced the decision to continue battle.

Akouso and Haron returned to the palace.

"What did you see?" the king inquired.

"Disobedience."

"There is more to it than that," pronounced the king. "You saw a man who is the center of his own thoughts, one who is more concerned about what others think of him than what I think. I cannot have such a man leading my forces.

"I am sorry now that I picked him. Take Haron. He will lead you to find a replacement. When you find the man, take this golden goblet and give him a drink from the fountain in the courtyard."

Haron and Akouso traveled west from the capital city to the city of Tikto in the coastal plain. There they were met by the elders of the city, who bowed low to the ground.

"The king is seeking brave-hearted soldiers for his royal forces," Akouso announced. "Bring me all the young fighting men in your town who are eager to enlist. I will examine them in the fields outside the town tomorrow afternoon."

When the appointed time arrived, Akouso found many men he gladly conscripted for service in the king's army, but not one met with Haron's approval as a replacement for Gaon.

However, the next morning Haron led Akouso to a field on the backside of the city where a young man hosted a morning cookout with little boys from the city. It was a poignant and peaceful scene until an angry man approached.

"What do you think you are doing, Peytos? Those kids belong in the city at the Boys' Home doing chores. Not out here."

The young man looked up. "We are just having a cookout, sir."

"Get them back in there at once. They do not need to be spoiled eating that kind of food!"

"This is my time with the boys, and I am free to spend it how I choose. That is what the king himself decreed when he commissioned the Boys' Home. I will bring them in after we have our celebration," Peytos said with steadfast conviction.

Haron pecked gently at Akouso. He was the one they were sent to find.

Later, Akouso sought out Peytos.

"Do you know who I am?" Akouso asked.

"Yes, sir," said Peytos, bowing low to the ground.

"I am on an important matter for the king. He is looking for a successor for Gaon, captain of the royal forces. I believe that you are the person who is to fill that role. When the time is right for you to take up the post, you will be summoned."

Peytos replied, "Whatever the king commands, I am ready to do."

"Please kneel," said Akouso.

Akouso poured the liquid of the fountain from the flask into the golden goblet and gave it to Peytos to drink.

As Peytos drank the liquid, Haron flew over and perched on his shoulder. A word formed in Peytos' head, repeating itself over and over again.

"Batah."

CHAPTER 13

L ooking up from the scroll, I saw Avi staring intently at me.
"What did you see?" he asked.

"Who are they?" I blurted out. "The people in the story, are they real?"

"Yes, of course. They lived in this land a long time ago."

"Did this really happen? Did Peytos become captain of the royal forces? What happened to Gaon? How did Akouso do the things he did? Who was Haron? Are we living in Sebi now?"

Avi patiently answered my questions. Peytos became a famous warrior. Gaon fought to retain his role as captain, but he was eventually forced to relinquish it. Akouso was something called a Naviro, a unique type of warrior, imbued with special powers. Naviro were able to hear, see, and understand things that were not revealed to others. Because Haron was a bird, he especially fascinated me, but Avi couldn't tell me anything more than what I picked up from the story. I wondered if Haron had any connection to my bird. And, yes, the land I was in was called Sebi.

"Why do you think you were given this story?" Avi inquired.

"What do you mean?"

"You could've been given a different story. Why this one?"

"I have no idea."

Our conversation was interrupted by a knock on the door. It was Emma.

"We have to go. We've been here too long. If the Elder comes looking for Rom, we'll all be in trouble."

"Think about it," Avi urged as we finished our conversation.

Outside, Emma concealed me in the cart. She tried talking to me as we traveled, but I evaded her questions. I should've told her what happened—after all, she was the reason I met Avi and was able to read my scroll—but I was so consumed with wanting to process my own thoughts at that moment that I didn't stop to think that she might want to know what her sacrifices and service had accomplished for me.

After reading the scroll's story, my own story started to make a little more sense. I drank from a goblet when I first awoke, just like Peytos did when he was selected Captain of the Guard. Maybe I'd been selected for something, I reasoned. Akouso was led around by a bird, who then connected with Peytos. My bird led me to Lithown.

Did my bird lead me here so I could meet Avi and read my story? Why would the Elder not want me to hear this story?

The rickshaw stopped. Emma lifted the cover and whispered, "We're almost to the Quarry. It's time to get out and walk the rest of the way."

"I don't know how to thank you, Emma. You're risking a lot to help me, but I'm so grateful you took me to see Avi."

"You should remember that the next time I ask you questions instead of pretending not to hear me," she said with a smile. "Avi's a great man. Whatever he told you, trust it. Now, let's check you back into the Quarry."

As usual, Josef was at the door. Emma ignored him and said to me, "Stay out of trouble, but don't let them bully you. And remember, you've been healed."

"I will remember," I said. "Thank you, Emma."

Back down the uneven stone steps and into the pit I went. I realized I hadn't seen Timela since she transformed. I didn't even know how long I'd been gone, but from the looks of it everyone was down by the rock pool. I made my way that direction, looking for Esah, Domi, or Rabah. Catching sight of Esah, I quickened my pace. But before I reached him, Plute cut me off.

"Stay right here, Rom. Everyone is getting out of the pool in just a moment for an announcement." Then, calling out in a loud voice, he said, "We're done swimming for the day. Please get out quickly and gather over here. I have something important to share."

Everyone clambered out of the pool and reassembled in front of Plute, waiting for the arid climate to quickly dry their clothes. Plute allowed me to stand with my friends, but Jaykah stationed himself right behind us, which prevented me from sharing about my adventure.

"This evening we'll take a special trip," announced Plute. "The people responsible for setting fire to the Elder's office have been apprehended, and they'll be brought to justice in front of the whole city. The Elder has decreed that attendance is mandatory."

Jaykah grabbed my arm. "You get to watch this too, Rom. Let's go."

I felt sick. Esah looked terrified.

Who did they catch?

When evening came, we walked together out of the Quarry gate, but we didn't walk far. West of the Quarry, opposite Emma's house on the main street, was an arched stone tunnel. Proceeding through the tunnel, we came to an open wooden door. Plute stood guard against it in his normal attire. After Jaykah and I passed, Plute left his post and filed in behind us. I was sandwiched in: Jaykah in front, Plute behind.

The tunnel opened into a giant theater. We entered the theater midway up the theater's bowl. Like the Quarry, the main portion of the theater was below ground level. Long, continuous, semi-circular stone benches formed rows of seating, most of which filled quickly with people. At six evenly spaced intervals, there were aisles of steps leading down to the theater floor. We walked a few steps down one of the aisles and filed into our seats. The center of the theater was open air, but our seats were covered by an awning, which decreased the already dim sunlight even more. The relative darkness of our seats focused attention on the brightly lit center stage.

I took my seat between Plute and Jaykah and took in more of my surroundings. The theater was sparsely decorated. Orange and brown tapestries hung on the back wall of the stage, each one with a picture of the book called *The Law of Lithown*, which I'd seen in the Elder's office. The remainder of the theater was just bare rock. The Elder sat just behind center stage, flanked on both sides by serious-looking officials seated in formal chairs.

As the final observers entered the packed theater, all attention centered on the Elder. He rose from his seat and stood center stage on a cylindrical platform that was raised a foot or two off the ground. Anticipation silenced the crowd.

"Fellow citizens of Lithown. I've called this assembly because, as you all know, a few days ago some vandals broke into my office and set it ablaze. Since that time, I've worked tirelessly to discover the identity of these miscreants. Such wanton evil must be punished publicly so that we might discourage others from engaging in rebellious behavior."

The sickness in my stomach grew worse. I tried to reassure myself the Elder couldn't be talking about me, since Plute said they'd apprehended the guilty party, and I was sitting in the audience.

"A number of you have been most helpful in my quest to ferret out the perpetrators," he continued. "We were told by many that two salt runners were responsible. These were important and valuable leads, for which I'm grateful."

The tension in my stomach started to lessen, but my guilt would not allow me to truly relax.

"But I can confidently tell you that the perpetrator is not a salt runner. It's much worse than that. He's a troublemaker, sent here to sow discord and wreak havoc among us."

My whole body tightened as the Elder's voice rang out over the hushed silence.

"The troublemaker's name is . . . Rom!"

As soon as my name left his lips, Plute and Jaykah transformed into Stone Guardians and grabbed me by my wrists. They stood up and dragged me down the stairs toward the stage. I was screaming, crying, and fighting to get free, but it was no use. My hysterics only sealed my guilt.

At the bottom of the stairs, I was hurled onto the stage floor. Towering over me was the Elder, now the Iron Guardian, his stocky build having morphed into solid moving metal of gigantic proportions. His eyes blazed red with the vengeance of justice. In place of his right hand was a sledgehammer, four times as wide as any sledgehammer I'd ever seen before. He raised the sledgehammer far above his head, blocking the sun, and with dizzying speed, brought the mallet down upon me like a meteor. I jerked my head and torqued my body just as the hammer cratered the stone floor where my head just was. Shards of sharp stone shot across my face as I rolled away.

He's trying to kill me!

Pure fear lifted me to my feet. Stumbling, I sprinted toward one of the exits, but the whole stage was encircled by a phalanx of Guardians who'd emerged from the audience, filling the aisles and blocking every exit. I felt imprecatory anger emanating from the crowd around me, craving for me to be caught and beaten.

The Iron Guardian moved more purposefully as he approached me the second time. His massive weight caused tremors with every step, as if the earth itself would give way beneath his crushing weight. The sound of iron crashing against stone echoed throughout the theater.

No one else in the whole theater moved. The Iron Guardian slowly maneuvered to corner me against the wall of Guardians. I felt them at my back as I cautiously retreated.

Suddenly he lunged forward, swinging his iron hammer. I jumped back. The wind from the missed swing blew me back against the Guardians stationed near the eastern exit. Stone fists clamped down on my arms and hurled me back into the fight, but they threw me too far, and I flew over the giant's hammer, which was still lodged in the ground. When I landed, my momentum carried me forward, and I half dove, half fell through the Iron Guardian's legs. He reached down with his free hand and grasped for me, but I escaped, scrambling to the other side of the stage for a few seconds of safety.

He turned to come after me as I stood still in the dim sunlight. It was hopeless. I couldn't escape forever. The weight of despair made my legs buckle, and I went down to my knees as if begging for mercy. My torso swayed forward, and my head felt dizzy as I awaited my execution. The Iron Guardian strode toward me, harshness etched into his iron face.

This is it. Whatever dream-life this is, it's over. Whatever I was supposed to do or be or become, I've failed.

Batah.

Out of nowhere, the word from Peytos' story popped into my head.

"Batah," I whispered as I awaited my fate. The word filled me with defiance and hope, and I lifted my woozy head to stare defiantly at the Iron Guardian.

"Batah!" I shouted with all the strength left in my aching body.

At that moment, above the Iron Guardian's right shoulder, something came hurtling toward me, like a tiny star shooting out of the sky. It blazed past the Iron Guardian before he took another step and came straight at my chest. At the last second, I recognized the outline of a bird, its wings locked behind its head, like the tail feathers of an arrow.

It hit me on the left side of my chest, a projectile shot at my heart. But instead of knocking me over, it absorbed into me, like a raindrop being swallowed by a lake.

A surge of energy like I'd never felt before gushed through my entire body. It began in my chest and raced outward in every direction. When it reached my hands, it felt like power was exploding from my fingertips. My legs felt like compressed springs uncoiling with tremendous force. A bone-rattling roar formed deep within my soul and forced its way past my lips.

The giant was upon me. His hammer hand traced a life-extinguishing arc over his head, falling from the sky toward me.

My uncoiling legs launched me into the air. Shockingly, I heard myself yell "Thureos" as I leapt over the falling hammer, alighting on the topside of the hammer for the briefest moment. It was my springboard for a second jump that propelled me toward the giant's stooped head. Grabbing his head, I vaulted over him and felt the crowd gasping along with me.

How did I do that?

As I tumbled acrobatically back toward the ground, I saw above me a shimmering circle of light plummeting from the sky. Instinctively, I stretched out my hand to catch it. It was a shield!

The Iron Guardian spun toward me, swinging his hammer at my head. But I raised my glowing shield in front of my face. The force of the hammer was palpable as it neared, but there was no impact. Instead, the hammer came to a halt near the face of the shield and then shot backward with increasing velocity, as if repulsed by a magnetic force.

It catapulted him back toward the Guardians at the western side of the stage. He landed with a huge crash, the sound of cracking stone echoing throughout the theater.

As he struggled to find his footing, Stone Guardians cautiously moved toward me, unsure what to do.

Alive with energy, I felt a surge of power pooling somewhere inside my soul. The power swelled up within me, forcing its way into mouth. My lips couldn't restrain the strength within me any more than they could stop a violent sneeze. Like a blast of fire from the heart of a dragon, the word "Ischuro" shot from my mouth. Each passing syllable forced my lips to open wider and wider. The blast felt less like a word and more like a raging river sending a wave of almost invisible force hurtling toward the Elder, shimmering like a heat haze as it went. When it crashed into him, it threw him back onto the heap from which he tried to rise.

Can this be happening?

From his prostrate position the Iron Guardian bellowed, "Grab him!"

Guardians came rumbling from all directions.

There were too many. I blocked the attacks of the first few with my shield, but after a moment, I heard Plute's voice in my ear.

"Remember," he said as he rammed his stony fist into my back. Suddenly all the pain was back—the pain from Plute's first beating, from the thrashing when I tried to help Domi, and from Timela's unexpected onslaught. My shoulder, chest, head, and back seized up. I dropped my shield and fell to the ground. The surge of power was gone. Plute raised me above his head. A tremendous cheer went up from the crowd.

My spirits flagged.

Piercing through the noise, however, I heard a sweet voice call out "Eleos."

"Eleos." The gentle word cut through the chaos.

When I heard it again, I instantly recognized Emma's voice. But that time it pierced my mind.

"Rom, you've already been healed of these wounds."

This is the pain from old wounds. Healed wounds. They have no power over me. Energy rushed back into my body.

"Thureos!"

My shield flew up to me from where it had fallen. I swung downward with all my might at Plute's arm holding me aloft. His stone arm crumbled, and he screamed in agony. The roar of pain caught me by surprise.

All the Guardians near me shrank back in horror. Plute grasped at the place where his arm had been. Now it was a pile of stone rubble scattered on the ground.

Regaining my bearings and standing once more on the ground, I swung again, this time aiming for his chest. Hitting him full force, he staggered backward, and a crack zigzagged down his body like a fault line. I raised my shield, intoxicated with power and prepared to swing again.

"No!" the Iron Guardian yelled. He held a Guardian above his head and threw the enormous creature toward me. I dodged the stone mass as it landed a few feet from me, shaking the entire stadium. Turning my attention to the Iron Guardian, I cried out "Ischuro," but no power emerged from my mouth. "Ischuro," I shouted more loudly. Nothing happened. The Iron Guardian took a confident step toward me.

In a rage, I cocked back my shield and launched it at him like a weaponized discus. When it left my hand, it glowed white, but by the time it reached him, it was fiery red. Striking him between the neck and shoulder, it sliced into his iron body, leaving a deep gash. He cried out in pain and torment. His agony silenced the crowd, but it fed my swelling anger. I called the shield back to me. Again, I hurled it at him; again, it cut him deeply, this time on his left flank. I ran toward him, shield back in my hand, compelled by bitter hatred.

"I'll teach you to steal my scroll, imprison me in that dungeon of a Quarry, and try to beat me to death. You'll never do that to anyone else again!" I screamed.

From the crowd came a calm, authoritative voice. "Rom, that's enough."

Trying to ignore the voice and longing to give in to the rage, I drew back my red-hot shield until I heard again, more forcefully, "Rom, enough."

It was Avi. He was walking deliberately down the steps and onto the stage. I turned to face him. A bird was perched on his shoulder.

Emma was not far behind him. "Are you okay?" she asked anxiously.

I was sucking in deep breaths, seething with unused adrenaline. No one else in the theater moved. Avi walked over to me, his eyes expressing concern and conveying the seriousness of his words.

"Rom, we must leave. Now."

As he neared, the bird hopped off his shoulder and onto mine. It was my bird. I examined him more closely this time and noticed that the writing on his body was indeed the same writing from my scroll. Like the scroll, I could almost read it, but it was just beyond my mental powers.

"Ginoskete," said Avi, and the letters read themselves to my mind.

Rohka.

His name is Rohka.

Rohka dug his claw into my shoulder, and I felt intense joy surge through my body, washing out all the anger and rage.

Looking over at Plute, still grasping the stump where his arm had been broken off, I felt a pang of regret. I understood the implications of my actions. My days in the Quarry were over.

My mind turned to Esah, Rabah, and Domi. Scanning the crowd, I located them. I knew I couldn't acknowledge them in that venue or I'd implicate them in the raid of the Elder's office. Timela still didn't know they were involved—

Timela! I completely forgot. Where is she?

My eyes surveyed the crowd once more before I realized that she wasn't in the crowd. Instead, I saw her among the Guardians, where she'd taken her rightful place. Her stone body looked like her real body, but I couldn't describe in what way. Her bronze eyes shone with sadness as she stared at me.

While I gazed at her, I heard Avi speak to the Iron Guardian.

"Gaboah, you're wrong. This isn't the way to handle this. It was his scroll. You shouldn't have taken it. In fact, you should give back all the scrolls to their rightful owners. They won't open for you because you've forgotten what we were taught. Think of what would happen if we were to train them. Shinar itself would fall, for even Mot couldn't withstand their power."

The Iron Guardian's response was venomous.

"Don't lecture me, Avi. The boy is a troublemaker, and the evil must be driven from him before he contaminates the whole city. If you'd been with us from the beginning, you would know that this is the way it must be done. Power without control will destroy him. You shouldn't have helped him read that scroll. You don't know the curse you've called down on him. It was I, not you, who was chosen to be Elder here for a reason."

"I think it's better if I take the boy and go," Avi replied softly.

"Where do you think you'll take him? And why do you think we'd let you both leave?"

Avi remained calm. "Gaboah, have you forgotten what is written on your robe? Remember the power of those words. Or shall I read them aloud?"

Whatever those words meant, the Elder backed down at once. Avi looked me square in the eyes. "Rom, would you like to come with me?"

"Yes, please."

We walked toward the eastern exit of the theater. As we passed the row of Stone Guardians, Timela's eyes refused to meet mine.

I looked back to where my friends were seated. Their faces displayed a range of emotions, and a lump formed in my throat. Domi looked exultant, gloating over the Elder's humiliation. Esah appeared sad, like he'd miss me. I couldn't read Rabah. Part of me wanted to yell for them to join me. Whatever was next, I wanted to do it with them, but deep in my heart I knew it wasn't possible. It wasn't their time to leave Lithown, and I regretted that the friendships which had sustained me through the confusion of the past few weeks were ending so soon.

When my eyes found Emma's, I saw approval, and my heart filled with gratitude. Despite my sadness, I was excited to leave Lithown. I knew there were greater things in store for me, opportunities which Emma's sacrifices helped create.

Avi followed behind as I exited the theater. My shield had disappeared, but Rohka was on my shoulder.

CHAPTER 14

"Quickly," Avi said as we exited the theater. "We need to stop by my house before we leave. I need to——"

"What just happened?" I interrupted. I struggled to regain my composure amidst a tidal wave of cascading questions.

Avi didn't answer. Maybe he thought it was a rhetorical question.

"What just happened?" I said more forcefully. "Where did my bird come from? Where did I get that shield? How did I learn those words?"

I grabbed hold of his arm, halting him and forcing him to address my questions.

"And why are you helping me?"

The impatience on his face gave way to kindness.

"Rom, there will be time for questions later. But right now, we must get going. As for why I'm helping you," he said, eyes glistening, "it's because I'm also on a journey." He began walking again.

"What journey? Where are we going?"

"There's another city a few days' walk from here. I've been trying to gather information about it since Emma first told me of you. I visited it once a long time ago, but my understanding is that it's changed a lot since then."

The main street was empty as we hurried away, but I kept looking back to see if people would appear.

"Are you sure we're safe?" I asked.

"What you did to Plute will give other Guardians pause before they pick a fight with you again. Another shot into his chest and you might've killed him. Even Gaboah was no match for that shield of yours or the anger with which you wielded it. You not only damaged his body, you severely damaged his ego—"

"Wait," I interrupted. "Why do you keep calling him Gaboah? Isn't he supposed to be called 'the Elder' or 'the Iron Guardian'?"

"Rom, those who insist others call them by their title are usually the ones least worthy of having a title. His name is Gaboah, and as I was saying," he continued, "if Gaboah is smart, he'll let us escape from the city. Once we're gone, he can spin whatever story he wants about us."

"So why are we hurrying?" I asked, as Avi again increased our pace.

"Because in my experience a person whose pride has been wounded doesn't usually do the smart thing. We often take difficult events that could bring us the gift of humility and twist them into opportunities for further focus on ourselves—thinking only of how we appear to others, how we've failed, and how we can make things right for ourselves. My fear is that his pride will demand that he come after us."

"But my shield disappeared, and I don't remember the word I used to summon it. What would I use to fight them?"

"You have that bird with you, and he's far better than any shield," Avi said.

With that Rohka flew off my shoulder back toward the theater.

"Where's he going?" I asked.

"Didn't he tell you?"

"No. He's a bird. He doesn't talk, does he?"

"Well, in your scroll story Haron communicated with Akouso, so I assumed that your bird talked to you too. Either way, I'm sure he'll be back."

Avi's confident tone was contradicted by the fact that we were almost running. Passing the Elder's burned office, I asked, "Should we see if other scrolls are still in there?"

"It's a good idea, but there isn't time. My guess is Gaboah moved them by now anyway."

When we arrived at Avi's home, he told me to wait by the door. After only a few minutes, he emerged from the back room, a pack on his back. He was already prepared.

"Drink some of this."

He handed me a bottle, and I drank. I expected the brackish water from the Quarry, but it was more like the sweet liquid sunshine from the first day, though not as potent. The velvety liquid ran down my throat, filling me with warmth as the smell of fruit filled my nostrils. I drank and drank. It was heavenly. I soon emptied the bottle.

I felt amazing: hopeful, safe, and loved.

Avi watched. When I caught his eyes, guilt swept over me. *Was this for us to share?*

"Thank you," I said. "I wasn't supposed to drink the whole thing, was I? That wasn't your last bottle, was it?"

"It was my only bottle. It cost me greatly to procure it."

Why am I so greedy?

"I'm so sorry," I confessed as I handed it back to him. "There might be a tiny bit left," I said hopefully.

"It's alright, Rom. Consider it a gift—a sacrificial gift. A salve for your wounds."

"Wounds? But I feel fine."

"Not visible wounds, but invisible ones. Where do you think your red-hot anger in the theater came from? Legalism and rejection create some of the deepest and most difficult-to-heal wounds. Lithown is an appropriate name for this place because like a stone, it can be rigid and unyielding."

"What's so powerful about this liquid?"

"The power is not in the liquid so much as what it cost me to procure it and the sacrifice it was to give it to you. It will take some time, but Emma's compassion in healing your physical wounds opened a pathway for this elixir to begin to mend your internal wounds as well."

We quickly moved down the path toward the main city street when Rohka sped back toward us. He landed on my shoulder as we hustled toward the city gate. But before we reached it, Avi stopped.

"Something doesn't feel right about this," he said. "Do you feel it?"

"Feel what?"

"It feels like we're not supposed to leave. At least not yet. What does your bird say?"

I looked at Rohka, but he didn't say anything as far as I could tell. Not wanting to disappoint Avi, I lied.

"He thinks we should get out of the city as soon as possible. Head straight for the city gate."

Avi appeared puzzled for a moment, but on we went, north and then west toward the city gate. The market was empty as we hustled through the stalls. *They must not be coming. We're going to make it!*

"This still doesn't feel right," Avi called over his shoulder. "Are you sure we're supposed to go this way?"

"I think so."

After all, Rohka stopped me before I went into that dangerous valley. If this is wrong, he would do something, wouldn't he?

Main street dumped us into the town square in front of the city gate. The gate was unguarded, but the massive iron doors were closed. Avi and I raced across the square, and together we pushed open the smaller pedestrian door. Avi was about to step through when he stopped again.

"We aren't supposed to leave this way," he insisted. "Something feels completely wrong. I don't have peace about this."

"No, this is right. We made it. We can leave!" I jumped in front of Avi and pushed my way out into the wider world.

Freedom!

Avi had a hard time stepping over the threshold, and it occurred to me that I hadn't stopped to think about how long he'd been at Lithown and how hard it might be for him to leave.

That's why he believes we're doing the wrong thing. He just needs a push. I reached back through the doorway and grabbed his arm.

"It's okay. It's time to go."

He stepped through the doorway, still dazed. Safely out, I pulled the door closed. Just before it slammed shut, I heard muffled screams emanating from inside the central theater.

PART 3: THE CAVES

CHAPTER 15

As we stepped out of Lithown, early evening gave way to sunset. The dim sun was about to be swallowed by the distant horizon. Remembering the primal roar I heard on my first day, I asked, "Will it be safe out here at night?"

My question snapped Avi out of deep contemplation.

"We need to find a place to rest for the night and begin our journey tomorrow. As long as your bird is with us, I think we'll be okay," he said, casting a glance back the way we came.

I looked to my shoulder, but Rohka was gone.

"What if Rohka leaves while we're sleeping? Will we still be safe?" I asked.

"Rohka. Is that his name? Did he leave? I can't see very well in this dusky darkness."

"No, he's still here," I lied.

"Good. Come on, let's go," Avi said. "We can't stay near the walls of the city because there'll post guards soon. We need to find our way to another ridge and, if we're lucky, a cave in which we can sleep."

As we walked, Avi pulled out a scroll from his pocket.

"Illuminatio."

A beam of light radiated from the scroll. He shone the light all around, taking in our surroundings. When he aimed the light toward me, he paused for a moment on my bird-less shoulder but didn't say anything.

Then he started north, away from the city gate. I followed meekly behind and pulled out my own scroll. I muttered the same word, but no light came from it.

As we descended from the city, the walking became difficult because the ground was uneven, and the terrain was hard to see. Avi regularly swept the light left and right, searching for a place to sleep. We walked together in silence for quite some time.

"Look up there," Avi said after a while. He pointed the light to our right, zeroing in on a wide-mouthed cave. "That's where we should try sleeping tonight."

We made our way up to the cave. It was suitable enough, perhaps twice the size of my cave in the Quarry. From his bag Avi unrolled two mats, and we lay down to sleep.

I didn't sleep well that night. I kept hearing muffled screams as I drifted in and out of sleep, fighting with my thoughts and questions.

Did I abandon my friends to the Elder's punishment? Why did I lie to Avi?

* * *

The next morning, Avi and I set out, continuing east.

"Where are we going?"

"Julat. It's a city much larger than Lithown and in a greener, less rocky part of the country. I've heard rumors of happenings there. A while ago, a mighty warrior arrived. He's said to be a man of great power, and I'm hoping we can learn something from him."

"What do you mean by 'great power'?"

"Rom, everyone has power of some sort. Emma has the power to heal; I have the power to help people understand; what you were doing in the theater is the first glimpse of your power, which looks like the power to fight. But you need training to use it correctly. Everyone does. It's clear that you'd never receive the training you need if you stayed in Lithown."

"Where did I get this power?"

"Your power seems connected to Rohka, your bird. That's why it's so interesting that you carry a scroll with the story of Akouso and Haron. Akouso's power was also connected to his bird. I've seen others with animals like you have—dogs, cats, birds, and more—and in each case the animal seems connected to their power. I've never had an animal myself, though I did enjoy having your bird on my shoulder in the theater.

"For me it's my scroll. When I have my scroll with me, especially in my hand, I feel power flowing into me. For Emma, there is something in her eyes. They flash red when she exercises her power, as if her eyes were windows into another world. How it all works, I don't understand yet. Perhaps we'll learn something in Julat that will help answer that question."

"What happens if you lose your scroll?"

"I can't. It's hard to explain, but it's always with me, or at least always nearby. Others can bring it closer to me, but no one can take it from me. What happened with your scroll and the Elder can't happen with mine."

"Haron was the king's bird and the king sent him with Akouso, but no one sent me Rohka. And now he's gone, so does that mean my power is gone too?"

"Rohka left?" Avi asked almost innocently. "When?"

I felt the blood rush to my face as I realized my lie had been revealed.

"Rohka confuses me. He seems to come and go as he pleases. He led me to Lithown but then abandoned me there. And he doesn't talk to me the way Haron talked to Akouso."

As soon as I said the words, I realized I exposed more of my lies since I claimed Rohka told us to leave Lithown. But Avi didn't seem to notice the slip.

We walked in silence. The landscape gradually began to change. Patches of green peeked out of the hardscrabble brown stone like the splattering of green paint on a brown canvas. The sun made its way toward the center of the sky.

"You said Rohka doesn't talk to you," Avi noted, breaking the stillness. "But how did you know the word to summon that light shield?"

"I'm not sure. It all happened pretty fast. The words were just in my head, so I said them out loud. I thought maybe you could help me make sense of it."

"I might be able to, but perhaps the best thing for me to do is to tell you my story and see if there is anything helpful in it for you."

Avi's words provided rhythm as we walked together toward Julat.

*   *   *

"I'm not from Lithown, nor even from the land of Sebi. I'm from a small village in another region altogether different from Sebi. My life there was very…"

Tears formed in his eyes as he struggled to find the words to use.

"Life in that village was miserable. I think I'll leave it at that. I desperately wanted to get out, but I didn't know how. One day, a group of young men from another village came by the tailor shop where I worked. After I finished mending their clothes, they invited me to join them for the evening. Harmless fun became not so harmless, and I found myself the target of increasing harassment and hostility as I objected to some of their activities. I tried to get away, but they locked me in the back room of an old abandoned house. Though they meant it for evil, it turned out to be the best thing that ever happened to me. In the house, I discovered a treasure trove. Not of money, but of books—a greater treasure by far. There were hundreds of books, some were dusty and ancient;

others were crisp and fresh. As a tailor I hadn't spent much time reading, but that afternoon I dove in. I don't remember what I read first, but it was intoxicating.

"Even after they let me out, I returned again and again to the abandoned house. Whenever I could spare an hour or two, I snuck back to the house to read. My tormentors must have moved on to new trouble in new places, leaving me in sole possession of the priceless collection. I suppose I should've just taken some books with me instead of returning to the house, but for all my other faults—and there are a lot—I didn't think of myself as a thief.

"I devoured the books, reading everything I could get my hands on in my new secret library. Mostly history, but also books of wisdom on topics such as human behavior, government, and engineering. The more I read, the more I craved reading. My mind began to wake up and stretch itself from the slumber of my provincial life. Then the inevitable happened. All my reading created an intense longing to get out of my village, to set out on an adventure. And more than that, it created a desire for truth—truth that couldn't be had where I lived and how I was living. My life felt more and more like a prison and truth the key that would set me free.

"One day I came across a book in the stack that was written in a strange, unfamiliar language. Not able to read the book, I originally left it aside, but the more I read other books, the more I longed to read that one. Time and time again I found myself cradling the soft leather-bound book with gilded edges, smelling its sweet, musty odor. Opening the crinkly pages, I found myself staring at the unknown language, willing myself to understand what it said. Yet all my desire to read it didn't help me. Repeatedly I returned to the book, only to throw it aside in frustration and disgust. Finally, when I resolved never to look at it again, I heard a voice—whether audible or not I don't know—say, 'Take up and read.' Shocked, I picked up the book out of obedience, not expecting anything different to happen. But that time, the impenetrability of the words that had plagued me for so long melted away. The words began to reshape themselves in my mind until I could understand them.

"It turned out that the language of the book was the language of Sebi. The book itself was a map of sorts. There were no pictures, but it described a journey, one that began from that very house where I was reading! The first thing the book instructed me to do was to utter the word 'Eleuthero.'

"When I did, a tiny scroll appeared, no bigger than a thumbnail, and it's been with me ever since. Over time, though, it has grown. Every word of power I've learned is written in this scroll. I used to worry that it would become too big for me to carry, but somehow, as it grows more dense and bulky, it becomes lighter and easier to handle."

At this he pulled out his scroll and lovingly held it in his hand. It looked far bigger and heavier than mine, but somehow it fit perfectly in his hand.

"I set out, taking the book and scroll with me, to follow what I read. The words led me over mountains, across several rivers, and through a desert until I arrived in Lithown.

"That was eleven years ago. At the time, the Elder in charge of the city was a man named Lukas. Gaboah, the current Elder, ran the Quarry, much like Plute does now."

"Is Gaboah from Lithown?"

"That's a good question," Avi replied. "I believe he is. He was there a long time before I got there at least. But, yes, if I remember right, I think he's from Lithown, which might explain what I'm about to tell you.

"When I arrived, I caused a bit of a stir, because I was clearly from another place. My clothes and my mannerisms at the time were quite unusual, and Lukas was summoned to the city gate to meet me. He wore the robe of the Elder, the one that Gaboah wears now. As he drew near, I was intrigued by the words from the ancient language that were written on his robe. Innocently, I read them aloud: 'Belonging to the one who wields the iron scepter.'

"As soon as I said those words, a large iron scepter, weighing several hundred pounds, materialized six feet off the ground and came crashing down, lodging itself in the stone pavement at Lukas' feet. Then an iron manacle mysteriously emerged and fettered Lukas' right arm to the scepter as if it were a giant ball-and-chain.

"No one was more surprised than me, and all eyes moved from the scepter to me and back to Lukas. Lukas' countenance was at once both frightened and focused as he stared at the iron scepter. Dropping to one knee in front of it, he stretched out his right hand and began mouthing silent words. The iron scepter quivered slightly, stalled, and then tipped into his hand. Standing to his feet, he attempted to lift it. At first it appeared to be too heavy, but then the front end rose off the ground and he held it aloft single-handedly. When it reached its zenith, it flashed brightly, synchronized with a flash of bright light from his robe. Then the scepter disappeared, manacle, chain, and all.

"Relief flooded his face, as if he'd passed a great test. Immediately he walked straight toward me. He asked who I was and how I was able to read what was written on his garments. When I told him my story, he welcomed me in. Over time, Lukas taught me most of what I know about Lithown. He helped me to hone my gift of reading and understanding. He brought me scrolls to read and stories to translate, and then would explain what the stories meant. That's how I came to have the informal position of scroll-reader in Lithown. It was the happiest time of my life."

"What happened to Lukas?"

"Lukas was a good man and a good Elder. But over time he felt he'd outgrown the city. He longed to go other places. He talked more and more of how he had the potential to do so much more than simply manage Lithown. He disappeared for long stretches at a time, leaving Gaboah in charge. One day, a few years ago, Gaboah showed up wearing the Elder garment. No one has seen or heard from Lukas since."

"What's wrong with Gaboah?" I asked.

"That's a more complicated question. Gaboah was convinced he deserved to be the Elder. He was well-known by the people and worked in the Quarry, which is not only a place where young men and women are trained but also a place where people go to learn to be leaders, so they can earn higher positions of power. He dedicated himself to studying *The Law of Lithown*."

"Wait! What is *The Law of Lithown*? I saw a copy of it in the Elder's office."

"It's an ancient book that's been passed down for generations. No one knows exactly where it came from, but it's a strange mixture of rules, genealogies, and ancient myths. Lukas showed it to me on a few occasions, and the one thing I remember is that it contains way more material than you might think, given its thin size.

"Anyway, as I was saying before, although Gaboah was convinced he deserved to be the Elder, he couldn't read the ancient language of Sebi. The fact that I could bothered him. Before he disappeared, Lukas gave more and more responsibilities to me and confided in me in greater ways, which only caused Gaboah to become more antagonistic toward me. Pride and a competitive spirit go hand in hand. Wherever there is pride, there is strife.

"At one point, I sat down to talk to Lukas about Gaboah. In my mind, Gaboah was interested only in power and control, a shepherd who fed only himself. I discovered that he was trying to find the secret to becoming the Iron Guardian. Those secrets were hidden by previous elders, and I was concerned that Gaboah wanted those powers. It seemed to me Gaboah thought being the Iron Guardian would give him enough strength to lift the Elder's iron scepter, whether he was worthy or not.

"I tried to point those things out to Lukas, but he defended Gaboah. Perhaps he was afraid of the people of Lithown who embraced Gaboah. I don't know. But from that point on, it was clear Gaboah would be the next Elder, and I would be seen as the lesser light. When Gaboah assumed the role of Elder, I knew he wanted to exile me, but he needed me to read the ancient language for him—though he made requests for reading less and less over time. I thought of leaving for a long time, but I couldn't bring myself to do it. Lithown was my home in Sebi. It had been good to me and good for me. People who matter to me in Lithown, like Emma, held me in the highest regard, despite my failures and shortcomings—something I neither deserved nor wanted to end. I also thought maybe I could help protect Gaboah from himself and others from him.

"It was in the middle of that struggle that you came along. I found myself willing to leave if I could help you on your journey. I feel like I have a chance to give you what I was given in that priceless treasure of books—a chance to escape from a small life and journey into something far bigger."

While we talked, I noticed the landscape changed more dramatically. The green, gently rolling hills contained more trees and shrubs, but it still felt empty, void, and lonely. There were no animals or villages or roads or people. It was like walking through a landscape painting and the barren brown background had simply been repainted green.

As evening approached, we looked for a place to sleep. Unlike my cave in the Quarry or the cave in the side of the rock we used the night before, this new landscape only offered underground caves. This made it trickier to judge just how big the caves were, since the opening had little to do with the size of the space beneath. Exhausted from all the walking, I was glad when we found what looked like a suitable cave.

Avi was out right away. I heard his low, rhythmic snoring not long after we lay down. I was just starting to drift off, when I heard a sound coming from a tunnel within the cave.

CHAPTER 16

"Clip-clop, clip-clop, clip-clop."

The sound of hooves echoed throughout the cave, steadily growing louder and louder. The crescendo of the hooves indicated they were coming closer and closer. I was transfixed. Other than Rohka, and possibly some other birds flying over Lithown, I had not seen any other animals. I racked my brain to think of any dangerous animals that made such a harmless sound, and none came to mind. I assumed I was safe.

But what emerged was not what I expected. Out from the back of the cave came a man and a medium-sized goat.

The man radiated intensity. He had piercing blue eyes; a strong, muscular jaw; and high, visible cheekbones. He was clean-shaven, with a head of short, spiky, jet-black hair. His clothes hung loosely on his taut body. An aroma of earthiness filled the cavern. His eyes were locked on me. I didn't feel threatened, but I did feel totally exposed, as if I was a criminal he was investigating.

"Avi," I called out, not turning my face from the advancing man and his goat. "Avi, get up."

"Let him sleep," came the clear reply. "We don't want Avi to wake up. He had a long day journeying with you. Besides, he likes his sleep."

"Do you know Avi?" I asked.

"Avi is well-known to many. Everyone in Lithown knows who he is, for he has great power."

"Are you from Lithown?"

"I'm not. But I've spent enough time there to know who Avi

is. Has he not told you that he has great power to read and speak the ancient language? He's highly favored in this, which is why I'm surprised to find him out here with you."

"Why?" I shot back.

"From what I hear, you're a troublemaker. If Hudati had been doing her job at the gate, you would've never been allowed into Lithown in the first place."

"I'm not a troublemaker. I have power too, just like Avi," I boasted. "That's why we are leaving Lithown."

"If you have great power like Avi, why are you running away from Lithown? You could've stayed and helped the people there."

I turned to look at Avi, but he seemed farther away than I remembered, as if I'd been walking toward the man and his goat.

"Are you sure Avi wanted to leave Lithown? Maybe when you heard those cries at the city gate, you should've gone back to the arena."

"How do you know about that?"

"I, too, have power. I have the power to recognize lies. That's why I know you're lying about having power. You were able to fight in Lithown because Avi was with you. He's highly favored. It doesn't surprise me that he has access to a shield of light. Wasn't he the one who summoned it for you?"

Was he?

"If you have power, why don't you demonstrate it to me?" came the challenge.

"Alright."

"But first, come farther into the cave. You are standing too close to Avi; if there's power that comes, it won't be yours but his that I'll see."

I consciously took a couple steps toward the goat and the man. The man's eyes had not once left me. I pursed my lips and tried to think of the word I needed to say to summon a blast of force, but

I couldn't remember it. I tried to summon the shield again, but nothing came.

"There's a better test of true power—and if you could do it, a sign that you're not a troublemaker. Did Avi not reveal it to you?"

I looked back toward Avi but could no longer see him. It was like I'd moved to the very back of the cave. Without waiting for me to answer his question, the goat pawed the ground in front of me, and there appeared an iron scepter.

"The one who wields the iron scepter is one of the favored ones," the voice said.

Yes, that sounds right. Avi told me about Lukas and the iron scepter.

The moment my eyes fell on the scepter, a craving appeared in my soul, though for what—power? vindication? significance?—I didn't know.

The iron scepter wasn't large, so I assumed it couldn't have weighed more than ten or fifteen pounds. A child could have lifted it, I reasoned.

Yet I could not. It wouldn't budge. No matter how hard I strained or pulled, the iron scepter remained stuck firmly on the ground. I sat back, confused and embarrassed.

The man bent down and lifted the iron scepter with ease. He hurled it at the wall behind him, smashing through the stone wall as if it were pottery. He and the goat climbed through the opening.

Just like that, I was alone with my thoughts in the darkness. Despair and hopelessness knocked at the door of my soul.

Am I nothing?

I tried to remember what I'd been told. I turned to find Avi so I could ask him why he told me I had power when I didn't, but I couldn't find him. Somehow, I'd traveled too far into the cave. I was completely disoriented.

I laid down on the hard ground and tried to go to sleep. I was desperate to escape from the nightmare I was slipping into, but sleep wouldn't come.

CHAPTER 17

Darkness remained. If I slept, I didn't know it. It was impossible to tell if any time had passed at all, and I didn't feel rested.

"Avi!" I cried out. There was no response. I tried again and again. Still nothing. I laid back down and closed my eyes.

CHAPTER 18

When I opened my eyes, I saw nothing but darkness. Full of doubts about myself, my worthiness, and this strange journey I was on, I called out for Avi again, but my cry for help was met with silence.

When will morning come?

I groped around the ground with my hands. Everywhere and on every side was cold, hard, unspeaking rock. Seeing no other option, I stepped into the opening the man had made with the scepter.

Once in the new room, the darkness felt stronger.

This was a mistake!

I turned to walk back through the opening . . . and walked straight into a rock wall. Turning back to face the room, I somehow saw another doorway in the darkness, but it was about ten feet in front of me on the opposite wall.

That couldn't be the door I came in, could it?

Using my hands, I felt along the wall on my left. The wall guided me in an arc around the oval room to the only doorway in the room.

This must be the way back.

I walked through the opening into another dark space. Feeling my way around the walls, it felt like I entered an oval space exactly like the one I just left, but this one somehow also only had a single opening. It was to my right.

With no other choice, I went through the opening.

With each chamber I entered, I became more confused. I was

lost in utter darkness, and no matter how many times I called out for Avi, he never responded.

In one chamber, I stopped to listen and thought I heard voices, but they were gone when I went through the next opening. Sometimes the openings went left, sometimes right, and sometimes straight ahead. For a while, I hustled through opening after opening wanting to believe I was making progress. But eventually, futility overcame hope, and I slowed to a walk. When I grew tired, I sat down. When I tired of sitting, I got up and tried again. Sometimes I felt exhausted and laid down and closed my eyes to try to get a few minutes of sleep.

No matter whether I sat or walked, I couldn't escape my thoughts.

I was better off in the Quarry. Why did I ever leave? Why did I steal back my scroll? Why did I lie to Avi? I'm just a troublemaker. This is what I deserve.

Then, after I stepped into the eighteenth or eightieth or eight hundredth chamber—I don't know—I heard hooves clomping in the chamber ahead. I raced forward. There in front of me was the goat. Inexplicably, he was easy to see despite the darkness. He didn't illuminate the room, but he was clearly visible. Behind him was the man with the intense blue eyes.

"You look lost," came his condescending voice, which I realized was emanating from the goat and not the man.

"Please! Help me get out of here," I begged. "I'm ready to go back to Avi."

"Fool," said the goat. "Avi left a long time ago. It became obvious that he was mistaken about you."

"Why are you doing this to me?"

"What am I doing, except the kindest thing of all: telling you the truth? You think you are like Avi, but the sooner you realize he has something you'll never have, the better. There's nothing more dangerous than deception, and the worst kind of deception is self-deception. I'm doing you a favor. Who do you think made all these holes for you? If it wasn't for me, you'd still be trapped in the cave. If you weren't such a troublemaker, you'd be more grateful."

Instinctively I replied, "I'm sorry. Please help me get out of here."

"Where are you trying to go?" the goat asked in a probing tone.

"Julat. Have you heard of it?"

The goat paused. The man looked down and said, "Julat? Could it work?"

"It's dangerous," said the goat. "But, yes, it could work."

Turning back to me, the goat asked, "Do you know anything about Julat?"

"No."

"It's a much fancier place than Lithown. The people are successful, beautiful, and powerful. It's one of the more important cities in northern Sebi, so you certainly won't fit in as you are. Was that poor excuse for a tailor, Avi, going to sew you a new set of clothes?"

"I don't know. I assumed people in Julat would be dressed like I am."

The goat laughed scornfully. "They don't wear the rags you're wearing. But don't worry, I have something that can help. It's a treasure of great value. With it, your self-confidence will grow. And nothing is more important for success in Julat than self-confidence."

"What's the treasure?"

"You have to find out for yourself. The test of your worthiness will be whether you can find it. If you can, then you'll have rightly earned it. If I just give it to you, it would have no real value, would it?"

"Where do I find this treasure?"

The goat pawed the ground again. At his feet appeared a scroll. The man's piercing blue eyes flashed as he picked it up.

"I have a map that will lead you to it, if you are smart enough to figure it out and diligent enough to follow it."

"Please, I'd like to try," I said as I reached out my hand for the scroll.

"Hold on," said the goat. "A map of this value is not free. It'll cost you something."

"What?"

"Well, what can you offer?"

"I don't have anything," I said. "Other than the clothes on my back." And then, desperate for something of value to offer to him, I continued, "Oh, and my bird Rohka, except he doesn't seem to hang out with me much."

At the mention of Rohka, the man appeared to involuntarily shudder, but nothing I said had any noticeable effect on the goat, who continued to talk.

"That's too bad. My normal price is a scroll. I'm a collector of scrolls. I only give up a scroll if I get another to replace it."

Instinctively I reached my hand toward my pocket, but when the goat's eyes followed, I stopped short. Something didn't feel right.

After all I went through to get this scroll, should I give it away so easily?

"If the treasure is so valuable, why don't you get it yourself?" I asked.

At this, the man laughed aloud joylessly. The goat, however, simply replied, "Son, I have an endless supply of that treasure in particular. Though it would be of inestimable value for you, scrolls are what I collect. I'm willing to make a trade for the scroll you have in your pocket."

"I think I'd rather keep my scroll and take my chances in Julat without the treasure," I said, sounding more confident than I really was.

"Since I know you wouldn't last very long in Julat without the treasure, it wouldn't be right for me to take you there, would it?" said the goat. "You'll have to find your own way."

With that, he rammed into the wall behind him, creating a new opening through which he and the man disappeared. As they left, the goat called back, "If you change your mind, leave your scroll in the chamber, and I'll help you get to Julat."

"Wait! Please don't leave me here." I raced after them, but they weren't in the next chamber. Only darkness.

Hopelessness returned. I lay down, alone again with my thoughts.

What a fool I am!

One more time, I cried out for Avi.

I can't understand why he let this happen to me. I know I lied to him, but why doesn't he come help me?

No response.

What choice do I have left?

Sure of my newly resolved decision, I called out, "Here it is!" I laid my scroll gently on the ground, stood up, and walked through the opening in front of me.

I waited. Nothing happened.

Maybe the scroll needs to be in this chamber.

I tried to go back the way I came, but a wall of solid rock barred my way. The only opening in the room was on the opposite wall, just like it had been before. Sensing trouble, I ran through the opening into the next room, but it was utterly empty, except for another opening on the right-hand wall.

"No!" I screamed. My scroll was gone. The truth dawned on me. Even if I had given them the scroll when they asked, they would've left me trapped. I'd been deceived.

Bitter regret swept over me.

Why didn't I see what they were up to? The man's negative reaction when I mentioned Rohka should have been a clue.

Wait a minute . . . Why did the man react poorly when I mentioned Rohka? The goat tried to ignore it, but the man couldn't help himself. Avi's name didn't make him shutter, Rohka's did. That's it! The conversation about Avi was another deception. The goat doesn't want me to realize that my power comes from Rohka.

"Rohka," I called out. "Rohka, come help me. Please, if you can hear me, come help me. Come find me."

There was no response. I sank to my knees in despair.

As I did so, my left knee crunched down on something that wasn't stone. Leaping up, I searched the ground with my hands until they latched onto something.

It was a scroll, and as soon as I touched it, I knew it was mine. I longed to run my fingers over the letters once again, so I opened it. What I saw in the scroll, however, surprised me.

Instead of dark letters, I saw bright ones aglow in the darkness. They appeared lit from within the scroll itself. They didn't provide much light, but the surrounding darkness couldn't overcome the letters' light.

The strange markings were mesmerizing. I waited for them to rearrange themselves in my mind so I could read them again. But something was different as I examined them. The large, ornate first character was different than it was the last time I opened my scroll with Avi. And there was less writing than before.

Is this a different scroll? No, it can't be. It opened for me, didn't it? What's this new story? If only Avi were here to help me read this.

But Avi wasn't with me. I kept running my fingers over the letters, wishing against hope that I could read them. As my fingers caressed the letters, almost involuntarily I cried out, "If this is a message to me, I can't read it. Please, I need help."

What if I could remember the word Avi taught me to say when he helped me read? Come on, think! What was it again? Ginovar? No. Gintana? No. Ginosha? No. Ginoskete? . . . Ginoskete! That's it!

"Ginoskete," I said aloud.

The words on the scroll began to rearrange in my mind.

CHAPTER 19

S ometime after Peytos was selected to be the captain of the king's royal guard, he became disillusioned. Inexplicably, Gaon remained the king's captain, and Peytos struggled to eke out an existence.

From time to time, gifts arrived from the king providing Peytos with money to cover his expenses, although not much more. One day Peytos said to himself, "What if the king decides not to replace Gaon? If he was going to do it, he would have done it by now. And what if he stops sending me money? What will I do then? I can't wait for someone else to make my life happen. I have to take matters into my own hands."

Leaving his wife in charge of his duties in the village, Peytos set out to find work outside of Tikto. Traveling to the distant village of Yatza near the border of Sebi, Peytos procured a job in the local mining community. The owner of the mines, a man named Nun, took a liking to Peytos and placed him in the lucrative role of raider. As a raider, Peytos was responsible for disrupting shipments of various metals or stone coming from competitors' mines in the region of Yatza.

Peytos' experience as a hunter enabled him to excel. He quickly became the leader of his band of marauders, and his cohort became Nun's favorite and most trusted.

One day Nun assigned Peytos and his group the task of disrupting a large shipment of iron, copper, and stone from the mine of Nun's most hated rival. The shipment needed to be delayed at least one week. Peytos placed a trap on the suspected route.

As the shipment approached, the first scout returned from his post with highly unusual and frightening news: the shipment was being guarded by the soldiers of the king himself! Peytos realized that something valuable to the king must be on that shipment.

"If we are caught, we could be tried for treason," the men argued.

But Peytos overruled them. "This is our assignment. We cannot go back to Nun and ask for another."

The raiders succeeded in delaying the shipment six days, but on the last day, as the shipment neared the capital city, all of Peytos' men were captured. As they were transported to the capital, the men colluded together to blame Peytos for their actions, hoping to escape punishment.

When Peytos discovered their betrayal, he was distraught. He knew it wouldn't be long before his identity became known to his captors, the whole city, and—worst of all—the king.

"The king has ordered the leader to appear before him," came word from the royal steward. "The rest of the men are to be set free."

As soon as Peytos was ushered in to see the king, he fell on his knees, "I am so sorry. I should not have gone to Yatza. I have caused you great trouble."

"Indeed," said the king. But then he continued, "Peytos, do you know what was on that shipment that caused me to send my soldiers to protect it?"

"No, sire."

"This." The king held up a sack of gold. "This was on that shipment, bound for the palace, and then from the palace to Tikto to help an instructor of young men with his financial obligations until he can come to the palace to take up his role as captain of my guard. The iron ore, copper, and stone were all important, but this had to be safeguarded by my soldiers to ensure it reached its proper destination."

The king handed the gold to Peytos. "Here is the shipment that you were working so hard to delay. Use it to provide for you and your wife until I summon you for service as the captain of my guard. Though the call lingers, wait for it. It will not delay long," said the king gently.

"In mercy, I have chosen you for this assignment, so do not lose heart. Though you do not yet know me well, I know you. There is a reason you were named Peytos. It is because you are 'beloved.' Never forget this."

CHAPTER 20

"Y ou are beloved." I didn't so much as read those words as hear them.

And I felt them, though in truth it might have been the earth quaking that I felt. Not beneath me, but far above me. Fifty feet or so above my head, the cave roof split and a shaft of light broke into the chamber in which I was sitting. Down through the shaft of light came Rohka. Tears filled my eyes, and I sobbed with relief and gratitude.

I had no idea I'd descended so far. The openings I went through must have taken me farther and farther into the bowels of the earth.

Rohka descended, stopping on a ledge just above my head. Seeing him filled me with strength and hope. I scaled the wall of the chamber to meet him on the ledge. He chirped loudly.

"I'm glad to see you too." I desperately wanted to hug him. "How can I ever thank you?"

Rohka fluttered up to another ledge, and I climbed after him. On this ledge was a thick wooden door with ancient iron hinges. I pushed on it, but it didn't budge. Rohka jumped up onto my shoulder.

"Ischuro," I called, suddenly remembering the word. Power welled up within me. Placing both hands on the door, I shoved with all my might. "Ischuro," I yelled. A shimmering stream of force rushed from my mouth as if I was going to blow the door open with a mighty breath. The door resisted for a moment, but then it yielded. It swung, gaining momentum until it smashed against a stone wall in the adjoining room.

This new, large, expansive chamber also had shafts of light shining into it from the cracked earthen roof above. It also had stairs, but the goat and the man stood in front of them. The man looked furious; the goat burned with hatred.

The man effortlessly hoisted a large boulder and hurled it in my direction. Without hesitation, I called out, "Thureos!" Down through one of the cracks in the ceiling fell my light shield, but it was clear it wouldn't arrive in time. I leapt to the left.

Landing on my feet, I reached out to grab my shield. Just then the goat screamed, "Troublemaker! Liar! Fraud!" followed by a high-pitched torrent of words unknown to me.

The words felt like spears in my brain; pain shot through my head. My shield fell harmlessly by my side as I covered my ears to block the sound. I'd never heard a sound like that before, nor felt such pain. I clutched and grasped at my head, trying to rip the sound out, but it was no use. The pain was excruciating.

I tried screaming at the top of my lungs, hoping to block the incoming sound, but to no avail. I couldn't keep the goat's voice out of my head.

"Fraud! You're powerless! You're nothing more than a liar and a deceiver! Avi left you behind—that's why he's not here! Coward! Filthy, vile, lying, worthless coward. Did you act honorably in abandoning your friends in Lithown?"

I tumbled to the ground. "Stop. Stop. Please stop," I wailed as the accusations burrowed down into my mind. It felt like they were nesting deep inside my consciousness.

The goat continued to scream.

"Emma is a healer; Avi is a teacher; what value do you bring? If you hadn't deceived Avi he'd still be in Lithown where he belongs. You're a plague! You're worthless—less than worthless! Everyone would be better off if you were dead!"

Amid the chaos and confusion, I registered Rohka digging his claws into my shoulder. I heard my voice cry out, "Cobaqeren."

As I spoke, I convulsed violently, collapsed to the ground, and vomited uncontrollably. The pain in my head intensified as the goat's accusations continued to assault me, overthrowing my thoughts and filling me with self-loathing.

Suddenly, a glowing light thudded on the ground inches from me. Instinctively, I reached out my hand to grab it. My fingers wrapped around something solid, and I pulled it towards my prostrate head, which felt ready to explode. The object—a helmet—slid down over my head.

"Beloved."

The word echoed in my ears.

"Beloved."

The knives withdrew from my mind.

"Beloved."

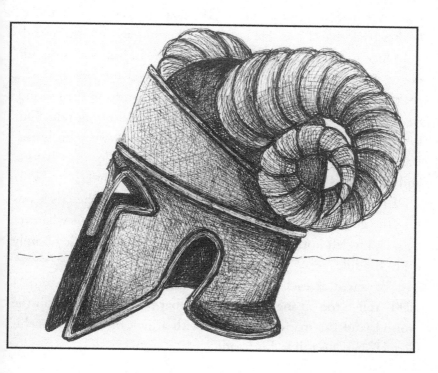

Quietness swept over me. Relief washed like water from my head down through my chest and into my arms and legs. If the goat was still screaming, I could no longer hear it.

Pulling myself up to my hands and knees, my eyes opened to see the enraged goat charging me at ramming speed. He was only a few feet from me, his head lowered and aimed at my side. I torqued my body to escape the blow but doing so threw my head into the path of attack. The front of his head met the side of mine. The sound was like a thunderclap. The impact wrenched my head, as if I'd been punched, but there was no pain. The goat staggered from the blow. Reaching my hand to my helmet to check for damage, I discovered horns like those of a ram. The goat backed up a few paces and charged again. Instinctively I lowered my head, leaned in, and braced for the collision. The clash of horns echoed throughout the chamber. My feet slid back from the force of his attack, but there was no jarring to my head. The goat, however, was knocked farther back than I was. He howled, either in pain or rage or both.

Once more, he charged. But my fear had given way to confidence. Crouching low to the ground, I braced my feet against a rock behind me, supporting myself with my hands on the ground. As he neared, I launched myself at him like a battering ram. Our heads aligned completely. I hit him dead center between his horns. Ram horns met goat horns. The collision was louder than before, and different. Instead of thunder, I heard a sickening crack.

I reached up to feel my helmet, though I knew the crack was his. The goat moved his lips, but my helmet filtered out whatever he said. His left horn was shattered. One large piece dangled limply off to the side.

We stared at each other for a moment and then he said, "I yield. You're too strong for me." The goat tapped his hoof on the ground, and the man walked over with a look of disbelief on his face. He had a scroll in his hand.

"If you'll let us leave, I'll give you the map to the treasure."

"Open it, so I know it's not a trick," I ordered. I had no idea what kind of trick I thought I might sniff out, but I felt triumphant, glorying in my newly won power and authority.

The man unrolled the scroll and showed it to me. I had no idea what I was looking for, but it had some writing on it, so I guessed that everything was on the up-and-up.

"Deal," I said.

The man, looking incredulous, handed the scroll to me.

"Thank you. You're free to go," I said, trying to sound authoritative, but my voice trembled and cracked.

The goat and the man walked across the room and climbed up the stairs. Just as they reached the top, I whispered, "Ischuro," blowing a wave of force at the man. It was just enough that he hit the edge of the arched doorway as he exited. Rohka chirped at me.

"What?" I said, laughing out loud in relief. "Come on, he deserved it and you know it."

I think Rohka actually rolled his eyes.

Fluttering off my shoulder, Rohka began to flit his way up the stairs. It was time to go. I slid the new scroll in my pocket alongside my old scroll. My shield disappeared. My new helmet was gone as well.

A broad smile spread across my face as I followed Rohka up the stairs. For the first time since I'd awoken, my mind felt settled, no longer churning with doubt.

PART 4: JULAT

CHAPTER 21

The doorway at the top of the stairs opened into a long, ascending path out of the cave. As far as I could tell, the goat and the man were long gone. The path was probably a few hundred yards long, and there was light at the end of it.

Emerging from the path, I felt reborn, as if the earth was giving birth to me. The daylight was blinding, but when my eyes finally adjusted, I noticed that I must've traveled some distance underground. The landscape was radically different. Lush, rich green dominated my vision: green trees, green grass, and green mountains. The terrain was still hilly, but not hardscrabble. The stony path I traversed meandered casually through the soft hills. Whereas the valleys near Lithown felt dangerous, these were inviting, but only visually. The surroundings were strangely silent with no discernable ambient noise at all.

"Hey, Rohka. How come you don't talk? The goat could talk, so why can't you?"

Rohka chirped.

"That's what I mean. Now would be a good time for you to say something like: 'Hello, Rom, my name is Rohka. I like to eat seeds. Sometimes I wish I was an eagle.'

"If you could talk to me, I could ask you questions like, 'Where are we going?' And 'Any idea what happened to Avi?' And, of course, 'How in the world did I get that helmet and the shield, and is there any chance I could get a bow and arrow or something like that?'

"Then you could say: 'Well, Rom, we're going to Julat. It won't be much longer. You don't need Avi anymore. You've proved yourself to be such a mighty warrior that you've earned the sword of power. Congratulations. I'm lucky to get to hang out with someone like you.'"

Rohka didn't seem to pay any attention to me.

"Maybe I could teach you to talk. What do you say, Rohka? Do you want to learn to talk?"

Nothing.

"Come on. To say yes, chirp once. To say no, chirp twice. Can you handle that?"

Chirp.

Chirp.

Chirp.

We walked on in silence. Up ahead I saw the outlines of a city, one that was much larger than Lithown.

"Is that city where we're going?"

Chirp.

"Is it Julat?"

Chirp.

"Rohka, are you actually answering my questions?"

Chirp. Chirp.

Crazy bird.

He flew up onto my shoulder, and we walked along the stone path together.

From afar the city loomed large. The closer we came, the more massive it appeared. It was probably four times as big as Lithown, if not more. Its gates were enormous, and the city within buzzed with energy, which was quite a contrast to the silent landscape we'd just walked through. I nervously watched Rohka on my shoulder as we approached the gates, but he didn't go anywhere this time. Two men and two women, smartly dressed as soldiers, were standing guard. At their sides were sheathed swords; their faces were stern and serious. Standing in front of the city gates, chatting between themselves, were two beautifully attired women. One was wearing a red, mid-calf length sheath dress; the other a similar style of dress in deep purple.

Before I could get close enough to engage them in conversation, someone came running out of the city gate, down the path directly toward me.

"Rom, Rom," he yelled. "It's you! You made it!"

It was Avi, beaming broadly.

"Every day for the past three months, I've checked in at the city gates wondering if you'd arrive."

"Wait . . . three months?" I said in disbelief.

"Yes. You've been gone a long time. What happened?"

I started to recount my adventures in the cave, but the shock of being gone for so long made it difficult for me to string together a coherent story.

"Come in, come in. We can talk more inside. Let me show you around Julat."

The beautifully dressed women seemed to recognize Avi. He commented that they were the prettiest sights to see in Julat. Both their faces registered casual acceptance of the praise, as if Avi was simply acknowledging what everyone should know to be true.

Avi playfully saluted the guards at the gate.

"I told you he'd come," Avi announced, as the guards waved us through, their faces showing no interest whatsoever.

"Guess who else is here?" he said as we walked into the city.

"Who?"

"Emma. When I couldn't find you in the cave, I first thought maybe you'd gone back to Lithown. I guessed that Rohka had led you back there to see if those we'd left behind were in trouble for helping us." Shame crept into my heart.

"In Lithown, I discovered that Emma was shunned for her relationship with you, so I convinced her to escape with me. She's quite a remarkable woman. I don't know that I'd fully seen that before. When I didn't find you back at Lithown, I thought maybe you set out for Julat on your own. When I got here and you weren't here, I didn't know what else to do except wait and hope. I must admit, I was beginning to believe you'd been lost or killed. I'm so glad you made it!"

I wanted to ask about Esah, Domi, and Rabah but was afraid of the answer.

As we entered the city, I noticed three soldiers corralling a disheveled-looking man with a noticeable limp who had been sitting just inside the gate perhaps begging for money. They appeared to be expelling him from the city. For a brief moment, our gazes met before he dropped his face in shame and disgrace.

Whatever you do, I thought, *do not fail.*

CHAPTER 22

Entering Julat was like entering another world. The main street bisected the center of the city and connected many side streets. Houses lined every street on both sides. And what houses they were! Mansions would be a better description. Whereas every house in Lithown looked pretty much the same, every house in Julat was unique. The exteriors were made of red brick, granite, marble, limestone, fieldstone, and other materials I couldn't identify. There were porticoes, pavilions, gated entryways, manicured gardens, fountains, porches, and more.

The center of the city was comprised of market stalls, public pools, and green space. The buzz of gossip filled the air. Although it felt vaguely familiar to me, like I'd been there before, it also felt strange. Multiple feasts were being held throughout the city at various houses. In full view of passersby, people were stationed around tables piled high with sumptuous food, but the food was mostly untouched. Loud talking with exaggerated gestures dominated the dinner parties as guests seemed far more preoccupied with what was going on around them than the food in front of them. The aura wasn't one of relaxation or joy, but of social climbing.

The most shocking contrast with Lithown was people's appearances. Julatians, on average, were tall. Most reached a height of probably six and half or seven feet. I was easily among the shortest. Everyone I saw looked athletic. The women had beautiful complexions, stunning eyes, and long, shimmering, jet-black hair. Some women wore their hair impossibly straight, like waterfalls of onyx cascading down their backs; others had thick, ringlet curls that hung like ornate velvet curtains round their necks and shoulders. The men oozed success and power: chiseled faces, winning smiles, immaculately coiffed thick black hair. Jewelry was everywhere. Gold bands encircled men's arms and women's necks. It was as if they were a different species than the people of Lithown.

While both Avi and I wore plain brown scrubs, the people of Julat were arrayed in royal splendor: reds, blues, purples, greens, and yellows; flowing dresses on the women, elaborate embroidered robes on the men. I hadn't been in the city long before I came to understand what the goat meant about not fitting in.

"Not everything is quite so palatial," Avi said as we arrived in a more modest section of town. "This is where I've stayed for the past three months. Emma isn't far from here. We should go visit her soon, but why don't you come in to clean up and rest first."

Avi's house was humble indeed, and he wasn't one for decorations. He had an extra mat, which he gave me to use.

"Avi, who are these people?"

"Julatians, with their physical advantages, are among the most successful people in all of Sebi. Everything here is about excellence, and I haven't found much that they don't excel at."

"I saw some of them eating. Do they need to eat?"

"No more than you and I," answered Avi. "From what I can tell, they eat because they can, not because they have to. Julatians love a good feast. They spend hours talking and debating, amid large quantities of food."

"Does it intimidate you to be around them?"

"Well, I wouldn't mind having what they have, if that's what you mean. Who wouldn't want to look like they do or have houses like most of them have? I sometimes wonder what might've happened if I'd taken a different path—if I'd ended up here rather than Lithown. Or even if I'd been born here. But a different path was chosen for me."

He grew thoughtful.

"Still, it's important to remember that things aren't always what they seem on the outside. I believe the people of Julat will spur you on toward greater things. Tomorrow, we'll find Ataymah, the powerful warrior I told you about. What do you think?"

I was intrigued at the prospect of meeting this great warrior Avi admired. My heart mulled over all the possibilities for me in Julat as I drifted off to sleep that night.

CHAPTER 23

Early the next morning Avi and I left his home and walked north down the main street. Rohka rode on my shoulder.

"Would it be all right if we stopped by to see Emma?" Avi asked, blushing slightly. "I promised I'd bring you to see her, and I don't want to disappoint her."

"That's fine."

Emma was staying closer to the main street, not far from Avi's house. It was good to see her again. When I probed about what happened at Lithown after I left, all she said was, "Those people have no class. No class at all. I'll leave it at that."

She turned to Avi. "Are we ready to go?"

Avi quickly turned toward me. "I invited Emma to go with us. I hope that's okay."

When we arrived at the city center, we came upon a large assembly gathered around a man giving a speech. Avi pushed his way forward so we could see what was going on. Many let us pass, seeing how short we were. Finally, the last row of large bodies parted like a curtain, and we stepped through. There before us was a breathtaking creature, which looked like a winged lion. He had a thick golden mane, emerald green eyes, and powerful wings, like those of an eagle, protruding majestically from just behind his shoulders.

Seated atop the winged lion was a man more handsome than any I'd seen in Julat. He had long, immaculately styled, light brown hair with bright green eyes. He wore a majestic purple cape over top of a silky, canary yellow shirt and a matching pair of pants. His clothes billowed in the wind and shimmered in the dim sunlight.

When he spoke, it sounded like he was singing, and he waved his hands dramatically with every phrase. Yet most arresting of all was the fact that his face glistened in a beautiful, but unnatural way.

"My friends, Ataymah here would have you think that we simply walked up to the fortress and defeated the horde of kunoi by accident," the beautiful man said, gesturing toward a tall man standing next to him. "Don't believe it! This plunder is hard won. Ataymah is a warrior without peer. Never have I seen such courage. Never have I seen such skill. Even Ramdon the Terrible couldn't stand against him."

Ataymah. He's the one we came to see. Stealing a glance at him, I was awed by his appearance. He was imposingly tall—almost as tall as the man atop the winged lion. He wore black, lightly armored battle gear and had short, neatly trimmed jet-black hair. He held a helmet in one hand and petted the head of a large black dog with the other. His face was friendly, his eyes youthful and energetic.

"Peris," Ataymah replied, "You're exaggerating. We were a team. You were just as responsible for our victory, and great as it was, there were not hordes of kunoi, just a handful."

Ataymah's voice was rich and powerful, yet warm and familiar. It wrapped itself around me like a blanket, as if I'd been hearing his voice all my life.

"Nonsense, Ataymah. You're too humble. The kunoi were quite a handful. Almost too much for us. It was a fearsome battle, but our bravery and excellence won the day. Let's not be afraid to say so. If we don't tell of our deeds, how will these fine people know what we've done? Our friends will think these riches grow on trees, and the Council will think that any warrior could go and collect them."

Motioning toward a wooden chest off to his right and a couple of guards nearby, Peris said, "Take these riches to the Council and tell them that Ataymah and Peris risked their lives for the coffers of

Julat." With a wink and smile he added, "And tell them that anyone who attains such plunder should be publicly honored."

At that moment, the glimmer on his face intensified and grew even more mesmerizing.

"The rest of you," Peris continued, "should know there are more riches to be had. We brought back only a small portion of the available treasure. Come back with us, and we can win the rest for ourselves. Who's with me?"

"If we come with you, can we keep some of the treasure for ourselves?" someone in the crowd asked.

"Yes, of course! The Council requires their portion, but I can promise that your share will be plenty. You deserve to be rich. Many of you have been to my house. Don't I serve some of the greatest feasts among us? If there's anything I know, it's treasure. Come and take for yourself that which you so clearly deserve."

"Peris, you might be overselling this," said Ataymah good naturedly.

"Don't be so droll, Ataymah. These people are like beautiful sheep. They just need a leader to guide them. No one wants to follow someone without the promise of great reward. Besides, when have I ever promised something and not delivered?"

Peris' face shimmered brightly in the pale ambient light.

"Will there be any more kunoi?" someone shouted from the back.

"We defeated those we faced last time. If any others show their mangy faces, Ataymah and I will be there to protect you. Aren't the people of Julat blessed? What bad can happen to you with us on your side? But if any of you are afraid to go, by all means, stay here. More treasure for the rest of us."

The last words sent a pulse of urgency through the crowd, as if the light shimmering from Peris' face lit a fire in them. People volunteered immediately lest they miss out. I tore my eyes from Peris' beauty to look at Avi and Emma.

"What do you think? Free treasure sounds pretty appealing to me."

"It might not be a bad idea to go," Avi offered. "After all, it would give you a chance to spend time with Ataymah and see him in action."

"But what about the kunoi?" Emma protested. "They're not as feckless as Peris says."

"What's a kunoi?" I interjected.

"It's actually 'kuno' in the singular and 'kunoi' in the plural, but they're usually referred to in the plural since they hunt in packs," Avi clarified. "But let's see. How would I describe kunoi? First off, they're like human dogs. They have hands and feet and can stand upright, but also possess the strength, speed, and ferocity of a wild animal. There are varying degrees of kunoi. In their least dangerous form, a pack of kunoi would probably leave a group of treasure hunters alone. If the kunoi were inclined to attack, they'd wait for one or two of us to get separated from the main group. These less vicious kunoi can sometimes even be domesticated to the point of serving humans. However, in their more vicious form—"

Peris' voice interrupted Avi, "So who's with us? We leave today at noon from this very spot. If you're not here, you'll be left behind, and your riches will go to another."

The crowd dispersed. Avi said, "I'll tell you more about the kunoi later. Right now, we need to decide if we're going along. If we are, I need to run back and get a few things before we go."

"It's not for me," said Emma. "I get the sense Julatian men think women have little to offer on such expeditions. As for you, Rom, I worry about someone so young going. But if Avi is with you, I'm sure you'll be safe."

"Sounds like a chance to prove myself," I declared. "I've made it through some pretty tough stuff already."

"Then it's settled. I'll go get my stuff," Avi said as he took off for his house.

"Wait, Avi, I'll come with you," Emma called out. "I want to give you something for the journey."

She held the backside of her hand against my cheek. "Be careful, Rom. Always stay with Avi."

After they left, I sat down on the ground to wait for Avi to return. A few Julatian men were standing nearby. Towering over me, one of them said, "Are you going with us, little man?"

It sounded jeering, but I couldn't be sure.

"I was thinking about it. Is that okay?"

"Sure, sure," he laughed. "It looks like you could use a few pieces of gold or a nice jewel. Would you like to see what I won on my first trip out?"

He sat on the ground next to me. Pulling a necklace from underneath his shirt, he showed me a beautiful emerald fastened to the end of a chain. The other Julatian men wanted to see it, and soon they were showing off their own jewels and gold, each with a story of how they got them. After a while it became a contest, as each tried to outdo the last.

As they talked, I was conscious of the fact that I possessed nothing of value to show them, which reminded me of the scroll I won from the goat.

Slowly, I rose from my spot and drifted away from the group. Reaching into my pocket, I unrolled the goat's scroll. It felt different in my hand than my scroll, and it wasn't written in the language of Sebi. Every word was crystal clear to me:

To locate the treasure of Jamish, travel to the City of Trees in the Plains of Orech. Hidden within the fortress lies the Red Tunnel. Follow the tunnel until it ends. When everyone goes right, go left. Ascend the incline. The Cavern of Contest is to

the east, though only one who surpasses them all may enter. Be forewarned, it is easier to find Jamish's treasure than to win it. Yet the one who wins Jamish's treasure will be second-to-none.

I reread it, then put it away. The names in the scroll were foreign to me, nonetheless, excitement gripped my soul. The Julatians could tell their stories, but if I could find Jamish's treasure, perhaps I'd be better than all of them.

Avi's return interrupted my thoughts. It was time to depart.

CHAPTER 24

About twenty-five of us gathered around Peris and Ataymah. After a few derisive comments about those who didn't join the expedition, Peris explained that we'd be traveling south from Julat, mostly by river, until we arrived at the fortress.

Peris took the lead, gaudily astride his sauntering winged lion. Ataymah was next, his dog marching smartly beside him. The Julatians who followed behind were by all appearances an impressive crew. Avi and I brought up the rear.

As we left, Rohka flew down and landed on my shoulder. "Glad you decided to come," I said. Rohka's on-time arrival transformed Avi's expression from serious to happy. His presence brought Avi a sense of peace.

"Have you ever heard of the Plains of Orech?" I eagerly asked Avi.

"I'm familiar with lots of places, but I don't think I've ever heard of Orech. Why?"

Feeling leery of talking to Avi about the scroll, I decided not to mention it. Instead I said, "I overheard a discussion and wondered where the name came from."

"Really? What was the context of the discussion?"

"Umm . . . I think maybe they mentioned something about traveling near them. Or something like that."

"Who was it? We could ask them if they're here."

"I'm not sure they ended up coming with us, actually. You know, I have a hard time making out the differences between Julatians. They all look so similar."

"Maybe Ataymah or Peris knows about the Plains of Orech," Avi suggested. "I was hoping for the chance to meet Ataymah. Let's go and ask him."

I was anxious to know where the Plains of Orech were, so I nervously made my way with Avi to the front of the group. Most of the Julatians we passed talked about how they planned to spend the plunder that Peris promised.

"Excuse me," Avi said, addressing Ataymah. "My name is Avi, and this is my friend Rom. We're wondering if we can ask you a question."

Ataymah inclined his head toward us as he walked. "That's a beautiful bird you have, Rom. Where'd you get him?"

"He found me, sir," I replied. Just then Ataymah's dog barked, and Rohka chirped loudly in return. It was as if the two were talking to each other.

"So, what's your question?" Ataymah asked.

"Have you ever heard of the Plains of Orech?"

"The Plains of Orech? Now that is a name I haven't heard in a long time. Where did you come across it?"

"Rom overheard someone in Julat talking about them. When he asked me, I suggested we ask you."

Ataymah registered surprise. "Someone in Julat mentioned the Plains of Orech? Who?"

He looked hard at me.

"I don't know his name, sir."

Incredulous, Ataymah called out to the group and asked if anyone knew of the Plains of Orech. No one had heard of them. Annoyingly, Ataymah's question focused everyone's attention on us. They all awaited an explanation.

"As fate would have it, we'll pass close by the Plains of Orech on this journey, although they haven't been called that for hundreds of years. Only the oldest scrolls that I have use that name.

The Plains of Orech surround the fortress of Liga, the very fortress to which we're headed right now."

"And what about the City of Trees?" I interjected, throwing caution to the wind. My question prompted a quizzical glance from Avi, and I suspected he knew I was hiding something, but my desire to find Jamish's treasure finally overrode any inhibitions about someone else finding out about the treasure scroll.

"The City of Trees is the ancient name for the city of Liga, which gave its name to the fortress. But no one has called it the City of Trees for hundreds of years. How did you come to hear these names again?"

"I thought I overheard someone use the terms while we were waiting to go. But that person didn't come with us," I said quickly.

"Really?" said Ataymah. "That would be shocking if true." But then he added, "I suppose it's possible. I wish you'd gotten his name."

Fortunately, at that moment, Avi chose to jump in with some other questions for him. Relieved, I drifted toward the back of the group.

So we'll be right there at the City of Trees in the Plains of Orech. How can I get away from the group to go exploring? Should I tell Avi?

While I was fixated on finding Jamish's treasure, a sinking feeling crept into my heart. *What if the plunder we're searching for is actually Jamish's treasure?*

After walking for a while, we came upon a narrow river racing south. The party boarded a large floating wooden platform docked along the riverbank. Setting off from shore, the current carried us briskly down the river.

The river journey was uneventful, except for the discussion about what to eat for dinner. The Julatians expected to eat a feast, but Ataymah seemed surprised anyone could think about food at such a time. Peris bragged about having brought food, but he only had enough to feed himself.

At some point we docked our floating platform and made our way back west from the river, with Peris again leading the way. The Julatians continued to talk loudly among themselves, but I noticed Ataymah was quiet. He appeared more tense and focused, as did his dog, whose ears were perked up and whose head was regularly scanning the horizon. This reminded me of an unfinished conversation with Avi.

"Avi, before we left Julat, you were telling me about kunoi. Wasn't there something about more dangerous kinds of kunoi?"

Before he could answer, Ataymah's dog let out a fierce bark.

"Quiet!" Ataymah yelled. It took the Julatians a minute to realize he was talking to them. I could tell they weren't happy about it.

Ataymah bent down next to his dog to figure out what he'd seen.

Something moved in the distance.

"Friends, it's time to take out your weapons," Ataymah said calmly but soberly. "I think there's a group of kunoi in the distance."

He drew an iron scepter from his side, brandishing it in his right hand. It was a mighty weapon, with four bladed sides and a pointed spear for a head.

Who is this man that he has an iron scepter? What I wouldn't give for a weapon like that!

Even with Ataymah's warning, some Julatians acted as if it were a drill. Some dug noisily through their supplies; others ignored the call to arms altogether; the rest perfunctorily grabbed jeweled swords, handsomely crafted clubs, or bows, all of which looked fashionable but not formidable in the least.

"Avi," I whispered. "I don't have a weapon."

"Don't worry. If the time comes, call for your helmet and shield. Besides, you have Rohka with you."

Avi didn't reach into his bag for a weapon.

"Go take a look, boy," Ataymah said to his dog. The dog ran forward a hundred yards or so, barked again loudly, and came straight back.

"There's a pack of kunoi coming toward us," Ataymah informed us. "But I don't think they'll bother us. Stay armed, though, just in case."

"Come now, Ataymah, you're scaring them," said Peris. "We'll be just fine. Friends, focus your attention on the treasure we'll get. Don't worry about the kunoi. They'll leave us alone."

The kunoi did indeed come close enough for me to see the pack myself. There were eight to ten grotesque, dog-like creatures walking upright on two legs. If I was alone, I would've been scared, but because we outnumbered them three-to-one, I didn't feel threatened. Their attention was on us, and ours on them, but no more than that.

We kept journeying along our path toward the ancient fortress of Liga, trading the lush green of the river valley for barren desert. Ascending slowly, I saw the city ahead, silhouetted against a backdrop of mountains. The fortress itself was surrounded by tall trees, an oasis of green amidst a canvas of desert brown. It was strategically placed on a high mound in the center of the plains overlooking the whole region.

As we continued, the pack of kunoi swung directly behind us, although still a good distance away.

Evening fell as we neared the ancient stone fortress. Peris was first to the gate. As he approached it, his winged lion ran forward, flapping his powerful wings. Leaping upward, the lion and Peris took flight, bounding over it in one smooth, powerful motion. When we reached it, we heard Peris' melodic voice from the other side, "I've disbarred the gate. Push it open."

A few from the group leaned into the wooden door. It creaked and groaned as it yielded to their strength. Together we stepped into an enormous courtyard. The fortress was empty and, oddly, appeared to be in pristine condition.

What little ambient light we had was rapidly being snuffed out. Ataymah suggested we set up camp for the night and begin our search at dawn's first light.

It was during our preparations for the night that we heard the first snarl from outside the fortress walls. Fear shot up my spine. The first snarl was soon followed by another and then another. We all turned to Ataymah and Peris. The looks on their faces were not reassuring. Ataymah had his iron scepter raised. Even in the descending darkness, I saw tension in his brow. Peris looked frightened. Everyone waited for someone to say what we were all thinking: *Something is prowling around the city.*

Rohka flew from my shoulder toward the top of the fortress walls at the spot from which the most recent snarls came. I lost him in the darkness. Ataymah's dog ran toward the same spot. I heard him bark at the wall, which only intensified the snarls. Soon his bark was drowned out in a cacophony of animal rage.

Suddenly a burst of flame shot into the air from behind the wall, illuminating the night long enough for me to see Rohka fleeing from the fiery blast.

"Avi, what's out there?" I cried out.

It was Ataymah who answered. "They must be kunoi, but not the ones that were following us. These are hellhounds. Depending on how advanced they are, we could be in some danger."

Ataymah's voice was thick with urgency.

"Listen to me, everyone. Gather your things. If anyone has light, we need it now. At the far end of the fortress are water caverns. We might be able to hide in those. Peris, fly above that far wall and tell us how many there are."

"Hide?" came the alarmed response of a Julatian near me. "You don't think they can get in here, do you? What about these fortress walls?"

It was strange to see someone who looked so tall and powerful shaking with fear.

"Won't we be trapped in the caverns if they come after us?" asked another.

A shimmer of dim light flickered momentarily across Ataymah's face. Shockingly, he looked unsure, and it appeared that he was reconsidering.

Avi spoke up. "It's a good plan. Let's do it. Come, follow me."

Julatians pulled out their lights as we retreated, heading toward what promised to be the underground water caverns. Peris rode his winged lion full speed toward the end of the fortress away from the noise. Gliding powerfully into the air, he hovered over the far wall and started to circle the fortress toward the kunoi. Peris had a light, so it was easy to follow his movement.

"They've got ropes!" Peris called out in a panic. "They're going to climb over!"

The snarling intensified once they spotted him. Then, suddenly, Peris' light fell from the sky.

"Peris!" Ataymah yelled. "Peris!"

We heard Peris scream, but his cries were soon engulfed in snarls, which came from higher up the wall.

The kunoi were coming over.

CHAPTER 25

P ut out the lights!" someone yelled. "They'll find us easily."

"No!" Ataymah shouted in reply. "We can't hide from them in the dark. They can still smell and hear and see us. We need the light to see them!"

Some lights went out. Others were cast in the direction of the kunoi coming over the wall. People scattered everywhere.

"Come to me!" Ataymah commanded. I ran to him. Avi was there, as well as a couple of Julatians.

"Illuminatio!" said Ataymah. Light shone from his iron scepter toward the wall.

"Illuminatio!" ordered Avi, and his scroll burst into a beam of light aimed at the same spot.

What came over the wall was something much more advanced and fearsome than the kunoi we saw earlier. The moment I saw them, I knew they were the more vicious form of kunoi that Avi warned of. These kunoi, like their tamer cousins, looked like a cross between a human and a dog. Except these kunoi were severely grotesque and deformed and worked together as a pack. They stood upright as they climbed over the wall, weapons slung over their backs. Their eyes glowed a poisonous yellow in the dark.

As soon as they hit the ground, they sprinted toward us on all fours. A few kunoi remained perched atop the wall, fitting arrows to bows. Volleys of arrows soon followed.

"Get behind me," Ataymah ordered. I obeyed. Avi yelled something and most of the approaching arrows fell harmlessly to the ground. Ataymah swatted away other arrows with his iron scepter

161

as if they were small insects. Other arrows, however, found their targets. Yells rose up all around. One Julatian near us took an arrow in the leg and crumpled to the ground.

Somewhere in the chaos my mind registered a chirp from Rohka.

"Cobaqeren! Thureos!" came out of my mouth. Out of the dark night sky, two balls of light hurtled downward, attracting attention as they fell. The snarls of the kunoi nearing us intensified. I stepped out from behind Ataymah's protection, thrust my hand into the air, and caught my light shield. At the same time, I felt my helmet settle gently onto my head.

With my helmet on, the noise quieted some, and I was able to see the kunoi more clearly. Five of the advancing kunoi targeted us. As the first kuno reached us, Avi called out, "Phosphano." A blast of red light shot from his scroll, hitting the kuno squarely in the chest. The kuno thrashed about, as if fighting the red light enveloping him. Ataymah hammered the struggling kuno with his scepter before turning toward Avi to intercept the remaining four. Three accepted the engagement; one targeted me instead.

Everything else disappeared, and my world narrowed to just me and him.

The hellhound lunged at me, teeth bared. I fell backward, ducking under him. I extended my shield arm, hitting him in the chest as I crashed to the ground. The shield lifted his midsection, and together with his forward momentum, flipped him five feet behind me. He landed on his back. I rolled over. He leapt to his feet and pulled out a spiked club. I scrambled to get up.

The kuno advanced quickly, swinging his club and snapping at me with his razor-sharp teeth. The first and second time his cudgel came, I blocked it with my shield. The third time, he dove at me, swinging. My shield caught his club, but his teeth sank into my left shoulder.

Fire shot through my bones. I felt as if I was being burned from the inside out. I shouted in agony. Instinctively, I smashed my helmet into his face. He released his bite, and I stumbled backward. He lunged again, this time for my neck.

Just then I felt wind on my left cheek. An iron scepter swung just short of my face and crashed full force into the kuno. Bones cracked like an eggshell being smashed. He sank to the ground and did not rise again.

My shoulder stung like mad. Wisps of smoke rose from it, as did the smell of burnt flesh and blood. I knelt, trying to summon the strength to block out the pain and return to the fight, but it was too much.

Yet Ataymah and Avi, fighting together, made short work of the remaining three kunoi. As soon as they finished, Avi ran over to me, pulling a bottle out of his pocket. Ripping back my shirt, he poured a soothing, oily liquid on my smoldering shoulder. The pain lessened, and my shoulder softened.

"Emma gave this to me. Did he get you anywhere else?"

As he spoke, his face contorted in pain. An arrow pierced his calf. I jumped in front of him with my shield to protect him from any more arrows.

"We've got to get those archers off the wall!" Ataymah said as he bent down to yank the arrow out of Avi's leg.

Just then we heard a snarl to our left, and Ataymah turned to fight.

"Ischuro," I cried out, blowing a wave of force toward the distant archers. But they were too far away, and the wave dissipated before it reached them.

Senselessly, I took off running toward the wall.

"No!" Avi yelled.

I ignored him. My attention was focused on the four archers. As I neared, I called out, "Ischuro!" Strength pooled in my lungs even as I started panting for breath. With one great exhale, I cried "Ischuro" again, and force flew from my mouth. The kuno drew his bow. The arrow hurtled toward me as the wave accelerated toward him. Losing sight of the arrow in the dark, I raised my shield blindly over my face and chest. I heard the blocked arrow drop harmlessly to my feet.

Opening my eyes, I saw my assailant fall. The other three scampered down the wall and galloped toward me. I froze.

A bark rang out to my right. Ataymah's dog raced to intercept one of the kunoi. Rohka swooped down to engage the other. Rohka was like a hornet, darting in and out and stinging the kuno with his beak. I turned to engage the third but immediately regretted the rashness of my decision. Within seconds he was upon me, teeth bared and aimed at my jugular. I shrank down, cringing in self-defense. His jaws struck. But where my neck had been, the top of my helmet was. The horns of my helmet caught him straight between the eyes. With a sickening crack, his neck broke, and he fell dead at my feet.

Ataymah's dog and Rohka were in a standoff with the other kunoi, who were warily sizing them up. As I cautiously approached the standoff, searching for a way to help, a beam of red light wrapped itself around the first kuno. As Rohka and the dog backed away, I saw my opening, but suddenly Rohka flew into my face and the dog impeded my path. As the first kuno wrestled with the light, I saw Ataymah dispatch the second. Ataymah twirled toward the first kuno and, with one more swipe of the iron scepter, the fight was over.

* * *

The chaos gave way to an eerie calm. It was time to assess the damage.

Avi, Ataymah, and I gathered together.

165

"How's your shoulder?" Avi asked.

"It'll be okay." I felt the healing oil working. Rohka was back on my shoulder again, perching himself near the wound.

"How's your leg?" I asked Avi.

"I just need to rub some of this balm on it. It'll be fine."

"Good, I'm glad. Ataymah, you're amazing!" I gushed. "How you made short work of those kunoi was unbelievable!"

"And you, Rom," he replied, "are quite foolish. Why would you run off into the darkness by yourself?" He frowned.

Expecting praise, I was taken aback. "But I wasn't alone. Your dog and my bird helped me."

"Yes, it worked out this time, but next time it might not," he scolded harshly. "I will admit that your bravery helped, but you need to be smart," he added in a softer tone.

Avi got out his light, as did Ataymah. During our first sweep of the grounds, we found sixteen Julatians dead and two wounded. Four more of our group had managed to get inside the entrance to the water caverns and stay hidden long enough to survive. Peris, his winged lion, and three others were unaccounted for.

We also found a few dead kunoi at various locations around the fortress.

It was deep into the night, but no one could sleep. The mood was part terror, part somber resignation. Someone suggested leaving immediately, trying for home, but it wasn't practical. We agreed together that we needed to make it through the night and figure out what to do in the morning.

So, huddled in the darkness we sat, drifting in and out of sleep, while Ataymah and Avi took turns keeping guard. Rohka also stood guard, perched on a wooden post, shining in the darkness.

CHAPTER 26

The next morning, the battered and exhausted remnant discussed our options. Still shell-shocked from the night before, the six remaining Julatians insisted on returning to Julat immediately. Watching them as they made their case, they no longer seemed as tall to me. It was as if the experience had literally cut them down to size. Although Ataymah retained his exalted height, he did look shaken, as if he felt responsible for the men's deaths. Our expedition may have been a coalition of the willing, but everyone knew that Ataymah was the leader. I imagined that the Council in Julat would demand an explanation of what happened.

When the men spoke of leaving, Avi tried to suggest that the worst had passed, so why not collect some treasure before returning to Julat. But the others were irrational, unwilling to countenance the idea of staying one extra minute in that place of suffering. Surprisingly, Ataymah, whose initial comments conveyed that his sympathies were with Avi, backed down in the face of the united will of the remaining Julatians.

It was decided that Ataymah would return to Julat with the others while Avi and I stayed to look for treasure. I don't think the Julatians cared whether we came back or not. Ataymah, on the other hand, was anxious that we should return to Julat, but my mind was fixed on Jamish's treasure. There was no way I wanted to go back while there was still a chance of obtaining it.

"The last time we were here," Ataymah informed us, "there was treasure at the bottom of the water cavern system. It shouldn't be that difficult to find. I think there's plenty left."

* * *

After saying goodbye, Avi and I descended the stairs into the first cavern. The caverns were a sight to behold: gigantic, interconnected cisterns whose smooth, plastered walls were immaculate. The fact that the gargantuan open spaces were hewn out of solid rock was breathtaking. In their day, the caverns must have held an unimaginable quantity of water.

After exploring the floor of the first cavern and finding nothing, we ascended the stairs, crossed the wooden rope bridge that was three-quarters of the way to the top, and entered the next cavern, which was similar in size to the first. We searched but found nothing of value and no red tunnels that might lead to Jamish's treasure.

We searched two more caverns. With light from his scroll, Avi augmented the ambient light coming from openings in the upper sides of the caverns. In the fourth cavern, Avi's light reflected off something shiny in the back of the cavern. It was a small, golden medallion. Avi was overjoyed. I told him he could have it for himself.

This can't be Jamish's treasure. Being second-to-none requires something much grander.

The fifth cavern was narrower than the first four, and it turned out to be the last cavern in the system. There was no rope bridge and no exit on the other side. As we began to descend the stairs, Avi's light reflected off something at the bottom. My heart began to race, and Avi began to pick up his pace.

We hit the ground and ran forward as Avi's light hungrily scoured the cavern floor. Reflected light sparkled and glittered on the walls of the cavern. My breath caught in my throat. *We found treasure!*

Peris had greatly exaggerated the vastness of the treasure, but there were seven small, knee-high mounds of gold, silver, bronze, and reddish medallions. They reminded me of the last depleted piles of snow as winter gives way to spring.

Whoever was there before made off with most of the gold and silver medallions, though a few remained. The bronze and reddish medallions dominated the loot.

I grabbed one of the reddish medallions off the nearest pile. "What's this?"

"That's red granite, which is quite rare and quite valuable in larger quantities. I'm not sure why someone would make all these red granite medallions. They are pretty, but not very practical. I wonder how they got here?"

While Avi spoke, it hit me: *Bright red medallions must mean this is the red tunnel. This is the treasure of Jamish! But where's all the rest?*

Avi happily scavenged through the piles searching for more gold and silver medallions. He talked about how just the precious few that he found would make a world of difference to his life in Julat.

I should have been happy with even one gold medallion, but compared to my vast expectations, the treasure was a huge disappointment.

This can't be Jamish's treasure, can it?

I decided to pull out the goat's scroll and read it again.

Unrolling the scroll, I immediately noticed it contained only one sentence, and it was in the ancient language—*I've got the wrong scroll!* But before I could exchange scrolls, it dawned on me that if this was my scroll, something new must have appeared on it. Intrigued, I quietly spoke the word that Avi taught me, "Ginoskete." The ancient language rearranged itself in my mind until it read:

Put down the beast in the reeds; when humbled he will bring great treasure.

I read it again. *Are the kunoi the beasts among the reeds? If they are, then doesn't that mean that this is the great treasure? But then why does it say "beast" singular, and where are the reeds?*

I got out the goat's scroll and reread the directions:

Hidden within the fortress lies the Red Tunnel. Follow the tunnel until it ends. When everyone goes right, go left. Ascend the incline. The Cavern of Contest is to the East, though only one who surpasses them all may enter.

"Rom, what are you doing? Help me collect this treasure!"

I walked over to Avi, still deep in thought.

"Dig through the bronze and red ones in that pile over there. There might be more gold or silver hidden in the pile."

His instructions refocused my attention. Finding a red granite medallion, I took it in my hands. It was polished stone. On one side was a beautiful geometric pattern, and on the other was a picture of a lake with tall grass growing along the side.

"Avi, what's engraved on the back of these red ones?"

Avi stopped to look. "Looks like a lake of some kind."

"All the red medallions have the same picture, don't they?" I grabbed more of them to confirm my theory. "But only the red granite ones are engraved with a picture. The others just have geometric patterns on them."

"I've never seen anything like these medallions before," Avi said examining one more closely. "Why would someone engrave this picture on a medallion? Maybe this lake is important."

"What lake is it?"

"I can't tell. There's just water and all these . . ." Avi started to chuckle.

"What's so funny?"

"Maybe it's nothing, but if you look closely at the engraving, it's not the lake that's being emphasized but the plants in the fore-ground."

"What difference does that make?"

"Well, if I'm not mistaken, the plants are reeds. If reeds are being highlighted, then that makes this a red, reed medallion. It's funny because in the ancient language there is great confusion between the words "red" and "reed." In some cases, the words overlap so that when you think you should have the word 'red,' you actually have the word 'reed' and vice versa."

My brain began to race. *This can't be an accident. The goat's scroll says that Jamish's treasure is at the end of the Red Tunnel, but that could mean the end of the Reed Tunnel. My scroll talks about a treasure from the beast in the reeds, but that could be the beast in red. And here we have red, reed medallions. I can't figure this out without Avi's help.*

"Avi. I've got to show you something." I pulled out my scroll and showed Avi what it said:

Put down the beast in the reeds; when humbled he will bring great treasure.

"When did this appear?" Avi asked. "Where's the story of Peytos?"

"It's gone. I found this in its place. But I just noticed it right now." I had his attention. "Could there be a greater treasure hidden somewhere here?"

"Let's think about this. We're in a water cavern. If this was filled with water, it would look like a lake, right?"

That sounded right to me. "Would it look like the lake on the medallions?" I wondered aloud.

Avi grabbed a red granite medallion. Twisting it around, he tried to orient the image to the place where we were.

"It could very well be," he exclaimed. "If this were the lake, then the reeds would have to be either on this side or that side," he said, pointing to the two shorter sides at the front and back of the cavern. "But what if you were standing in the entrance?" Avi continued, thinking aloud.

Running to the entrance, Avi reoriented the medallion again. "If this were a map of this room, the reeds would be there." He pointed to what was the short back wall of the cavern.

We both hurried over to the wall. Illuminating its surface with his lit scroll, we searched for anything out of the ordinary.

"Wait a minute," Avi exclaimed. "This wall isn't plastered like the rest of them!"

I was so used to seeing stone walls that I stopped paying attention to the plastering. But he was right. The wall was rougher than the other three, as well as all the other cavern walls we had seen.

Running my hand along the wall's bumps and crevices, I searched intently for anything unusual. As my hand passed along the surface, my index finger slipped into a darkened spot on the wall.

"Avi, come here!" I said excitedly. "Doesn't this hole look like it was carved out of the wall?"

As his light illuminated the surface, I saw more clearly a thin rectangular slot about chest high, obscured by minor protrusions around it. If I hadn't been searching for it, I wouldn't have noticed it. It was four or five inches long and maybe a half an inch wide.

"Something must go in here," Avi conjectured. "Maybe there was a lever or something."

While he talked, it hit me.

"It's a token slot."

"A what?"

"A token slot; something you put tokens in to activate."

Avi was bewildered.

"Never mind. We just need to find the token." It only took a second to realize exactly what the token must be. "It's the medallion. Put one of those red granite medallions in this slot."

It fit perfectly. As the medallion dropped into the slot, it made a clunky rolling sound. I heard it winding its way into the inner recesses of the wall.

Then the wall began to open.

CHAPTER 27

I stepped into the breach. Avi followed.

"Illuminatio."

The passageway in the rock was narrow. I searched for somewhere everyone would turn right, but the tunnel was, for the most part, straight, with gentle twists and turns here and there.

Avi wore a big grin, and his eyes were wide open. He jabbered on about how much fun we were having and how glad he was that we hadn't gone back to Julat. As he hustled ahead, I thought about how to ensure I was the one who discovered the treasure, rather than Avi, so I could become the one who was second-to-none.

We walked through the tunnel for a long time. As the light shone ahead, we approached what looked like a dead end. But when we got there, we noticed a sharp right turn after which the tunnel opened up into a larger space. I stopped.

"What's the matter?" Avi asked. "Let's keep going."

This must be the place where I turn left while everyone else turns right, but how? All that's in front of me is a stone wall.

"Why don't you keep going to the right. I am going to stay here for a minute."

"What? Why?"

"I just am."

"Okay, I'll wait with you."

"Avi, there might be treasure up ahead. You can start looking for it. I'll catch up."

"Rom, what's wrong? I already have plenty of treasure. The great thing for me is that we're on an adventure together. I don't mind waiting."

My strategy wasn't working. It was time to try a different approach.

"Avi, for some reason I just don't think that I'm supposed to go right. I know that it looks like a dead end, but it just feels like we are supposed to go left."

We searched the wall on our left for a slot or some other sign that it was a façade. But it felt like a real wall. Avi told me to stand aside. He put his ear up to it and said something under his breath.

I waited.

"It sounds like there's running water on the other side!" Avi said with surprise.

This news lit a fire in my soul, and I searched intently in every nook and crevice for anything unusual. Avi stepped back to survey the wall from a distance.

"There's something about the protrusions of rock on this wall. Something's unnatural about them. But I can't quite put my finger on it. They don't look random. Rather, it's . . . it's . . . it's almost like they spell something." Avi continued, his words gaining speed as he spoke, "Rom, come here and look at this!"

I stepped back and stood next to Avi.

"Doesn't that protrusion look like the downward stroke of a pen? And that one there look like another?" Avi asked excitedly.

I stared intently at the wall, but I didn't see any pattern.

Then I heard Avi say with great satisfaction, "Ah, I see it now. Ginoskete."

He turned to me and said it again. In my mind the protrusions of the wall rearranged themselves into the word "scroll."

"Avi! You're a genius. But what's that at the end of the word—that horizontal line thing? It looks like an arrow. Do you see it right here?"

"I think it *is* an arrow," Avi replied. "I bet we have to place a scroll at the end of the line. Try yours since it talks about great treasure and the beast in the reeds."

Although Avi meant my scroll, I thought better of this and pulled out the goat's scroll, holding it against the wall at the end of the line.

The outlines of the word "scroll" lit up, and that portion of the wall swung open to reveal a flight of stairs. We climbed up the steps to what I was fully expecting to be the Cavern of Contest. As we climbed, I thought of what it meant to be one who "surpasses them all," if that was indeed a condition of entry.

Reaching the top of the incline, a path opened to the east. At this point, I wanted to look for the treasure by myself.

"Avi," I said, "I wouldn't have made it this far without you, but I want to see what is ahead by myself. I don't want to do it together."

"You don't want me to come with you? Why not?" Avi was confused and hurt. "Did I do something to upset you?"

"No, of course not. It's just . . ." I couldn't think of any reason to give him, which frustrated me.

"You wouldn't understand," I snapped. "This is my chance to do something for myself; to make a name for myself. You were the one who suggested I come to Julat with you to become a mighty warrior. How can I be a mighty warrior if I don't tackle whatever is coming by myself?"

"But haven't I been helpful?" Avi pleaded. "There's no reason to go on alone. What if whatever is ahead is too much for you?"

"It won't be," I said arrogantly. "I'll come get you if I need you. But I'm ready to tackle this on my own."

"You want me to just wait here?"

It sounded ridiculous when he said it like that.

"Yes," I admitted.

"All right."

He's agreeing to wait?

For a moment, I wondered why he would do something like that. Such an attitude was foreign to me, but the anticipation of what was inside pushed aside any self-reflection or empathy. I buried the growing feeling of disgust with myself and pressed on.

As Avi sat down on one of the boulders near the stairs, I started walking into the wider expanse, not knowing what to expect. After about twenty paces, my knee hit an invisible barrier. Both of my feet sank about five inches into the ground, as if I'd stepped into a muddy bog. I couldn't move. I was about ready to swallow my pride and ask Avi for help when I heard a voice address me.

"Do you wish to enter the Cavern of Contest?"

I couldn't identify where the voice was coming from—it may have been inside my head—but it sounded like it was coming from underground. Either way, I don't think Avi heard it.

"Yes," I replied back quietly. "I wish to enter the Cavern of Contest."

"Only those who surpass all others are allowed to enter."

I replied, "I've come alone, haven't I? Others started with me, but I alone am here."

"Are you willing to leave your companion behind?"

Shamefully I said, "I am."

With that, the ground sucked me down and spit me out into an underground river. The current immediately whipped me forward in a torrent of racing water. Before I knew what was happening, I cascaded down a waterfall. It slammed me into the water below and then pressed heavily on me, as if the water was dunking me and holding me down. Panic seized me, but my wild, flailing limbs somehow moved me out from under the water's grip. I pulled myself up to the surface. Blinding mist surrounded me. Disoriented, I lunged back toward the thundering waterfall, thinking I was escaping. The water hit me square in the back. Down again I went, breathless, swallowed by the water.

Help! Help! Help!

"Ischuro!" came my remembered reply, creating bubbles under the water.

The blast that came from my mouth propelled me backward just enough to escape the downward thrust.

"Ischuro!"

Upward I went until I burst from my watery grave back into the air. I blew back the mist with another wave of force. At last I could see my way out. Yet when I tried to propel myself forward using the power again, curiously, no force came from my mouth. Instead, I threw my deadened arms in front of me and swam weakly toward the rock shore. When I reached it, I hugged it dearly.

Standing up, I surveyed my surroundings. I had cascaded over a waterfall into a small lake bordered on all sides by a dense thicket of reeds, like a lion's mane encircling his face. Remembering what was written on my scroll, I became alert to the possibility of a beast among the reeds and the fact that I wasn't carrying a weapon.

From the thickest patch of reeds adjacent to me came a voice, "Have you come to win Jamish's treasure?"

"I have," I replied, hoping to sound brave.

Those same reeds began to rustle. Slowly something emerged. But it wasn't a wild animal, at least in outward appearance. It was a woman. A mesmerizingly beautiful woman with enchanting blue eyes, light caramel skin, and thick brown-blonde hair. She was dressed in flattering, tightly fitting red pants and a red shirt. Even the most elegant and attractive women of Julat paled in comparison. All I could do was stare, bewildered by her beauty.

"I was expecting a warrior," she said, playfully laughing. "You're just a boy. Are you lost? Jamish's treasure is not easily won. Only one who is second-to-none can ever hope to earn it."

Her laugh was intoxicating. Whether I was qualified or not

didn't matter. I had to have the treasure, if for no other reason than to impress her.

"Quiet resolve?" She winked at me. "That's quite attractive. But are you smart enough? The one who wins the treasure must be second-to-none in intelligence, so answer me this riddle:

The more I am fed, the hungrier I become.
The more I am wounded, the stronger I get.
The more I forget what should be remembered,
The more I remember what should be forgotten.
What am I?"

I struggled to clear my mind, which still felt drunk with the sight of her beauty. All I wanted to do was tell her how gorgeous she was.

"Could you tell me the riddle again?"

She smiled seductively as she replied, "The more I am fed, the hungrier I become; the more I am wounded, the stronger I get; the more I forget what should be remembered, the more I remember what should be forgotten. What am I?"

What is she even talking about? Come on . . . think harder! Failure is not an option.

My brain churned. I pressed my fingers against my forehead. I closed my eyes. Nothing came.

It's time to give up. I'm not smart enough to figure this out.

"I don't know the—hey, what's that?"

Something vibrated against my leg. It felt like it was my scroll.

"I don't know the . . . the name of what I'm trying to say," I blurted out, trying to recover. I unrolled my magic scroll.

"Ginoskete," I said as the woman in red wore a puzzled look.

CHAPTER 28

After Peytos repented of his marauding ways, he returned to Tikto to find honest means of supporting himself and his wife. His experience as a marauder made him highly qualified for the role of private security, so he soon found himself in the employ of a wealthy spice merchant named Mori. Whenever Mori was away peddling his spices, Peytos' job was to guard his storehouses. Whenever Mori was around, Peytos functioned as a sentry during negotiations. Peytos' fierceness as a fighter quickly earned him a reputation as a man to be feared. That reputation provided cover for Mori, who became more and more reckless in his dealings with others, trusting that Peytos would protect him from all retribution.

Several months passed. As Mori tasted more and more success, he soon forgot Peytos' contribution and became convinced that his material success was due to his superior negotiating ability. When some quietly attributed his success to Peytos, he began to despise him openly. Yet even as Mori's treatment of Peytos grew worse, Peytos refused to skim goods when Mori was away, a typical practice. Instead, the worse Mori mistreated him, the harder and more honorably Peytos carried out his duties.

Over time, Mori, filled with the pride that cannot share glory with another, fired Peytos. When Peytos received the news that not only was he fired, but Mori was refusing to pay him any portion of his current month's salary, he grabbed his sword and prepared to take what was due him by force.

"Beloved," his wife said to him, "do not do what you're planning. The king promised to make you the captain of his guard. When he does, you will not want to be remembered for this act of violence. The king's captain is too good for such things. Forget about the money and your wounded pride. When you are captain of the king's guard, we will have plenty of money and recognition."

"But I am not yet captain, and I do not know how long it will be," Peytos argued.

"True. But can the king be trusted?"

"Yes."

"Did he promise to make you captain of the guard?"

"Yes."

"If his promise is true, then aren't you as good as captain of the guard already? Is not that money as good as ours already? It is only a matter of time."

The beautiful woman in red watched me intently. "I need an answer."

"The more I am fed, the hungrier I become; the more I am wounded, the stronger I get; the more I forget what should be remembered, the more I remember what should be forgotten. What am I?" I repeated, buying time.

"I have it," I boasted. "It's pride."

"'Pride' is the correct answer. Well done. You are brilliant indeed. Very few have ever solved that puzzle."

"Did I win the treasure?"

"Not yet, sweet child. Jamish rewards not only intellectual superiority, but physical as well. One must excel at both to be second-to-none."

She continued, "As for the test of physical superiority, do you see that high place there?" She pointed toward a ledge some forty feet off the ground on the far side of the cavern.

"You must catch me before I make it around the lake and reach that high ledge. Do you understand?"

"I think so."

"Good. Ready? Go!"

With that, she bolted away. Registering what this meant, I sprinted after her. Slim and athletic, she was the picture of grace in motion. A strong desire to catch her welled up within me, but she was fast. I trailed by twenty paces or so as we rounded the lake behind the waterfall. By the time I reached the cavern wall, she scampered up the face like she was climbing a ladder. I took much longer to get to the top, afraid at first of pushing my still-healing shoulder too hard, but even after it proved strong, I wasn't as fast as she was. When I arrived, she was sitting on the ledge with her back against the cavern wall. Her legs were crossed, and she was neither sweating nor breathing heavily.

"You failed," she said mechanically.

"It's unfair," I protested. "You knew the course we ran, but I've never been here before." I hoped I wasn't whining.

"What do you propose?"

"That we run again. But this time, I have a chance to practice before it's official."

She looked at me with her sparkling blue eyes. "I hope you do catch me. Because of all the people who have come here, you might be my favorite. Yes, you may practice if you like."

Her words were like honey, sweet and smooth, causing my chest to inflate and my brain to swim. I walked back to the start in a daze, determination growing within me.

Hopeful that she was watching me, I raced along the path. Familiarity with the course let me concentrate more on running. I didn't want her laughing at me as I practiced, so I ran with abandon. When I reached the cavern wall, I studied the rocks. I climbed up and down again and again. She didn't say how many times I could practice, and she didn't stop me. I stole glances at her whenever I could. She appeared to be occupied with something in the reeds where I first met her.

As I practiced, the rock wall became familiar, as did the path. Strangely, instead of feeling worn out, the more I practiced, the more energized I became. All I thought about was the desire to show her how great I was.

Finally, after much practice, I brimmed with confidence. My body felt cloaked with strength, sculpted and chiseled. I strode back to her at the reeds.

"I'm ready."

She looked at me, as if truly seeing me for the first time. "You look taller and stronger than before."

"I'm ready whenever you say go," I told her.

My muscles tensed.

"Go."

Like a red flash, she was off. I was but a moment behind. My eyes fixed on her as I ran, willing my legs to pump faster and faster. She was a step or two ahead of me. Past the lake we sprinted, toward the cavern wall. I leaned forward. Just a few feet more and I would catch her. I extended my hand to tag her in the back. Three feet from the wall, she leapt forward and scampered up it in one beautiful motion. I, less gracefully, attacked the wall, climbing furiously up my practiced path. Her foot was inches from my hand as we scaled the wall in unison. Diving up onto the ledge, I tumbled after her. My hand was on her foot. I caught her!

But she had made it to the ledge first.

"You failed again. I was so sure you were going to be the one to win the treasure."

I was sure I was too. The disappointment was crushing.

"One more time," I begged.

She smiled, but it was a different kind of smile, not flirtatious or alluring, but cold and distant. "What would change this time? Wasn't that your best effort?"

Defeated and humiliated, I made my way out of the secret underground portion of the cavern, back to the place where Avi waited.

CHAPTER 29

D id you find treasure?" Avi asked, springing to his feet from the rock on which he sat.

"No."

"Where did you go?"

I explained as briefly as possible—and probably quite rudely—about the underground cavern and the challenge. Then, with great embarrassment, I admitted that I failed.

Avi had a compassionate look in his eyes. "If it means that much to you, why don't you try again?"

"What do you mean?"

"Try again. Go down the same portal and give it another try."

"But what would be different this time?"

"Everything could be. You won't know unless you try." He then added. "Would you mind if I came? I won't interfere."

Initially my longing to be alone with the beautiful woman in red made me want to refuse, but my guilt over how supportive and encouraging he was stayed my tongue. He could have demanded that he give it a try instead of me. He certainly had earned the right.

"That would be great," I said, hoping it counted as an apology.

Back into the portal I went.

"I have come alone, haven't I?" I said when the voice asked me about being one who surpasses others.

"Have you? Will you not leave your companion behind?" the voice asked back this time.

"No. I'm the only one competing, but he's earned the right to be here to watch."

Down through the portal I went, back into the water. Ready this time, I dove out from the waterfall as I went over to avoid the spray. I looked for Avi, but he wasn't coming through.

"I'm up here!" I heard him yell. He perched on a nearby ledge, able to watch the whole thing.

Over to the reeds I went.

"I've returned to win Jamish's treasure, and I'm not giving up until I have it."

The beautiful woman in red rose from the reeds. I was ready with my answer, but the question never came.

"Welcome," she said, playfully laughing. "Beware that Jamish's treasure is not easily won. Only one who is second-to-none can ever hope to earn it."

Doesn't she recognize me?

"I'm ready for the challenge," I replied.

"The one who wins the treasure must be second-to-none in intelligence, so answer me this riddle:

What brings tomorrow into today,
not in fullness but only part way.

This riddle seemed more confusing than the first, but immediately I unrolled my scroll. It was still the same story of Peytos and Mori.

Does pride bring tomorrow into today? No, that can't be right.

And then my eyes fell on the end of the story.

"A promise," I exclaimed. "A promise brings the future into the present! That's why Peytos can begin acting like the captain of the guard today. It's because the king promised it to him."

The woman looked bemused as I blurted out my thinking along with my answer.

"That's impressive," she cooed. "'Promise' is the correct answer. Well done. You are brilliant indeed. Very few have ever solved that puzzle. Do you think you can handle a bit of a physical contest?"

"Show me the treasure first," I demanded. "How can I truly compete if I don't see what I'm competing for?"

"Don't you see it right now?" she asked seductively.

"No. You're not the treasure. You don't ever leave this cavern, do you? Show me the real treasure. The treasure of Jamish."

The woman walked over to a section of the reeds. Bending over, she lifted a small ornate box. Opening the box, I peered in. There, lying on a bed of soft green velvet, was an enormous red ruby. It was like a bright, perfectly shaped strawberry hidden among leaves of green, big enough to fill my palm. The medallions we saw earlier looked worthless in comparison. Nothing Ataymah and Peris brought back could come close to this magnificent prize.

No one who has this jewel could be considered a failure. I must get that jewel.

While she put it away, she explained the course again. I didn't bother to listen.

I must get that jewel.

"Are you ready, handsome?"

I must have that jewel. I must.

At the word "go," I was off, my adrenaline pumping. My legs swallowed the ground in front of me like a tremendous machine. The landscape blurred as I raced faster and faster, visualizing the jewel just in front of me as I ran. The cavern wall ran toward me as quickly as I ran toward it. In one bound I was on it. I shot up onto the ledge as if I'd flown.

Only then did I stop to look around. I heard Avi yelling. The woman in red was just now ascending the cavern wall. At the edge of the ledge, I reached my hand down to help pull her up.

"No one has ever run that fast before," she gushed. "You win Jamish's treasure. You're second-to-none!"

At those words, I shouted aloud. Avi cheered as well. The woman and I walked back to the reeds. She was talking, but I wasn't listening. She handed me the ornate box. Taking the ruby into my hand, it felt heavy and light at the same time. The surface was smooth, like polished rock, and I couldn't stop my fingers from running over it again and again. It smelled like roses. Unable to help myself, I kissed it. It tasted like honey.

Under the stone was a gold chain meant to hold the ruby. The woman in red slipped it around my neck. Though it was a substantial stone, my neck felt lighter while I wore it. I raised my head high in triumph.

* * *

Avi loved looking at the stone as well. As we collected some golden coins and red medallions for him, we talked about what a magnificent stone it was. I wished I could share the moment with Esah, Rabah, and Domi.

On the way back to Julat, Rohka made an appearance.

"Hey, where have you been?" I jokingly chided him. "Why do you always disappear at the important times? You missed my great triumph." I showed him my ruby necklace. He chirped a few times and then settled in on my shoulder for the journey back.

Ha! Even Rohka is impressed.

CHAPTER 30

My re-entry into Julat was triumphant. Right away Ataymah came to visit Avi and me. He was duly impressed with the jewel. He didn't ask much about our adventures in getting it, as if having the jewel itself was all that mattered.

Emma too came for a visit. She was relieved I returned with only slight injuries, but her first concern was clearly Avi. I sensed they wanted to spend time together alone, so I went to explore the city and my newfound fame.

Everyone I met over the next several days wanted to hear the story of our battle with the kunoi and our hunt for the treasure. Forgetting—or not really caring—that many Julatians died during the battle with the kunoi, I was happy to oblige.

No one had heard from Peris since he disappeared that night, and while it was no loss to me, many Julatians were heartbroken, unable to mention it without weeping profusely. Others were angry with Peris for leading such a foolhardy expedition and wanted all mention of him erased from the records of Julat. Ataymah was especially burdened by the loss of Peris, but his own status among the people had increased greatly. And rightly so. He was a fighter beyond comparison, the mightiest warrior in the city—some said the mightiest warrior the city had ever known. It was hard for me to imagine anyone greater.

The Julatians hung on Ataymah's every word, and he was the subject of seemingly every conversation. They were convinced that Ataymah was the key to expanding the city's influence and power. The Council may have held the institutional power in the city, but

Ataymah was the true driving force. Everyone wanted to spend time with him.

Including me.

Ataymah was regularly found in the city center, where I first encountered him and Peris. He would hold court, taking questions from Julatians and waxing passionately about a wide variety of subjects. He had an answer for every question, yet he wore his learning lightly. I made it a point to be in the city center to hear him as often as possible.

One day, having finished answering a question about the value of the iron scepter, there was a lull as he calmly and confidently waited for the next question.

I was about to ask where he got his iron scepter when someone jumped in with a question regarding reasonable prices for fruit. A younger Julatian of slightly smaller stature standing close to me stifled a laugh at the silly question. His reaction loosed a laugh from deep within me that I couldn't stop.

People shot daggers in my direction as I backed out of the group, barely containing the tidal wave of giggles—disproportionate to the actual humor of the situation—that welled up within me.

"Next up, an impassioned discussion of the color brown," chortled the young man who followed me out of the crowd.

That did it. The dam burst, and I howled with laughter as we hurried quickly out of hearing range.

"Gaius," he said with a huge smile on his huge face.

"Rom," I responded. "I'm an aspiring fruit vendor vexed by price fluctuations."

Gaius' laughter shook his thick black hair that sat like a helmet atop his rather large head.

"Hey, you're the guy who won that jewel. Can I see it?" he said, pointing inquisitively at the prize that hung around my neck.

"That's quite the rock. Even Ataymah the Great seems to be impressed with it. I've heard him tell the story of how you won it. That's impressive."

I liked Gaius immediately.

"You're obviously not from here," Gaius said kindly. "Where are you from?"

"Well, I came here from Lithown."

"Lithown? That's a tough place. Hey, I know someone who lives in Lithown. His name's Esah. Know him?"

"Esah? I know Esah. We're friends. I tried to get him to come with me to Julat, but he wouldn't leave."

"Esah wouldn't leave? Did he know you were coming to Julat? I thought he'd jump at the chance to come back here."

"He's been here?"

"He's actually from here. But that's a story for another time— Hey, do you want to come to lunch with me? I normally go to the house of a man named Vish. I'm sure you can come with me. I'll introduce you to some people. And it's a pretty sweet house."

Not needing food to survive had diminished my thoughts about food, but I was curious to see what it would be like to eat something. Plus, Gaius' personality was warm and welcoming, so I eagerly accepted the invitation.

Vish's house was indeed a palatial estate befitting a man of high standing in Julat. Oddly, Vish was not at the lunch feast, but Gaius said that was not unusual. His home was open to Julatians whenever they wanted to come together.

When we arrived at his house, we sat down to a sumptuous banquet of mostly fruits, breads, and meats. Everything tasted familiar, but I couldn't remember where I'd eaten such things before. I wasn't hungry when I started eating, and I didn't feel full when I stopped eating. Eating was nothing more than pure pleasure.

During the introductions, Gaius was quick to boast to the others that I was the one Ataymah had mentioned. Everyone wanted to hear the story of my adventure in Liga and see my prize jewel. I was glad to oblige. A jolt of excitement shot through my body any time people talked about the jewel and how impressive it was. Their affirmation and approval fed me more than the food.

Though they talked about the jewel for a long time, none of them asked about Rohka, even though he sat on my shoulder the whole time. Whereas I loved talking about Rohka with Avi when we left Lithown, I didn't mind that no one noticed him now. The jewel was what I'd become proudest of, not for being some guy with a bird.

Unfortunately, at some point the conversation turned to other topics and, try as I might, I couldn't steer it back. Since there wasn't anything else I wanted to talk about, I left Vish's house. I took some bread with me and tried to feed it to Rohka, but he kept chirping and pecking at my necklace.

"You want to see the jewel again, don't you? I don't blame you. It feels amazing."

I held up the jewel for him to see. He pecked at it and chirped loudly. I assumed he was as happy as I was to bask in the glow of such a gorgeous jewel.

* * *

The next day, back at the city center, Ataymah invited me to join him as he addressed those who gathered for the morning conversation.

"Rom is one of the budding warriors who will bring Julat great fame," Ataymah bragged.

A question rang out from the crowd, "Rom, where will you go for your next quest?"

All eyes were on me. I saw Gaius in the crowd, waiting expectantly for my answer.

What kind of hero doesn't have his next adventure picked out?

So, I said the first thing that popped into my head: "I'm thinking about going to the Valley of Salt."

It was a total lie. I hadn't thought about the Valley of Salt since Lithown. But as excitement rippled through the buzzing crowd, I knew it was a good answer.

Ataymah put his hand on my shoulder. "The Valley of Salt would be quite the challenge indeed. I've never been, but I've heard stories. Are you sure you wouldn't want to try something a little less dangerous first?"

"No. To become a great warrior, you have to rise to great challenges."

The people cheered.

"What's your great quest in the Valley of Salt?" The question came from a man named Noch.

Why do I do these things to myself? I don't know anything about the Valley of Salt.

All I knew of the Valley of Salt was that there were salt runners who went to trade for salt.

"It is a quest that has something to do with salt mining and trading. I can't tell you more now."

I searched the crowd eagerly for approval. I saw tacit acceptance in the eyes of many, so I reasoned that it was also a good answer.

To my surprise, Noch continued. "Excellent. I'd like to talk to you about your quest in more detail when you have the chance. I have something to do with salt trading here in Julat."

With that, my interview ended, so I stepped off the stage and re-entered the crowd. Noch tried to make his way toward me, so I slipped out the other side, heading away from the city center toward where Emma was staying. I knew she and Avi would be the right people to talk to about the Valley of Salt.

Even as I left, many Julatians broke away from the crowd to wish me well.

The whole city is interested in me and my plans! That goat was right about this place being intimidating, but with the treasure of Jamish, I'm second-to-none.

The only distraction from my good feelings was Rohka, who kept chirping incessantly and tugging at my jewel necklace.

"Not now, Rohka. I don't have time to show you the necklace."

But he wouldn't leave it alone. I swatted at him to shoo him away, embarrassed that others might see him acting strangely.

Finally, to my relief, Rohka flew off. As I continued toward Emma's place, I mentally scrolled through all the people I met in Julat.

They're all better looking than I am; wealthier than I am; better relationally than I am; but I'm the greatest warrior among them. I'm not anywhere near Ataymah's level, but I'm still developing. These people can keep their beautiful houses and their beautiful faces. I have something most of them could never dream of having. If only they understood how great this treasure is. If only they understood what kind of hero it took to win this great treasure. It's only a matter of—

Wham! I was stopped mid-thought, knocked backward by a jarring force.

CHAPTER 31

I staggered up from the ground. *What happened?* Trying to get my bearings, I saw Rohka streaking toward me like a bolt of lightning.

He's coming to help. I must be in great danger!

Opening my arms to receive him, Rohka hit me square in the chest.

It was like colliding at full speed with another person, except I was the only one knocked back. I tumbled to the ground again, the breath knocked out of me. Pain radiated from my torso out to all my limbs. Confusion and fear ruled my mind. The truth awakened in me with a shock.

Rohka knocked me to the ground! Twice.

I rolled over to my side and saw him circling above me. While I watched him, he morphed from his tiny shape into a much larger bird—an eagle or something like an eagle. I got up to run, but he swooped down and slammed into me again, knocking me back to the ground. His talons grabbed at my chest.

"Ischuro," I yelled. Nothing happened. "Thureos!" No response. "Cobaqeren!" Again, nothing. Rohka grasped at my chest. I threw my hand over my ruby and rolled out from under his clutches. He flew into the air.

"Rohka," I gasped up in the sky after him, "what are you doing?"

He screamed and then dove toward me at an alarming speed. Two feet from me, he spread his wings, screeching to a stop. His head and body stopped almost instantly, though his talons swung toward my chest like an eagle snatching a salmon from the surface of the ocean. They locked onto the ruby hanging round my neck. Rohka's momentum shoved me backward, while at the same time, his wings flapped powerfully, yanking him, his talons, and my ruby in the opposite direction. The chain holding the jewel snapped.

"No!" I yelled. I propelled myself forward to tackle him. "That's mine!"

I lunged at my jewel in his talon, catching one of the ends of the necklace. He flapped his wings, and we rose into the air a few feet while I fought to get my jewel free from his grip. But his talon was like an iron vise. With all my strength, I couldn't pry it open. Suddenly, we plummeted back to the ground. My knees absorbed the heavy shock as we landed, and they crumpled awkwardly beneath me. Rohka pinned me to the ground as I struggled to squirm out from under him.

He pecked at my right leg. Immediately it stiffened. Then he pecked at my left leg. It froze also. Two pecks to my shoulders quieted my flailing arms. I was immobilized. Terrified, I watched Rohka step away, still clutching my ruby in his talon. Laying the stone on the ground, he squawked twice angrily. Then he lifted his right leg and stomped on the face of the ruby.

It shattered underneath the force of his blow, like a fragile ornament crushed beneath a heavy boot. I wanted to shout at him to stop, but I was too frightened and confused.

When he lifted his foot, smoke rose from the crushed ruby. It reeked of burnt, rotten eggs. The smell was nauseating. Rohka flapped his wings, blowing the odor in my direction. Involuntarily, I inhaled and, turning my head to the side, immediately retched. Rohka kept flapping his wings until the smell was blown away, replaced by a sweet, almost lemony aroma.

Still immobilized, my eyes followed Rohka as he flew away toward the southern gate. I lay on the ground, humiliated, hoping that no one would see me.

After about five minutes, Rohka returned, carefully carrying a goblet in his talons. Easing down next to me, he picked up large shards of the ruby and placed them into the goblet. Each one dropped in with a splash, causing small droplets of red liquid to spill over the rim. Finishing the work, Rohka flew over to me. He pecked at my arms and legs, releasing them. I sat up cautiously as Rohka looked at me, his eagle eyes boring into my soul. I knew what I needed to do. Slowly, I reached into my pocket and pulled out the scroll that contained the instructions to finding Jamish's treasure.

Rohka screeched. Wrong one. I rolled that scroll over toward Rohka and pulled out my scroll. "Ginoskete," I commanded as I unrolled it.

The words on the scroll read,

> **With pride comes opposition; with humility comes help. The willing will eat well; the unwilling will reap destruction. In this is the seed of great wisdom; when planted, it will grow into a weapon of incomparably great power.**
>
> **Here is a mystery hidden from long ago. In the place of reeds lies the root, and the root will grow until red washes away red and white makes white. For this reason, the red seed will take root, and one day all will become clear.**

Shame and embarrassment came over me. The words about pride dug into my soul. I realized my fight with Rohka wasn't really because of the jewel. The jewel amplified and focused what was in my heart and mind.

I didn't have a word for how the rest of the reading made me feel; some combination of hopeful, confused, and unworthy.

I looked up from reading to find Rohka transformed back into his smaller form. Standing next to the goblet, he spread his little wings and knocked it over. Red liquid spilled onto the dry ground, which drank it down thirstily, leaving behind a red stain and three small red seeds. They resembled sunflower seeds still in their shells.

Rohka reached down and took a seed in his beak. One by one he brought them to me and dropped them into my extended hand. He then flew off, leaving me to ponder what had just happened.

Clutching the seeds in my hand, I proceeded to Emma's house, knowing I needed her help. She didn't seem surprised when I asked her for assistance in planting the seeds even though, out of embarrassment, I never told her where they came from. She gave me some potting soil, talked to me about frequent watering and sunlight, and sent me on my way.

Returning to Avi's house, I planted the seeds in the potting soil, hoping all would become clear once they took root. I'd not seen such rich, loamy soil anywhere in Sebi as what Emma had given me. It smelled muddy and stuck to my fingers as I sank the seeds deep into it. The black dirt happily swallowed the bright red seeds. There wasn't much sunlight in the room, but there was one exterior window, which I hoped would prove sufficient.

* * *

Days passed. I tried to avoid Gaius as much as possible. My wounded pride couldn't stomach him introducing me to others and asking to show off my red ruby. I didn't see Avi much either, which I think hurt his feelings, given that he seemed to want to spend more time with me than I wanted to spend with him. Still, I made regular visits to Ataymah's sessions, trying to learn as much as possible. Emma never asked what I was trying to grow, but my mind was never far from the potted seeds. I couldn't shake the feeling that everything about me being in Julat was wrapped up in those seeds. I'd grown accustomed to constantly talking to others about my jewel and quietly comparing myself to them. Now, when those thoughts came, I thought about the seeds instead or remembered the warnings and promises on my scroll, consciously willing myself to drown out the constant chatter of proud speculations in my head.

What will these seeds grow into? Were they inside the jewel the whole time? I wondered. *Any good from winning that jewel is going to come from those seeds.*

Rohka encouraged my preoccupation with the seeds, as I usually found him standing guard over the seed pot. At times he perched on top of the soil and dug his feet into it, chirping happily.

One day, I returned home, and Rohka flew to my shoulder as soon as I opened the door. I hurried over to the pot. The first signs of a seedling poking its head up from the dirt were visible. I

couldn't tell what was coming, but something was growing, and it was definitely red.

Day by day, I examined the plant—though it wasn't like any plant I'd ever seen before—and it fascinated me. Even the beautiful jewel from which it came did not hold my attention like the plant did. As it grew, it remained red, like the color of the seeds and the ruby before it, but it took on a new richness and depth of color. If I looked at it from different angles, its translucent, ruby-red color changed slightly. The material itself was strange to me. I longed to touch it, but the one time I tried, Rohka didn't approve, so I left it alone. The material looked as though it wanted to be amorphous, but its shape was perfectly cylindrical, a rod with a diameter of about two inches rising out of the dirt. The nearest thing to which I could compare the texture was solidified honey.

Soon, tiny scratches appeared on the inside of the rod. After it grew more, I realized the scratched were letters inscribed inside the rod. The best that I could tell, they appeared to spell out the word "debashadom." Nothing magical happened when I pronounced the word, so I assumed this was its name, which I promptly shortened to "Shadom."

One morning I awoke and Rohka was standing on my chest, his fiery eyes locked onto mine.

"What is it, Rohka?"

He flew over to the Shadom, but this time he perched on top of it.

"Is it time? Can I touch it?" I was fully awake, hustling over to the pot.

Rohka chirped once.

Slowly reaching out my hand, I let my finger poke the cylindrical growth. It was as hard as glass, and as solid as a rock. Watching Rohka, I pulled back my hand.

He chirped twice and then fluttered over to guide my hand

back toward the Shadom. Grasping his intentions, I wrapped my hand around the top end of the stick.

The craziest sensation followed. A sweetness came over me like I'd never felt before. The only thing comparable was the nectar-water I drank twice prior. But the taste in my mouth was more like honey. Immediately, instead of feeling satisfied, I felt a deep, unknown craving. Not for the food, possessions, or praise of Julat, but for the taste that washed over me in that moment.

Meanwhile, my hand sunk into the rod. The once-hard substance enveloped my hand, though I still grasped something solid and firm. When I pulled back my hand, the red rod popped out of the dirt. It felt like an extension of my arm, as if I gripped a sword or a hammer, yet it was as light as air. The arm that contained it felt stronger than my other arm.

What is this? Is it a sword?

Immediately, the rod reshaped itself into a double-edged sword. I sliced through the air with precise control, as if the sword was pulling my hand.

"Rohka, this is amazing!"

I wanted to hit something, but the only object near me was the clay pot in which the Shadom had grown.

More fitting for a hammer than a sword.

Suddenly the sword reshaped itself into a war hammer, still light as a feather. Unable to resist, I swung the hammer with such power that the pot burst into tiny pieces and sprayed dirt everywhere. Rohka shook his feathers to clean himself off.

How do I get my hand back? I wondered.

With that thought, the hammer melted. Instinctively, I turned my palm upward to catch the liquid-like material before it spilled to the ground. But nothing dropped onto the floor. Instead, my hand absorbed the red liquid. When the liquid disappeared, the only trace that remained was a reddish glow on my right arm.

"Rohka, how do I get it out?"

Instantly, the flow reversed, and the rod popped out, extending upward from my hand.

"Can I throw it like a spear?"

Rohka chirped. The rod reshaped into a spear and I hurled it deep into the wooden wall.

How do I get it back?

Without delay, it flew back from the wall into my hand.

"Rohka, are you seeing this?"

If birds can laugh, his chirped response sounded like one.

"This is the weapon of incomparably great power that my scroll was talking about, isn't it?"

As soon as the word "scroll" was on my tongue, my scroll tore free from my pocket and shot into my hand. The Shadom enveloped the scroll, catching it from the air and simultaneously draining back into my forearm, leaving my right hand holding it. Yet while I held the scroll, it felt like I was still holding the Shadom, as if the scroll and the Shadom were two parts of a greater whole.

The sense of wholeness between the Shadom and the scroll made me feel complete, as if my purpose in Julat was fulfilled. When I opened my scroll, I knew before I saw it that something new was waiting for me.

CHAPTER 32

In those days, the king of Sebi summoned Daybe, the head of the royal treasury, saying to her, "Daybe, I have heard rumors that the Salt Reapers in the city of Arritu have been cheating on their taxes, misappropriating money that should rightly be given to the royal treasury. Take one of your best accountants, pose as merchants, and investigate these allegations."

So Daybe called her deputy chief. "Make arrangements for us to travel to Arritu under the guise of establishing a contract to purchase salt from the Salt Reapers. In the course of our business transactions, we will request to examine their financial records."

Once arrangements were made, Daybe and her assistant traveled to the city of Arritu. Soon they were engaged in the process of negotiation with the officials.

"We would like to see your financial records as a show of good faith," Daybe requested.

"Rest assured. All our finances are in order. Come back tomorrow, and we will have all the records to show you," one of the officials assured her.

Daybe and her assistant spent the night in the city. When they returned the next morning, the owner of the business himself presented the records.

"Here are the financial records. And here are the names of our clients who have been with us for many years and can attest to our financial integrity," he asserted.

Daybe and her deputy looked through the records. Everything did seem to be in order.

"We need more time to study these documents. Give us one more day to look through them, and we'll be ready to sign a contract with you," Daybe said.

As the two women returned to their lodgings in the city, a man approached them from the shadows outside their door.

"My friends, I must speak with you," he whispered. "I am one of the accountants in charge of taxes. May I come in to speak with you in private?"

"We cannot invite you into our lodgings at night," said the assistant, alarmed by his presence. "It would neither be safe nor proper."

"It's okay," Daybe said, waving off her assistant's objection with her hand. "Come in," she invited.

Once safely inside, the man began, "I know you are here on the king's business to investigate false dealings."

Daybe wanted to protest, but the matter-of-fact way in which he made his assertion gave her pause.

"And rightfully so. We heard rumors that the king was cracking down on fraud, yet we continued to underreport our income. I myself have been the cause of some of the improprieties. Tax accountants are considered a necessary evil by our management, and we are expected to supplement our low salaries by skimming tax money that belongs to the king."

"But why did the financial records look so clean?" Daybe asked. "I would expect the owner to overstate his financial position to gain new business, not deliberately understate it."

"Why? Because everyone knows you are spies for the king. The owner announced it to all of us even before you arrived. We've been working overtime to prepare for your coming."

Daybe looked at her assistant and wondered how it was possible that the owner could have known this. Daybe was sure that her assistant could not and would not have alerted him.

Turning her attention back to the informant, Daybe spoke up, "Why are you telling us this?"

"In hopes that you will show me mercy and put in a good word for me with the king," the man replied. "Perhaps he will look kindly on my willingness to help."

"He will. I have worked for this king for some time. He is always merciful to those who seek his mercy."

"Please tell the king that I am ready to repay all that I have stolen from him. And when you go back to the Salt Reapers tomorrow, I strongly urge you not to let on that you know their records are false. Give the slightest hint that you are on to him and the owner will ensure that you never return to the king."

"Thank you," said Daybe. "What is your name so that I might tell the king about you?"

"My name is Zan. And it is I who must thank you." The man bowed low and exited.

The next day, Daybe and her assistant were able to convince the owner that they believed his ruse. Returning to the king, Daybe requested an immediate audience.

"Daybe, did you find that the Salt Reapers have been stealing from me by giving my tax money to others?"

"Yes, my king," she said. Although it seemed that the king already knew what she was about to tell him, Daybe *went through the whole story.*

"Prepare the penalties for the management of the Salt Reapers," said the king sadly. "As for Zan, tell him to give those reparations to the poor and invite him here to join the royal accountants. Make him feel welcome and never mention his fraud to him or anyone else."

"Yes, my lord," Daybe replied. "One more thing. How could the owner know that we were coming? I did not tell anyone, and I cannot possibly believe that my deputy did either. I have worked with her a long time, and she is completely loyal to you. There is no way she could or would have alerted the owner. Is it possible that someone knew about this other than the three of us?"

"No," said the king. "Just the three of us knew. But do not worry, I am perfectly aware of who leaked the information."

"You are?" Daybe said, astonished. "Who was it?"

"Me."

PART 5: CINDROPOLIS

CHAPTER 33

When I told Avi that it was time for me to leave Julat and journey to the Valley of Salt, he didn't appear surprised. At first, I thought he'd come with me, but Emma didn't want him to go. She was convinced that I needed to do it by myself, and Rohka appeared to agree with her because he became agitated when I tried to talk Avi into going.

I could tell my departure was bittersweet for Avi. On one hand, I knew he wanted me to stay in Julat with him, Emma, and Ataymah. On the other hand, I knew he was proud of me for going on an adventure by myself just like he had done when he journeyed to Sebi. Likewise, part of me was scared to do it without him, and part of me was glad for the chance to spread my wings.

When I found Ataymah in the city center, a crowd was gathered around him as he led a discussion. I waited impatiently amidst the townspeople for a chance to tell him I was leaving. At one point, the conversation settled on the subject of Julat's future.

"Rom, come up here for a moment, please," Ataymah called out. "People like Rom are the future of Julat. Many of you may know that Rom is planning an adventure to the Valley of Salt."

A murmur of approval rippled through the crowd.

"Rom, tell these fine people what you learned on your last adventure when we traveled together to the Fortress of Liga."

Trying to think quickly on my feet, I replied, "Well, I learned about kunoi. I came face-to-face with some hellhounds. That was frightening. I saw what someone with an iron scepter can do. You were amazing."

I turned to the crowd, unsure of whether I should talk to Ataymah or the group.

"I mean, Ataymah was amazing. I've never seen anyone wield a weapon like that! Umm . . . what else . . . well, I guess I learned about red granite medallions."

"That's what you experienced, Rom. What did you *learn*? No adventure happens by accident, and it's worth pondering what you're meant to learn each step of the way. After all, you never know when someone is going to call on you to recount your story in front of others."

Ataymah smiled, the crowd laughed, and I grew more nervous.

"More importantly," Ataymah continued, "a warrior's skill does not consist of his honed abilities but the cumulative power of the lessons he's learned in life. An unexamined adventure is a wasted adventure. So, what did you learn during your time in Liga?"

That was a harder question.

"I guess I learned something of the power of submission. The Julatians who obeyed your orders during the battle fared far better than those who panicked and tried to save themselves in their own strength."

"Is that why you ran off to fight the kunoi archers on the wall when Avi told you to stay put?" Ataymah prodded gently.

"I didn't say I knew this *before* we went," I retorted with more intensity than I would've liked. "Besides, I had Rohka with me. I knew he would bail me out."

"Don't make the mistake of thinking that your bird is insurance against foolishness. It doesn't work that way. But go on. Is there anything else you learned?"

Thinking of the adventure in the Cavern of Contest, I continued, "I also learned something of the value of help. Encouragement from others can help us reach our goals, especially when we're afraid."

"That's why it's called 'in-courage-ment'" Ataymah opined. "Because it puts courage into you. Every journey we go on is a journey into fear. No one can make it through fear to the real destination without being regularly refilled with courage."

* * *

Gaius thought I was crazy for heading off into the unknown. To sum up his attitude: If there isn't treasure involved, why go? But treasure wasn't really what I longed for. I longed for success. I longed to be a hero, to be highly esteemed, to matter. To be wanted, not just tolerated.

I said goodbye to Avi and Emma, not thinking to thank them for all they'd done to help me on my journey. Instead, I packed my few meager belongings and began the journey to the Valley of Salt.

The directions I'd been given took me west through lush green rolling hills bordered on the south by brown, stony ridges like those of Lithown. The journey was uneventful, which gave me plenty of time to think and to practice with my Shadom.

I loved the feel of the Shadom as it burst from my arm into my hand with a crisp, satisfying pop.

What about a bow and arrow? I wondered on one occasion during the journey. Sure enough, the thought created the action, and the Shadom reshaped into a bow.

"Look at that, Rohka! Pretty cool, huh? Umm . . . where do I get arrows from?"

Rohka looked at me like I should know the answer without asking. I didn't, but I pulled back the bowstring anyway. The string yielded to my touch with hardly any resistance, which was good since I had to use my left hand to draw the bow. As soon as the draw began, a red arrow formed. Releasing the bow caused the arrow to fly toward a nearby tree at breathtaking speed. The only problem was my aim. The arrow flew off to the left, bounced off a rock, fell to the ground, and disappeared with a pop.

I pulled back the bow again. Another arrow. Another errant shot. Another vanished arrow.

"Is there a limit to the number of arrows?"

Rohka chirped twice.

Cool.

"Sword," I called out. The Shadom became a sword again. "Spear. Axe. Halberd." As fast as I spoke the words, the great weapon re-formed. Then an idea dawned on me.

"Iron scepter." Nothing.

"Scepter." Nothing.

"Become a scepter." Nothing.

"Rohka, why won't this become a scepter?"

He gave me a blank stare.

"Well, it's still a great weapon, even if it won't transform into a scepter."

I loved having the Shadom in my hand. Turning it every which way while I walked, I casually inquired of Rohka, "Was the ruby always supposed to become this great weapon?"

I didn't really expect an answer, nor did I receive one, but asking the question gave form to what had once been incoherent thoughts.

"What I don't understand," I continued, "is the fact that I got the ruby from the scroll the goat gave me. How could that vile creature be the source of a gift of such blessing? He meant the ruby to be a stumbling block to me, a source of pride, but without pride driving me to work hard and succeed in the Cavern of Contest, I wouldn't have received the Shadom. That's so puzzling to me."

If Rohka was also puzzled, he didn't let on.

"And why did the ruby have to be broken for the red seeds to emerge? And what was with all the other stuff on the scroll about red and white?"

I was lost in my own thoughts.

* * *

Fortunately, Rohka led the way, since I was deep in thought and had lost any sense of where we were going. After many miles of traveling, we crested an inauspicious dry desert hill to find a large valley below us that could only be the Valley of Salt. The whole valley glistened white. If the sun had been brighter, the white gleam would have been blinding. The white salt gave the impression of being soft and powdery like fine sand, but it was solid, hard as a rock, and sharp as nails. I was glad I wore my sandals, as no one could've walked barefoot on the salt for very long.

"Battleaxe," I called out. My red forearm extended the Shadom as it reshaped itself into an axe. Swinging at the ground, I chiseled off a piece of salt. I recoiled as a stinging bitterness assaulted my mouth when I touched it to my tongue.

In the middle of the valley was a large city, much larger than Julat and far larger than Lithown. It had no walls, and the houses and city structures seemed to emerge gradually out of the salt itself.

The city sprawled out into four main clusters. The largest was in the center, with two clusters to the north and one to the south. They looked like a flattened "S" lying on the ground. In the center section, a gigantic blue tree towered over the entire city, dwarfing all else like a man standing among boys.

From where Rohka and I entered the valley, the blue tree was directly in front of us. As we neared the center section, I noticed what must have been salt-runners. People were leaving the city and the valley, heading in all different directions with salt loaded on sleighs that were pulled by large beasts of burden—animals which looked like a cross between a horse and an elephant. The sleighs were like ice skates, skimming across the hardened salt on sharpened blades.

No walls meant no gate, so Rohka and I entered the center section of the city unnoticed. My first impression upon entering the city was that it was far more diverse than Lithown or Julat. Some people looked Lithownian; others Julatian; still others were similar to Avi in outward appearance. My second impression was that there were many more buildings than houses in the city, and while the structures were not as luxurious as the houses in Julat, they felt much more important, befitting a center of commerce.

In the center of the city, it was impossible to ignore the enormous blue tree. It dominated everything else. Roads led away from it in every direction, like spokes from a hub. The diameter of its trunk must have been at least thirty feet, perhaps more.

Engraved in large bold letters in the middle of the tree were the words: Welcome to Cindropolis.

"Rom? Is that you?" a voice called out while I was gawking at the tree. Surprised to recognize the voice, I turned.

"Rabah? It's great to see you! What are you doing here?"

"I'm a salt runner for Lithown," Rabah replied, with perhaps a touch of embarrassment. "What are you doing here?"

"It's complicated. I guess I'd say that I'm on a journey." It sounded pretty dumb when I said it out loud.

"A journey? What happened to you after that day in the Lithown assembly? People still talk about what you did, although we do it in secret because the Elder forbids us to discuss it. Where—hey, is that a bird on your shoulder?"

"Yeah. Like I said, it's complicated."

We spent the next several minutes catching up. I told him some bare essentials from my story: moved to Julat, was involved with an expedition near Liga, and just arrived in the Valley of Salt. I carefully avoided the embarrassing episodes of getting lost in the caverns outside of Lithown and being attacked by Rohka.

"What about you?" I said to Rabah. "How did you get here?"

"Well, the Elder was pretty mad at us after you left. He never found out that we helped you, but we got branded troublemakers anyway," he said. "Esah and Domi are still working in the Quarry, but Timela convinced the Elder to let me try being a salt runner."

"Yeah . . . about that," I tried saying, but Rabah interrupted me.

"Where are you staying?"

"I don't know. We just got here."

"I can show you a guest house that's open to those here on business if you're interested."

"Sure. Thanks."

Rabah and I headed away from the giant blue tree on one of the paths leading south.

"Hey, Rabah, what's the deal with the blue tree?"

"The tree marks the center of Cindropolis. It was here long before any of these buildings were. Legend has it that it goes back even to the ancient times when there was another city in this place.

"What city?"

"I'm not sure. You'd have to ask someone else. But as I was saying, every month the leaves fall. Then they're gathered up, dried, mixed with salt from the valley, and ground into a fine powder, which is called Gibra. I'm sure you'll get a chance to try some. It's amazing. People can't really agree on what it tastes like. To me, it's an in describable mix of salty and sweet. But others swear that it's fruity or meaty tasting. People drink it in water, inhale it, or take pinches of it in their mouth. Some people bake it into a hardened form and suck on it. Technically, there are laws in Lithown about salt runners abstaining from Gibra, but everyone I know sneaks a little here and there." His eyes lit up while he talked about it.

"Hey, that reminds me of an old saying," he continued. "I first heard it when I started this job. If you want to keep a Lithownian salt runner from taking Gibra in Cindropolis, send another Lithownian with him."

I stared blankly at him.

"Don't you get it?" he asked in the face of my silence. "The only thing stronger for a Lithownian than the desire for Gibra is the desire for approval from others."

Oddly, as he recounted the saying, his face glistened for the briefest of moments. It reminded me of what Peris' face looked like in Julat, and Ataymah's in Liga. But then it was gone.

While we conversed, we arrived at the short-stay hostel at the eastern end of the center city. Rabah was heading back to Lithown that evening, so I helped him load his salt sleigh. As he departed, we agreed to try to get together the next time he was back.

By then Rohka had flown off to do some exploring, so I settled down in a room in the hostel by myself. My thoughts turned to the story of Daybe as I remembered that she was sent by the king to expose a fraudulent business scam. Tomorrow, I reasoned, I would begin the search for my great adventure.

CHAPTER 34

When I awoke the next morning, Rohka wasn't back yet. Since I couldn't figure out why everyone in Julat thought the Valley of Salt was so dangerous—it seemed harmless enough to me—I decided to explore on my own.

As I walked into the lobby of the hostel, the same person from the previous night was at the front desk. She smiled as I approached.

"Good morning. It's Rom, isn't it? Did you enjoy your evening here?"

"It was fine, thank you. Can I ask you a question?"

"Sure."

"Have you ever heard of a company or a group of people or something called the Salt Reapers?"

"Salt Reapers? No, sorry. But there's a company here called Salt Works. Perhaps they're related. Salt Works is housed just a couple blocks south of here. Why don't you check them out?"

"I will, thanks." I turned to go.

"Are you leaving? Do you want your ration of Gibra? It's free for all who spend the night here." She held up a small vial containing bluish powder.

"Sure."

"How do you want it?"

I must have looked confused, because she quickly added, "First time? Why don't you try it in some water?" Opening the little vial, she poured it into a glass with water, stirred it, and gave it to me to drink.

The water tasted salty-sweet, which reminded me of how Rabah described it, but it also had a bite to it, which I wasn't expecting. All in all, it tasted quite good and went down easily.

The young woman pointed me south, and I arranged to stay back at the hostel again that evening.

Soon after I left, I started feeling unusually energized. My senses drank in my surroundings. My brain accelerated. My body tingled. I felt alive in a new and fresh way, wanting nothing more than to sprint all the way to the Salt Works.

* * *

The Salt Works building was the tallest in the area, making it impossible to miss. Three guards were stationed at the front entrance, but what caught me completely by surprise were the three kunoi standing guard with them. Startled to see such beasts in this setting, I stopped in my tracks. My erratic behavior drew the attention of the human guards, and all three placed their hands on the hilts of their swords as the kunoi glared wildly at me. Tension filled the air. My mind reached out for the weapon in my arm, but as I did, I felt a peace wash over me. Rohka settled onto my shoulder. If the guards noticed his presence, it didn't show, but the kunoi most definitely did.

"What business do you have here?" one of the guards asked in a surly voice.

"Have you come seeking employment?" asked another in a more welcoming manner.

"I think so."

"Follow me," said the friendlier guard. The kunoi sniffed in my direction but made no move to hinder me from following. The other guards moved aside, and we passed into the entrance hall of the large building. "Wait here."

The guard soon returned with a smartly dressed young man.

"Welcome to the Salt Works. My name's Mikra. I'm told you're interested in a job. Is that right?"

"I guess so."

"Great! Our salt mines are fully staffed, but we have a new iron and copper mining operation that needs workers. Would that interest you? The work is not too difficult, and the daily pay is two vials of Gibra and one silver, plus free housing." Without giving me much of a chance to think about it, he added, "Why don't you come with me. That way you can look at the operation and decide for yourself. Okay? Great. Let's go."

Instead of heading into the building, Mikra walked quickly past me to go back outside. I turned and followed. We passed the guards and headed toward the giant tree in the central green.

"Where are we going?"

"To the work site. That building was the barracks where we provide housing for workers. If you take a position with us, you'll stay there. Most newcomers find the community there to be quite pleasant."

We walked briskly past the giant blue tree, heading north. Along the way, the man spewed facts about the Salt Works. He droned on about the different kinds of workers and different levels of opportunity.

When we arrived, I wasn't prepared for what I saw. Kunoi were everywhere. Not just tame kunoi, but hellhounds. In one area, hellhounds breathed fire to heat a huge cauldron, which contained what looked like molten copper. Less fierce-looking kunoi scurried everywhere, some carrying crates of materials from station to station, others foraging through crates at various stations and sorting materials. Among the kunoi, there were also humans working side-by-side.

The man explained the layout to me. In front of us was the main building of the Salt Works' copper and iron mining operation. Behind the main building was open space with green plants growing in walled rectangular plots of land that had been cleared of salt. A path led through the green field toward mining facilities nearer the upward slopes at the edge of the Valley of Salt.

While we stood there, my guide hailed a baby-faced man entering the building near us. "Jethera! Come here for a moment." As Jethera approached us, Mikra whispered in my ear, "What's your name?"

"Rom."

To Jethera he announced, "Rom here is ready for a job at the Salt Works. He's been briefed on the wages. You just need to show him what his responsibilities are."

Jethera looked as if he couldn't care less that I was there, but he said, "Come with me, and I'll show you to your spot."

As Jethera turned to leave, Mikra coughed loudly and held out a small pouch.

"Oh yeah," said Jethera, and he dropped something into the pouch.

"Come on," Jethera mumbled as he led me through the building toward the green field.

"You'll be starting in the fields like everyone else. When you've cleared your plot of salt, you'll get the mining equipment. I'm not sure what Mikra told you, but the pay for field workers is one bottle of Gibra per day. It raises to two once you start the actual mining."

He led me to a small patch of hardened salt on the edge of a series of grapevines. Many of the grapevines had people tending them, but there were also groups of people gathered together in open spaces not doing much of anything. Jethera handed me a shovel and a pickaxe and pointed to a ten-foot by twenty-foot rectangular patch of salt enclosed behind a six-foot high wall.

"Here's your spot. You can start work anytime you want."

Apparently, he thought I'd taken the job.

To my left was a young woman tending to a small vine. I

watched her work for a while. Noticing me, she turned.

"I'm Cora," she said.

"Rom."

Though Cora had a friendly smile, she had sad eyes which drooped downward. Her perky nose disagreed, pointing up slightly at the end. She was petite and cute, with small hands. She smelled vaguely like cinnamon.

"The first thing you do is dig up all the salt. It takes a while, but once you're done with that, you can plant your vine," said Cora.

I grabbed a pickaxe and took a swing at the hardened salt. The salt parried the blow and stinging reverberations raced up my arms. I barely dented it.

No, thanks. I'm not interested in this job. Maybe there's some other way to find out if Salt Works is running a scam.

I abandoned the plot and wandered toward one of the groups gathered near the pathway to the mines. Rohka hopped off my shoulder and stayed back at the salt patch. He seemed preoccupied with watching Cora's vine.

As I walked by vines in various states of growth, I felt someone come up alongside me.

"Hey, Captain. I'm Stig. Are you going up to check out that group over there? I'll go with you."

"Captain?" I replied.

"You look like a captain, so I decided to call you that."

Stig was a balding young man, whose remaining wispy blonde hairs fanned out in an attempt to conceal a massive scalp. He had unusually muscular forearms and a semi-permanent sly smile etched onto his face.

Stig and I arrived at a group of about fifteen men and women standing along the pathway. They were playing a game called Spinning Crystals, in which they spun an enormous polished crystal of salt—kind of like a top—and placed bets of silver coins on where it would fall over and land on a mat.

"Let's give it a try, Captain," Stig said joyfully, as if we'd been friends for years. He placed a silver coin on one of the open spaces.

"I don't have any silver," I admitted. People all around stared at me like I was an idiot for showing up to a gambling game without money.

Stig handed me a silver coin. "Here, I've got an extra one. Make your bet."

After watching for a bit, I came up with an idea of how to rig the game so I could win. I placed my bet on a square opposite of where I stood. This elicited a few stares, but Stig thought it was funny. The person in the center gave the crystal top a spin and moved out of the way while we all watched it meander its way around the board. As I'd hoped, the top began inching its way between me and the square I'd bet on. Whispering ever so softly under my breath, I muttered the word "Ischuro." The wind forced the spinning crystal over into my square, where it soon fell. I collected eight silver coins. I gave Stig back two of them and pocketed six.

"Let's try again," I said. "Better stick with my lucky square."

Lest it be too obvious, I lost that time. And the next. On the fourth, the crystal meandered toward Stig's space, so I let him win. He was ecstatic, and everyone laughed good-naturedly at him. He gave me one of his silver coins.

"I think you're good luck."

As we prepared for a fifth game, a loud-mouthed girl bullied her way into our circle. The expression on her face was joyless and bitter, the irises of her eyes unnaturally black.

"Silver coins? Mot's monkeys! Last week this was a Gibra board, and now we're playing for silver coins? Come on babies, let's play for Gibra." She plopped down a vial on one of the spaces. Tension rose. If anyone wanted to object, no one dared. Even still, no one placed a bet.

"Come on! Is this a game or what? Okay. Let's play for shares. Surely you babies can do that, can't you?" She whipped out an empty vial and poured a fraction of her Gibra into it.

Shamed into it, a couple people poured portions of their Gibra into the vial and then selected their square with their remaining portion.

The girl confronted me and Stig. "Come on," she bellowed. "Place your bets."

Stig looked at me.

"I don't have any Gibra," I admitted.

"I'll sell you a portion for the three silver coins you won," Stig offered.

"Sure. Why not?"

He poured in two portions. I picked my same spot. Stig chose a new one.

The croupier sent the crystal spinning. With higher stakes, I had to be careful because people were watching more closely. "Ischuro," I muttered ever so softly and exerted a tiny push. The crystal started wobbling but surprisingly stayed upright. In fact, it spun more quickly as it meandered toward the loud-mouthed girl's square. So, I quickly blew again. This time the crystal almost fell into my square, but then it suddenly recovered.

All the gyrations heightened the excitement, and people cheered wildly. Stealing a glance at the loud-mouthed girl, I noticed her eyes fixed on the crystal and her lips moving ever so slightly.

Concentrating more intensely, I sent a third wave of whispered force, greater than the previous two, toward the crystal, which fell unnaturally into my square.

Stig yelled out, "Way to go, Captain!" as he slapped me on the back. "We should call you Captain Luck," he chortled. "Yeah, we'll call you Cluck for short." He laughed, amused at his own wittiness. "Good job, Cluck. Go get your winnings."

The loud-mouthed girl shot daggers at me with her eyes. "Double or nothing," she insisted. "Just me and him, half the board apiece." She slammed down another vial of Gibra.

Someone in the group protested, "But, Rhea, his is a mixed vial, and yours is pure. No one is going to take that bet."

Rhea put a second vial down next to the first.

"Two for one, then."

All eyes turned to me. She clearly wanted the vial I just won. I hadn't yet come to understand the depth of her desire for Gibra and, at that moment, infuriating her in front of everyone felt better than winning more of the bluish powder.

"No thanks," I said as sweetly as possible. "I got lucky once. I wouldn't want to tempt fate." I grabbed my newly won vial and left her fuming, as if I'd robbed her of a prized possession.

Stig followed me, chuckling to himself as he walked. I slowed down to walk with him.

"That was great. She's a real hellhound. Are you going to drink your Gibra now or later?"

"Do you want to split it? After all, two shares in here came from you."

Stig gave me strange look. "You're new here, aren't you? Have you ever had Gibra before?"

"Yes, I'm new. This is only my second bottle. I drank my first one last night, and it was pretty good."

"Thought so," Stig laughed. "You wouldn't normally ask someone to share a bottle of Gibra with you. It's too personal. Besides, you paid me for my shares so they're yours now."

"Last night when I tried it, I had it with water. Is that the best way?"

"My favorite way is to pour the whole vial under my tongue and hold it there for as long as I can."

Stig watched amusedly while I tried his method.

That Gibra tasted different than the one before. It was still somewhat salty and sweet, but other unidentifiable flavors appeared also. All in all, it added up to a much fuller, richer flavor. I wondered how much of the flavor came from how I ingested it and how much was because it was a mixed vial.

Reluctantly, Stig said he needed to get back to his work so I walked him to his patch of ground. However long he'd been at it, only about half of the hardened salt was cleared away.

At that moment, something in me made me want to get back to my plot of salt. The tingling sensation of being alive had returned, and I felt nervous excitement well up in me as I thought about my plot.

What if I can get the patch cleared before Stig does? I'm behind now, but maybe I can catch up. I only gave it one swing the first time around.

As I approached my plot, an official-looking man was standing in front of Cora's area with two rather menacing kunoi next to him. Rohka was nowhere to be found. The man wore a harsh scowl on his face, and Cora's sad eyes were fixed dejectedly on the ground in front of her. His lips were moving, but I couldn't make out what he was saying.

I entered my walled-off space. The man with the kunoi soon moved to stand in the entrance to my plot.

"Are you the new guy? Rom, isn't it?"

"Yes."

"I'm Shafat. You haven't done any work," he said gruffly. "You're an employee of the Salt Works now. You were hired to work, so get to work. If you don't work, you won't get paid any Gibra." With that, he left.

Strangely, I felt both a desire and a compulsion to obey.

With the tingle of Gibra still in my mind, I reached for the Shadom, willing it to emerge as an axe. I sliced and hacked away at the hardened salt floor. The Shadom was far superior to the pick-axe they'd allotted me. It was as light as air and stronger than steel.

Soon I switched to a war hammer, and with shattering blows I assaulted the salt floor until it heaved and cracked. For the whole afternoon I worked, sweat trickling down my brow as I vigorously cleared a small portion of my plot down to the soil beneath. I felt driven by a combination of the desire to succeed, the growing longing for more Gibra, and the satisfaction of doing something to free the ground from its salt prison and enable it to be productive.

As evening rolled in, Stig invited me to head back to the barracks with him. Cora was still working on her plant when we left. As we exited the area, I stole a glance at Stig's plot. He had more cleared than I did, but I smugly concluded that my day was more productive, and it was only a matter of time until I surpassed his progress.

As we walked, Stig and I joked together about Rhea, the loud-mouthed crazy girl from the Gibra game. Stig nicknamed her the Cursed Spinster. At the barracks, I received a boxy room in which to sleep, not far from Stig's. Since my possessions consisted of the clothes on my back and the scroll in my pocket, there was nothing to retrieve from the hostel or to unpack in my new room. Somehow Rohka was already in the room when I entered. With him perched near my head, I drifted off to sleep, wondering if this was indeed the start of a new adventure.

CHAPTER 35

The next several days proceeded in roughly the same way. Mid-morning, Stig and I would make our way to the work area, and Cora was usually there when we arrived. We worked separately for a time, usually meeting up in the early afternoon to socialize. Stig and I wandered the Salt Works' grounds meeting the craziest people. Often, we played Spinning Crystals. I won enough and helped Stig win enough to keep it fun for us, though try as I might I couldn't motivate anyone to bet Gibra portions again.

To me Gibra was bottled happiness. Each day I took my vial of Gibra in the afternoon after socializing. I liked taking it then because the afterglow kept me focused and humming along until the workday was done. All morning long I anticipated taking it.

I also learned that Shafat, the supervisor, stopped by at the same time every day.

"I've never seen such speed!" he remarked effusively one day. "You might set a record for clearing the salt in the shortest amount of time."

Such comments felt like taking a dose of Gibra. My section was almost clear and I was rapidly gaining on Stig, who didn't seem to care one way or the other. Shafat usually yelled at him for being lazy, but he just laughed it off.

Cora, however, was different. Even though she was further along in the overall process than both me and Stig, I heard Shafat berate her every day for her lack of progress. I hadn't to that point found evidence of corruption and fraud at the Salt Works, but they certainly were relentless with people they didn't think matched up to their lofty standards.

One day when I arrived at my work site, I noticed a kuno sitting outside of Cora's space, so I walked over to see if she was all right. Having grown accustomed to kunoi in Cindropolis, I was taken aback when this kuno growled and bared his teeth as I neared. I chose to go back into my plot and yell over the wall instead.

"Cora, are you okay?"

"I'm fine."

"Do you need some help?"

"Leave me alone."

So, I left her alone and got to work on clearing more salt.

Somewhere around the middle of the workday, Stig wandered over.

"Hey Cluck. What's with the kuno?"

"I don't know. It was here when I got here. Cora doesn't want to talk about it." I tried to say it loud enough so she could hear me.

"Have you downed your vial of Gibra yet?"

"No, why?"

"I hear one of the groups is betting Gibra today. It would be great to win one of those mixed vials. Do you want to go and play?"

A surge of excitement shot through me, but I tried to play it cool. "Sure. Why not? Which group is it?"

"I think it's the group that's normally over by Stina's land. You know, the group with that Wicki guy with the big eyes and the two noisy girls."

"Is Rhea playing?" I asked, trying to sound nonchalant.

"I don't think so. Why? You don't want to take her Gibra again?" he said with a big, goofy grin on his face.

"Something about her feels dark to me," I admitted.

"Maybe she's a Power," Stig replied, laughing as he said it. "Cindropolis is supposed to be filled with Powers. Maybe finally found one!"

"What's a Power?"

"It's mostly just stuff people make up to try to scare each other. Powers are supposed to be . . . um . . . a thing with special powers. I don't know. It was supposed to be a joke."

* * *

The entire time we played Spinning Crystals, Stig kept up a running dialogue with himself about all the people he knew who could be a Power. After we both won mixed vials, I returned to my plot.

It was quite late by the time I got back, but I wanted to finish clearing the salt that day, if possible, so that the next day I could bask in Shafat's praise.

I had just summoned my axe for work when I heard the faint sound of crying emerging from Cora's area.

"Cora? Is that you? Are you all right?"

The crying grew louder. I poked my head out to investigate, but the kuno still guarded her entrance.

"Cora, come right up next to the wall. We can talk through the wall. What's the matter?"

"I just don't understand," she said, trying to stifle her sobs. "I do everything these people want me to do and all that happens is I get yelled at. I even gave some of my Gibra to Shafat to try to get him to like me, but it just seemed to make him despise me more. You're not even here half the time, yet somehow you're making great progress, and you seem to be having the time of your life. I don't understand. What do you have that I don't?"

Somewhere deep in my soul, I think I knew the question she was really asking. She felt lost and needed a guide for the journey, but I was afraid to talk to her about such things. So, I tried to cheer her up instead.

"Cora, you're doing fine. Shafat's a jerk. He doesn't like anyone."

She started to cry again. "You don't have a kuno sitting outside of your door growling at you constantly. And all Shafat ever says are positive things about you."

I wasn't sure what to say. Shafat said positive things about me, I reasoned at the time, because I was a hard worker. The Cavern of Contest had taught me that: set your mind on what you want and don't stop working until you get it. Up until then I assumed arrogantly that if Cora would just work harder, she would succeed.

"Rom, maybe you could come and help me. I'll give you some of my Gibra if you do." Her voice sounded desperate and hopeful at the same time.

Something in the way she asked confirmed the realization that her need was deeper. She needed rescue the way that Rohka; Avi and Emma; and Esah, Rabah, and Domi had rescued me. I imagined the stone walls around her plot feeling like the walls of the Quarry in Lithown and the kuno guarding her plot like Josef or Plute—though in truth, her plot may have had more similarities to the barren wilderness I was in before I arrived at Lithown.

Suddenly, I thought of an idea to help her escape from the kuno, but I quickly pushed it away.

To do such a thing would change everything.

As I fought against the idea, I noticed a flutter of wings, and Rohka settled on the wall between us. His eyes glowed, and as I met his gaze, I felt a strong impulse to reread my scroll, which I hadn't opened since arriving in Cindropolis. Unrolling the scroll, I half expected to find something new, but it was still the same story of Daybe and Zan.

What am I supposed to make of this? Rohka still stared at me, as if expecting me to understand. *I'm looking for corruption in Salt Works, but what about the fact that Zan helps Daybe accomplish her mission?*

"Rom? Are you still there?"

I knew what had to be done to help her. "Cora, I'm not sure you really want my help. I'm not that good at helping people."

"I do want your help. Please, Rom. Please help me. I'll give you as much Gibra as you desire."

Summoning my courage, I whispered, "Pickaxe." I smashed it repeatedly into the wall to create a toehold, and then jammed the Shadom into the wall above my head to pull myself up. I swung my body onto the top of the wall where Rohka was perched, and to where Cora was now looking with longing in her eyes.

"Take my hand," I whispered. "I'll pull you over to my side and get you out of here." Using my arm, she scaled the wall. I jumped back into my area and helped her down into it.

So far, so good.

"Come on. Let's sneak you out of here."

We moved to the back wall and I helped her up and over it. Staying low so the kuno wouldn't see her, she tumbled into the adjoining plot behind mine, which was empty because it was so late. I walked as casually as possible out of my entrance and headed back toward the main building at the edge of the field.

Just as we were about to leave Salt Works, I heard a howl. A stop-you-in-your-tracks kind of kuno howl.

Dread filled Cora's face. Knowing I had to act quickly, I ran a few steps toward the kuno. "Over here," I yelled. "She's over here!"

"What are you doing?" Cora gasped.

"We have to lure him away from your plot before help arrives. Otherwise it'll be obvious you're responsible."

"Responsible for what?" Cora wanted to know.

Without answering Cora's question, I shouted "Run!" and grabbed her hand because my plan had worked, so to speak. The kuno sprinted toward us on all fours. As soon as we started running, the kuno stopped to howl again and then launched after us.

Cora and I raced past the main Salt Works building back toward the central portion of the city. We headed into the open space that separated the mining area from the city. Other kunoi joined the hunt.

"Thureos. Cobaqeren." My light shield and helmet fell from the sky. I pulled Cora to a stop in the middle of the open space. "If we go too near the city, we'll attract unwanted attention. We have to make our stand here. Get behind me."

Four kunoi raced toward us. "Bow!" My hand shook as I pulled back the string, knowing that Ataymah and Avi were not there to help. I was on my own. Firing arrows as rapidly as I could, I pleaded with them to somehow find their targets. My trembling hands and pounding heart exacerbated my poor aim, and arrows sprayed everywhere.

A hand settled on my back. "Take courage," Cora said. "You can do this."

Her encouragement calmed me, and my next arrow hit a kuno in the face. The final arrow implanted in another kuno's leg.

"Sword," I yelled.

The first arriving kuno dove at me, but I deflected him to the side with my shield. Whirling around, I swung my sword and sliced through nothing but air. Cora yelled. Claws raked across my arm. Jaws lunged at my neck. Re-centering my sword I drove it straight up, skewering my attacker.

Side-stepping my falling victim, I cried, "Ischuro," and blew a wave of force at a second kuno, who was trying to pin a brawling Cora to the ground. I managed to knock him off Cora enough for her to give him a swift upward kick and break free. Howling filled the air.

"Spear!" I hurled my weapon toward him as he lunged at Cora again. It caught him in the back, but the howling continued.

Where is that coming from?

I searched frantically until I noticed it was the kuno with the arrow in his leg. I took three big bounds in his direction and dove at him helmet first. It smashed him in the mouth, silencing his howl. My sword pierced his side as I barreled into him. The fight left him as we landed on the ground in a heap.

"Cora, we have to get out of here! Now!"

Extricating myself from the mess, I ran with Cora as fast as we could into the outskirts of the city. Thankfully, it had grown dark. We found a large building and collapsed in exhaustion behind it.

Blood slowly leaked from the claw marks on my arm, but I was okay. I caught my breath more quickly than I expected. All the hard, manual labor clearing the salt had me in good physical shape. Cora was sore but in one piece.

A howl rose up from the site of our battle.

"We better keep moving," I said. We helped each other up and began making our way back toward the barracks under the cover of darkness. While we scurried along, I wrote off Cora's silence as shock.

And, to be honest, I was a little shocked too. I only planned to help her escape, but it escalated so quickly.

Why were they so desperate to keep Cora from leaving?

My gut told me that something more was going on in Cindropolis than what I saw with my eyes.

As we approached the barracks, I saw two kunoi guarding the door. Instantly it dawned on me, between the claw marks on my arm and the howls that pierced the night, the guards would never let me pass.

"Cora, I can't go back to the barracks tonight. My injured arm is too suspicious. You go ahead. I'll go spend the night in the hostel I used when I first got here."

Her eyes widened with fear. "I can't go back by myself. Please don't leave me alone."

So, we both headed to the hostel. Our rooms ended up being on opposite ends of the building. She went to hers, and I settled into mine, ready for some rest. Not much time had passed when there was a knock at my door.

"I forgot to give this to you," Cora said as she handed me a vial of Gibra.

"What's this for?"

"I promised you Gibra if you would help me," she responded.

I should have refused it, but my eyes lingered on the slender vial of powder. We hadn't gotten paid for the day, so I had none of my own. My heart beat fast.

"I'm not sure if what we did will actually end up helping, but thanks," I said and took the vial from her.

*   *   *

The next day, Cora and I determined that our best bet was to go back to Salt Works and pretend nothing had happened. I cleaned up my arm and hoped that anyone who looked at it would think they were cuts obtained while clearing salt.

As far as we knew, no one outside of the kunoi we fought had seen us, and they were all dead. Kunoi were a rough group, and Cindropolis was a rough place at times, unlike Lithown or Julat. Kunoi howls in the night were a regular occurrence, as were fights and brawls.

Still, I kept wondering what Shafat's response would be when he noticed that the kuno he left to watch Cora was no longer there.

How did I ever think that killing the kuno guarding her was a good idea?

"Rom, I'm scared," Cora admitted. "What's going to happen?"

"I don't know. But I'm here to help you. Don't be afraid." I tried to sound brave. We both took a dose of Gibra, which helped immensely.

Cora's plot was open. No kuno in sight. Seeing she was safe, I got to work on mine, the Gibra flowing through me and energizing me for the work.

It was my last day removing the hardened salt. I hurried to finish before Shafat came by.

Surely he'll have some over-the-top affirmative thing to say about me if I finish today. Maybe it will divert attention away from Cora.

Sure enough, when Shafat came by in the afternoon, he barely engaged Cora at all. He didn't ask where the kuno was or yell at her. He just looked around and continued over to my area.

"Rom, this is some of the best work I've ever seen. I can't believe you've completed this part already! If this is how quickly you're able to clear the land, I can't wait to see how large and fruitful your grapevine will be. Let me go and get you the best seedling I can find."

And with that, he left.

Still basking in Shafat's praise, I whispered over the wall, "Cora, did he say anything to you?"

"Nothing."

"I guess the plan worked."

"I guess so."

Shafat returned later that day with a grapevine seedling in a clay pot.

"This was the heartiest one I could find. I had to fight off others for it. I won by promising that you'd grow this vine into the greatest one here. When I told them how quickly you cleared the land, my claim triumphed."

"This seedling is the descendant of one of the most ancient grapevines in the valley, so you must take good care of it," he added. "That's another reason why everyone was fighting to get it."

The brown vine sticking out of the pot did indeed look healthy. Green leaves had already sprouted on the multiple branches, full and thick. Stig later told me he'd never seen such a large, healthy seedling in a starter pot before.

"Don't be surprised if some higher ups from Salt Works come by to see how you're doing," Shafat said. "They have high hopes for this seedling and the grapes that will come of it. Just make sure you don't let us down."

CHAPTER 36

The next day, when I got to my spot, Shafat was waiting for me along with someone I recognized as Julatian but couldn't place. His dark features contrasted his richly colored robes.

"Rom, you remember Noch, don't you?"

"Sure. From Julat."

How do I know him?

Noch spoke up. "I see that you did indeed seek out an adventure in the mining industry. I came to Cindropolis to conduct some business and thought I would look you up. Salt Works is a great operation, and Shafat here says you're doing wonderfully—so much so that they entrusted you with a seedling from the ancient Shinar vine!

"It's like you have access to a Book of Knowledge! Isn't that what you said, Shafat?" Noch enthused.

"It is," Shafat agreed. "But I'm sure Rom hasn't seen the Salt Works' Book of Knowledge. He may earn a visit, though, if he can get back to the progress he made at the beginning."

"Are you serious?" Noch said. "Could he really gain access to a Book of Knowledge? Rom, do you know what this means?! Do you know what you could do with a Book of Knowledge? Wow! That would change everything.

"Well, I'd better let you get back to work. You've got a lot to do. And a lot riding on this. I'll be sure to tell everyone in Julat that you're a rousing success in Cindropolis!"

* * *

As time passed, however, my seedling did nothing. It was no better than the day I planted it. I tried everything, but I couldn't make it grow. Watering with Gibra, like Cora suggested, didn't help. Watering without Gibra didn't help. Not watering didn't help. Breaking up the ground around the seedling didn't help. Ignoring it didn't help. Everyone had a different piece of advice, even Stig. He told me to try not caring, but that still didn't make my seedling grow.

"You do know that your chance to see Cindropolis' Book of Knowledge is slipping away?" Shafat said to me one day, wrongly thinking that my problem was a lack of motivation instead of a lack of help. A tutor was what I needed, not a taskmaster.

"Maybe if you let me see it now it would help me know how to get this to grow," I suggested meekly.

"Let you see a Book of Knowledge now? You've haven't done anything of value! A reading from the Book of Knowledge is only for the best and brightest. It almost guarantees you success."

"What does it do?" I asked.

"It gives you knowledge, moron. Why do you think they call it a Book of Knowledge? And knowledge is power, so anyone who gets knowledge gets power. Now get back to work."

* * *

When I thought about quitting, Rohka squawked. The story on my scroll wouldn't change. The conversation with Ataymah about the value of submission in Liga kept coming to mind. To scatter felt more dangerous than to stay and obey. The idea of earning a look at a Book of Knowledge had lodged itself in my head, though it was a fading flicker of hope. And some inexplicable craving tied me to the land and the work.

I was stuck.

The only bright spot was the time spent with Cora and Stig.

When we hung out together, we didn't talk about growing vines. Cora's wasn't doing that well, and Stig had just received his seedling but didn't care what happened to it.

I continued to receive Gibra every day and that was a source of happiness too. For the fun of it, Cora and I tried different ways of combining our portions to see if it changed the taste and how it affected us, but Stig mostly wanted to keep his to himself.

Yet even those bright spots were not to last.

* * *

One morning, when Stig and I arrived at the fields for work, Cora wasn't there and a kuno was stationed outside her plot. He stared angrily but did nothing to harass me.

Shafat arrived that morning for his daily harangue.

"Rom, that seedling hasn't grown! What's the matter with you? Don't you know how valuable that Shinar cutting is? What a waste it was, giving it to you!"

"I'm trying my best, sir," I said, ashamed because I knew he was right.

"Try harder," he barked, expressing explicitly the same harsh and condescending attitude I'd once had toward Cora. I'd judged her lack of success as laziness, back in the days when I cleared my plot with ease. My inability to make my seedling grow, no matter what I tried, helped me realize that her struggle may not have been because of a lack of effort.

"What happened to Cora, sir?" I blurted out.

Shafat turned on me in a rage. "Why are you worried about that worthless girl? I sent her to the dungeons. Did she really think I wouldn't notice that my kuno was missing? She'll pay the price for her audacity. Worry about your vine or you'll be next. Maybe I should leave a kuno here to watch over you too." Then, as if the idea just dawned on him, he smiled and said, "I think it's time for that."

True to his threat, a larger, more fearsome kuno than the one assigned to Cora's plot was waiting for me when I got back that afternoon from Spinning Crystals. The kuno moved aside so I could enter but then growled menacingly as he filled the doorway barring my exit. My only experience with kunoi was in combat. Now that I had the chance to study one up close, and it only increased my unease. Kunoi certainly were ugly creatures. Standing on his hind legs, he was taller than me. His gnarled black face had a hauntingly sinister feel. I kept worrying that I carried the stench of my previous kunoi battles, and one day my kuno guard would sniff me out. His bright yellow eyes never left me, burning a hole in the back of my neck while I worked.

I say "work," but there was nothing to do. I mostly sat and stared at my worthless, stagnant vine shoot.

More days passed. No matter what I did, I couldn't make the vine grow. I felt trapped and alone. Stig didn't understand. Cora was gone. Avi was back in Julat. Emma couldn't help this time, as was evidenced by how long it had taken for my clawed arm to heal. I hadn't heard from Rabah again. The frustration was so overwhelming that I'd long forgotten about the possibility of infiltrating Salt Works and discovering some great fraud. The hope of seeing a Book of Knowledge was extinguished as well.

If I can't even grow a grape vine, how can I hope to accomplish anything of real value.

The probability of failure was always with me, never far from my thoughts. Though it shouldn't have, the fear of failure overshadowed every success from the past.

I came to discover that misery loves company, but it never actually finds it because misery can't see anyone else's problems but its own. As I turned inward, I felt more and more alone.

It almost feels like when I was alone in those dark tunnels under-

ground on the way to Julat. It's that same claustrophobic feeling. I need help.

"Rohka," I cried out. "Where are you? Come help me." No answer.

The bird can't hear me. Why should he care whether this vine grows or not? Why do I even care?

But I did. Despite the illogic of it all, I cared.

Warm tears began to form in my eyes. Somewhere deep in my soul, I knew he could help me, if only he heard me crying. There wasn't anywhere else to turn.

What good is he if he won't come and help at a time like this?

"Please, Rohka," I whispered for fear of the kuno, "don't let me face my own ruin. I know it's just a vine and it shouldn't matter to me, but it does. I can't live with failure."

This is silly. He can't hear me. And even if he did come, how could he tell me what to do?

Somewhere in the midst of my tears and self-pity, Rohka settled onto the ground near the plant.

"Rohka!" The sight of him was like warm sunshine breaking through on a cloudy day. My fear and anxiety subsided.

Rohka walked around the vine seedling. I watched with trepid anticipation, wanting to believe that something would happen.

"Am I supposed to walk around it?" I asked aloud. "Is that what you're telling me?"

I scrambled to my feet and hurried to follow him around the little vine, taking care not to step on it. We must have looked quite silly, but at that point I didn't care. The only one watching was the kuno. I felt his eyes following me, but somehow he seemed oblivious to Rohka's presence.

While we were walking, Rohka began to sing. The notes of the song lifted the limp and drooping leaves just slightly. I tried to whistle what I heard, but my rendition wasn't even close. Whistling made me feel better, though, so I kept it up. It was all we did that day.

When I arrived the next day, the kuno was there waiting for me, and Shafat still yelled at me, but the seedling's leaves had retained their newfound life. Shafat may have missed it, but I'd studied that dumb plant long enough to know that something had happened.

"Rohka, where are you? Come back and help me. I know there's more to do."

Silence.

"Rohka, I know you want to help. I'm not doing anything else until you show up."

So, stubbornly I sat down and waited, but thankfully not long. Rohka appeared and landed next to the seedling. This time, instead of walking around the plant, he dug into the ground as if looking for a worm. I drew close to watch him. When I neared, Rohka touched my right forearm with his beak. Out popped my Shadom in the form of a sword, digging deeply into the ground. I worked out what he was telling me to do, so I dug a trench all the way around the seedling, about a foot back from the plant. Anticipating what Rohka might want next, I pulled out a vial of Gibra to pour it into the trench. I saw others do something similar to fertilize their plants.

Rohka screeched.

"Not Gibra? What then? Water?"

Rohka seemed much happier with this suggestion.

"I'm going to get some water," I said to the kuno, who growled as he moved aside.

When I returned, Rohka flew to eye-level and hovered in the air, impeding my progress toward the hole.

"What?"

Rohka flew to the top of my head and started tapping. *What does this mean? Use my brain? No. Oh, I bet I know.*

I set down the water.

"Cobaqeren," I declared, and my helmet fell from the sky into my waiting arms. It took a minute, but I figured out I was supposed to pour the water into the helmet. As soon as I did, Rohka began to slosh around in the water, using his wings to splash the water onto the insides of the helmet, as if he was washing it. Using my hand, I did the same. Strangely, the more the water washed up against the sides of the helmet, the cleaner the water felt.

The time came to pour the water into the trench. As it flowed into the ground, a burning and hissing sound rose up from the fledgling vine.

When I left that evening, Rohka stayed behind. I was anxious to get back the next day to see what happened. Shamefully, the fact that Cora was exiled to a dungeon barely registered with me. I'd become so consumed with the hope that I might succeed so I could get on with my next assignment that I forgot about her.

The next day, the vine was bigger still.

"Rohka, it's working!" I filled my helmet with more water, purified it, and poured it into the trench. I tried whistling something at the plant while I worked.

"What's next?"

Rohka flew level with my eyes.

"Rohka, I know there's more. What else do I need to do? I'm ready to learn," I implored. Abruptly, Rohka flew straight at the kuno guarding my door, smashing into his ugly snout. The kuno yelped in pain and turned toward me, teeth bared.

Instinctively, I called out "Thureos," and my light shield fell from the sky as I prepared for the battle that Rohka initiated. Except the battle never came. The kuno calmed down and only stared in my direction with a puzzled look. It was as if he couldn't see my shield. In his dazed and confused state, he returned to his post as if nothing had happened.

I searched for Rohka. Above my head I heard his wings flapping. Around him was a beam of light that fell directly on my shield, which hung on my left wrist. Finally it dawned on me: the purpose of my almost-confrontation with the kuno was simply for the purpose of summoning my shield.

The reflected light coming off the shield was brighter than the ambient light. I moved closer to the vine until it basked in the reflected glow. As when the water went into the trench, the same hissing and burning sound emerged from the plant as the light shone on its leaves. This time, though, wisps of smoke rose up off it. The smoke was putrid, like the smell of burnt leaves that had once been moldy and wet. Something in the revolting smell was familiar, though. Almost like a bittersweet saltiness.

At first, I thought the leaves themselves were burning, but it was a darker film on top of the leaves. It burned away like paper over an open flame. What remained when the film was gone were the deepest, lushest green leaves.

By the next day, the vine was nearly twice its original size and had twice as many leaves. I continued to work, asking for Rohka's help every day. Seeking help was a lesson I'd learned with Avi during the Cavern of Contest, but the more I got used to seeking help, the more I found it, ironically, liberating. Receiving help made me feel much less alone. In a week, I started building a trellis system to support the vine.

"Well done, Rom," Shafat cheered. "I knew my blunt chastisement and a kuno guard would encourage you to work harder. That's what I'm here for—to unlock your potential so you can take that Shinar seedling and do something fantastic with it. I have to tell you, I was starting to get worried. Wait until the boss sees what you're producing here. She'll get off my back about you and probably reward me for the good work I've done with another glance at the Book of Knowledge. Let me know the moment a grape appears. By the way, I'll be reassigning this kuno to another slacker in need of some Shafat-style motivation."

Shafat could think what he wanted about how helpful his rebukes and the kuno had been, but I knew better. I knew Rohka made all this happen. There could have been a hundred kunoi guarding my door, and I still would've never solved the problem on my own. But with Rohka's help, I did it. With Rohka's help, I triumphed.

In another week's time, the first tiny grapes appeared. Shafat brought others to come and see my work, and they asked me for advice. Unexpectedly, I came to love taking care of the vine. For the first time, it felt like I had accomplished something; like I built something. The goat's accusations about my power and worth coming only from my connection to Avi rang more and more hollow, as did the Elder's assessment that I was a useless troublemaker.

The first seeds of purpose began to sprout in my mind, and with that emerging sense of direction came the reminder that I was in Cindropolis to discover what was truly going on at Salt Works.

CHAPTER 37

When the first budding fruit appeared on the vine, I brought it to Shafat's attention. It was still green, but I was hungry for more affirmation. The vine itself had doubled in size again, so I was forced to spend as much time rebuilding the trellis as I did caring for the vine.

"Great job! It looks like you're ready for your worker," Shafat announced. "I'll bring him by tomorrow so you can begin to train him. Keep this up, and I'll talk to the higher ups about letting you visit the Salt Works' Book of Knowledge."

The next day Shafat arrived with a small burlap bag tied gently at the top with a red ribbon.

"Hold out your hand."

Shafat loosened the strings and turned the bag over. Into my hand dropped a tiny milky-white snake covered in wood shavings. Along with the snake came four nuggets of copper and a square chunk of wood.

"Here's your miner, Rom." Noticing my confusion, Shafat continued. "This snake is going to be the one who retrieves the copper from the ground for you. He's young and impressionable, so take these copper nuggets and use some of the grapes from your vine to teach him to retrieve the copper. He'll learn to love the fruit of the vine as a reward for retrieving copper and will be motivated to serve you in this role, just as you have been motivated to serve Cindropolis in your role. When he's ready, release him into the ground, and he'll go and retrieve copper nuggets for you in exchange for the pleasure of more grapes.

"I should tell you that this snake is highly valued as well. His mother comes from the region of Shinar, the same region where your vine is from. Some even believe that he's a distant descendant of the Great Snake. Make sure you feed him nothing but grapes or this won't work. In addition, each day he needs to sink his teeth into this block of wood. It's a special piece of wood designed to absorb the venom he produces. He should already love the taste of the wood since he was hatched into these shavings."

In another day's time, a few of the grapes ripened, turning deep reddish purple and smelling quite delicious. I took one and offered it to the baby snake. He flicked his tiny forked tongue at the grape, which was nearly the size of his head.

"Rohka, he's not doing anything with the grape. What should I do?" I was growing accustomed to Rohka answering me when I asked for help. Sure enough, he flitted over to the snake, whose forked tongue began to investigate him. Rohka could have picked him up like a worm, but instead he punched at the grape, piercing the skin. Drops of juice flowed down the side.

I positioned it so the tiny snake's tongue would taste the juice. Once he tasted it, he opened his mouth to ingest the whole thing. As he digested it, I placed the copper nuggets in front of his mouth to try to develop some association between the grapes and the copper. His little fangs were hardly developed, but when I placed the wood chunk near his tiny mouth, he gladly sank his teeth into it.

Stig came by while I worked with my snake.

"Hey, I got one of those snakes too. Does yours like the copper? Mine keeps banging his head against the nuggets. You should come see it."

Instead of leaving, though, he kept talking. "Have you tried some of the grapes yet? They're really sweet."

"You ate the grapes? Are we allowed to do that?"

"Why not? From the looks of it, you're going to have way more grapes than that little snake is going to be able to eat. Shafat would never know if you tried one of them. I heard that if you mix them with Gibra, the combination is unbelievably good."

The grapes did look delicious and smelled even better. Remembering that the only thing I'd ingested to that point in Cindropolis was Gibra, I began to long for a taste.

"Maybe tomorrow if there are more," I said, trying to convince myself of the prudence of this line of thinking. "Right now, I only have another four. I think I need all of them for training my snake today."

"Here, try one of mine," Stig said, handing me a lightly colored red grape. It was firmer and smaller than the grapes my vine produced. I popped it into my mouth. My teeth sank into it, and it crunched satisfyingly and sweetly in my mouth.

"Wow, that's good," I effused. I hoped he'd offer another one, but he didn't.

I looked at my four ripe grapes. *I can easily spare one of these. There will be more tomorrow. And if I wait until after Stig leaves to try one, then I won't have to share with him.*

When Stig finally departed, I eagerly grabbed two of the four remaining grapes. I gave the first to the tiny snake, taking some of the juice and spreading it over the copper nuggets. The second I held up to my nose and took a long whiff. The smell was deep and rich, almost intoxicating.

I popped the crisp grape into my mouth and crunched down on it. The flavor was both sweeter and fuller than Stig's grape, though the taste was similar.

The after-effect, however, was completely unique. Almost immediately after swallowing it, a burning sensation tore through my chest, as if someone lit a fire in my lungs. I ripped off my brown tunic. Something like a fiery rash appeared on my chest.

Alarmed, I rubbed my chest to try to alleviate the burning.

Slowly the sensation faded, and the rash gradually disappeared. With its disappearance, though, came an inexplicable craving for Gibra. Still confused, I hurried off to collect my vial for the day, excited that I would soon be a miner and my allotment would double.

* * *

When I came back the next day, the grapevine had again almost doubled in size. By then, there were grapes ripening everywhere. Shafat warned me to keep my baby snake with me until he could be trained to stay at the plot, so I pulled him out of his travel bag. Rohka glanced over momentarily, but otherwise didn't pay him much attention. The snake also had grown considerably, though not as much as the vine. I took grapes and covered the copper nuggets with some of the juice as I fed him.

Shafat was beyond pleased during his morning visit and promised me that at the rate I was going, I would soon mine for copper.

Later that morning, Stig came by. I was almost finished tending the vine.

"Do you want to try one of my grapes?" I offered, curious to see how he would fare eating one.

"Sure," he replied good-naturedly. "I think you owe me a few."

"A few? I'd start with one if I were you."

"These smell great," Stig remarked. "Maybe I should try the trench thing with my vine."

I watched him closely as he popped the grape into his mouth. A look of delight settled on his face. His chewing slowed as he savored the flavor. His eyes closed.

"This tastes even better than mine," he said, opening his eyes as he swallowed.

I puffed my chest, feeling pleased with my work.

"You had to go and have a better grapevine, didn't you?" he

added. "I guess you deserve it after all that—Ow! What was that?"

As Stig clutched his chest, a pit formed in my stomach. "Ow! That burns!" He tried spitting the juice out of his mouth. "Something's wrong with your grapes."

"Try some Gibra. It made me feel better."

"You knew this would happen?"

"Well, I wasn't sure. I thought maybe it was just me."

Stig placed some Gibra between his gum and cheeks. He yelped a little when it first went into his mouth, but soon he flashed me one of his sly smiles.

"That's better," he said.

"Do you think my grapes are poisonous?"

"Did they hurt your snake?"

"I don't think so." I gave my snake another grape, and he happily downed it.

"Well, just don't eat any more, and hopefully your snake will still be able to do his job when the time comes."

* * *

A week or so later Shafat collected the wood block, saying mysteriously that the snake no longer needed to use it. Then he showed me to the mining fields. No longer a baby, my snake was three feet long and ready to work. And a good worker he was. We quickly fell into a regular routine; I fed him a few grapes in the morning to get him ready to go, released him into the ground, and he returned after a while with copper nuggets in his mouth, awaiting more grapes as his payment. The vine still required tending, but a majority of my time was spent mining copper.

I was Shafat's prized worker. He often brought people to see my vine since my snake mined more copper than most. Shafat grew quite friendly toward me, so one day I asked the question that had been nagging for so long in the back of my mind.

"Shafat, what ever happened to Cora?"

Surprise registered on his face, and then confusion, as if he was he scrambling to decide what to say. Finally, he replied, in a not unfriendly way, "She's in the dungeon. That kind of disobedience has to be punished."

"Are people allowed to see her?"

"Absolutely not." He sounded slightly perturbed. "That girl is getting what she deserves. No one is allowed to visit the dungeons."

"Can I ask a different question?"

"Depends on what it is," he replied.

"Where do the snakes go when they disappear underground?"

"It's not common knowledge, but the snakes travel through underground caves to get to the mining fields."

"Do people ever go down there?"

"I've never been through them, but there are hidden entrances that the mining planners use." He stopped as if shocked he had revealed so much to me. "But—but I can't tell you anymore, and if anyone ever asks, we didn't have this conversation."

Before he left he said, "I'm coming by early this afternoon with officials from Salt Works' leadership. Make sure your snake is here. They specifically asked to watch your snake leave and return, so don't send him again until we arrive."

Salt Works officials? Is this my chance to find out what's truly going on with this company?

"Great. Will I be able to ask them some questions?"

"What? No." Shafat said gruffly. "This isn't an interview. Just do what you're told!"

That afternoon, a large contingent of official-looking men and women arrived, guarded by a number of fierce-looking kunoi. I noticed that Rohka had made himself scarce just as they approached.

"Rom, is it?" said the person I took to be the leader of the group.

"Yes, sir."

"We'd like to watch your snake do his mining work, if that's okay. We'll mark your snake with a line of red paint on his back. The paint will be gone in a few days, whenever he next sheds his skin. In the meantime, the mark will allow us to identify him when he goes underground. We'll reward you with two extra doses of Gibra for your help."

A woman placed two fresh vials of Gibra into my hand as the man motioned to two others with him. "Mark him. Go and report what you see when the snake emerges underground. See if he heads down the G-4 tunnel." A man and woman left together.

"Rom, would you kindly go get some grapes so we can release your snake to fetch copper?"

As I turned to go back to my plot, I noticed that the man and woman headed west toward the building at the end of the vineyard plots. Upon my return, I caught sight of them again as they disappeared into a doorway I hadn't seen anyone use before. I marked the door in my mind and delivered the grapes to the delegation.

"We'll be back in a couple of hours. Please make sure you set aside the copper your snake brings back for us to examine."

The delegation departed back toward the main building south of the vineyards. As soon as they were gone, Rohka returned.

"Rohka, let's go exploring."

Onto my shoulder he flitted, as if he was thinking the same thing: the doorway was the curtain behind which we needed to peek. Hurrying away from the mining fields, I scanned for onlookers, and then, as rapidly and discreetly as possible, headed toward the door the man and woman from the delegation had disappeared into.

The door was obscured behind an overgrowth of bushes. I tried opening it, but it was locked. I peered through the slit between the door and the jamb, but it was dark.

"Rohka, I need some light."

Rohka lit up. Leaning against the door, I saw through the slit. Starting at the bottom and running all the way to the top of the door, there were ten wooden latches fastening the door shut from the inside.

"Sword," I said, and out came the Shadom. "Thinner," I said aloud, and the sword thinned. Starting at the bottom, I ran my sword all the way up the slit until all the latches released.

The door creaked open. I stepped into a dark and musty corridor. Rohka provided the only light. At the far end of the corridor was a stairwell descending into what looked to be a tunnel. Creeping nervously down the first few uneven steps, I listened intently for sounds of footsteps or voices.

Driven on by the desire for incriminating evidence, I descended the stairs further, until I reached the bottom, maybe forty or fifty feet underground. To my right was another doorway through which a faint light shone.

"Kala, is that you?" came a man's voice from far inside the doorway.

At that moment Rohka extinguished his light and dug his claws into my shoulder. My mind screamed, "Run," and I took off.

"Hey! Who's there? Kala? Is that you?"

Up the steps I sprinted, heart pounding. In the darkness, I stumbled on the uneven stairs, and my knee crashed against the ground.

Ignoring the pain, I scrambled to my feet and stole a look back. The light in the doorway grew stronger. I heard footsteps and a voice crying out, "Hurry! Hurry! Someone's in the stairwell!"

I flew up the steps, almost on all fours trying to feel the steps in front of me with my hands. Light emerged behind me, like the sun rising. I had ten more feet to go, but I wasn't going to make it in time.

Suddenly, the whole chamber flashed behind me with the brightest of lights. Seeing the stairs clearly, I leapt up the final few.

"Who is it?" a woman's voice called out.

"The light's too bright, I can't see!" came the man's reply. As I dove into the corridor, the bright light followed me. It was Rohka.

With the blinding light no longer hindering them, our pursuers resumed their noisy scramble up the stairs. I sprinted to the door. Throwing it open, I dashed into the open fields.

I saw a group walking toward the mining area and quickly joined them. I heard commotion behind me as I forced myself to ignore the strong urge to turn around to determine if I'd been spotted.

Slipping from group to group, I made my way back to the mining area seemingly unnoticed. There were no signs of any trouble when the delegation returned, but I reminded myself that they ignored what Cora and I did to her kuno guard for a long time before punishing her.

Even if I was seen, I have to find a way back down those steps as soon as possible before they come for me.

CHAPTER 38

The next morning, I arrived at my mining area, checked in with Shafat, received effusive praise for how well I'd handled the delegation, and listened in vain for talk about an unauthorized person in the mining area.

Impatience to return to the cavern gnawed at me. Every different conspiracy theory about Salt Works felt true after being underground. I was suspicious of everything and couldn't focus on anything except figuring out what was down those steps. In addition, my snake was growing rapidly, and I didn't know how long it would be until he shed his skin and the red paint would be gone. If possible, I wanted to be able to identify him underground. So, I fed him grapes and sent him to mine his copper. After I let him go, Rohka hopped onto my shoulder, and I made my way to the hidden door. Releasing the latches, I entered the same dark corridor. Down the stairs I went, feeling my way without any light this time, just to be safe.

When I reached the doorway, I entered new territory. Staring into the pitch black, I heard scurrying noises in front of me.

"Rohka, what do you think about a little bit of light?"

My breath caught as the canopy of darkness was pulled back. Illuminated in front of me was a vast underground cave that sloped downward to my left. Slithering up and down the sloped cavern floor were hundreds and hundreds of snakes.

Getting my bearings, I figured out where I was in relation to the mining fields and reoriented myself in that direction. Sure enough, I saw another slope higher up that was perpendicular to the one in front of me. The whole cavern looked like a backward "L," or the bottom, right-hand corner of a square. Snakes descended into the cavern down the stem of the "L" and then made a sharp, ninety-degree turn to my left to descend further into the copper mines. I searched everywhere for my snake with his red painted stripe but couldn't find him. Among all the milky white snakes, he would've stood out easily.

Then it dawned on me.

I'm not going to see him descend. I released him ten minutes ago. He would've already passed this point while I was still walking over here. I'll have to wait for him to ascend after mining some copper.

That made sense to me, but it raised a more puzzling question.

Why did the man and woman from the delegation expect to see him descend into the mines? They wouldn't have gotten here fast enough either, would they?

Perplexed, I absentmindedly watched snakes go up and down while I tried to figure out what I was missing. After some time, I was jarred out of my unfocused trance when I saw a snake with a red mark beginning to make the descent into the copper mines. He was about twenty feet in front of me, moving from my right to my left. Though he came close to me, he paid me no attention as he passed. After a few moments, he disappeared into the ground at the base of the wall to my left.

Even more surprising, he wasn't gone very long. Almost immediately, he returned from the underground paths carrying a large nugget of copper in his mouth. As expected, he ascended the slope in the cavern, turned left at the base of the backward "L" and ascended the stem until he left the cavern and returned to the surface above.

I raced out of the cavern, up the stairs, and back to my mining station. When I got there, he was waiting for me with the hunk of copper in his mouth. I took the copper, rewarded him with some grapes, and sat down to try to think it through.

If the mining space is really that close to the cavern, the snake should be able to go and return in less than half the time it takes him now. Why the delay?

I fed my snake more grapes and sent him off after more copper. I raced as fast as I could back down into the cavern, taking a bunch of grapes with me. I waited and watched. Again, after a considerable delay, my snake entered the cavern on my right, descending to the left toward the mines.

"Rohka, let's see if we can restart the process from inside the cavern."

I walked out onto the incline, carefully avoiding contact with other snakes, and placed a grape in my snake's path. Upon reaching the grape, he flicked his tongue, stopped dead in his tracks, and swallowed it. He then abruptly reversed direction and headed back up the incline. But instead of turning left and ascending the stem of the backward "L" back to the surface as he did when he had copper in his mouth, he kept going straight, disappearing through the wall on my right.

There's something on the other side of that wall!

With Rohka still radiating light from where he sat perched on my shoulder, I scrambled up the incline, keeping close to the wall to avoid the mass of snakes. When the top of the cavern was only a few feet above my head, it became clear what was happening. The cavern was shaped like an inverted "T," not a backward "L" as I'd assumed. Snakes descending into the cavern from the surface had the choice to go either to my left *or* to my right when they reached the bottom of the incline. Turning to my left led the snakes into the cavern where I stood and eventually to the copper mines. Turning to my right led the snakes somewhere else, and what I saw as I stood there is that every single snake turned to my right first.

From my position near the base of the inverted "T," I discovered a hidden path that would allow a person to follow them. Scrambling over the rocks in front, I passed through the cavern wall.

The path was longer than I expected, and it descended slowly as it went along. When I finally reached the end of the tunnel, I stepped out into a gargantuan open space, almost like another world underground. What lay before me looked like the ancient ruins of a city. In the middle was an enormous column holding up the earthen roof. The column was bathed in a faint blue light, the only light in the cavern besides Rohka. Snakes coming out of the wall streamed toward it. Other snakes slithered away from it, back toward the cavern from which I had come.

I made my way toward the column. The closer I got, the stranger it looked.

Suddenly, Rohka extinguished his light and darkness enveloped me. I opened my mouth to protest, but at that moment I heard the unmistakable growls of kunoi. They were coming closer.

My eyes searched for them, and I found a pack near the lighted column. In a short time the growls and grunts grew fainter. I realized the kunoi must be marching around the column.

Are they guarding something?

"Sword," I whispered and cautiously crept closer and closer to the column.

Except that it wasn't a column. It was the base of the trunk of an enormous tree. An enormous blue tree. The great blue tree of Cindropolis! At its base were enormous exposed roots, five to six feet apiece in height, spreading out far and wide. The roots effectively formed wooden walls, making the marching circumference around three or four times what it would have been around the trunk alone. It would take the kunoi some time to fully circle the tree.

I moved closer still. Snakes were all around me, but they ignored me on their way to and from the tree. Moving nearer and nearer, I finally discovered in the pale ambient light what the snakes were doing. As they approached the tree, they sank their fangs into its enormous roots, waited for a moment, and then left.

So that's what the wooden block is for—training them to empty their venom into the tree!

My eyes were drawn up toward the middle of the tree, where I was used to seeing the words, "Welcome to Cindropolis." Something was engraved in the trunk at the same height. I couldn't quite make it out, but I knew it wasn't those words.

My brain began to register the faint sound of kunoi growls, but I wanted to know what was written on the tree. Closer and closer I came. The growls grew louder.

"Ginoskete," I whispered, and the writing on the tree reshaped itself in my mind.

"Welcome to Arritu."

Arritu? That's the name of the city on my scroll! Could Cindropolis actually be built on the ruins of the place where the king sent Daybe to investigate the Salt Reapers? Rabah told me there was an ancient city here before Cindropolis, but he didn't know its name.

The intensifying growls snapped me out of my pondering.

Run!

But at that moment, a bright white light appeared, like a firework exploding in the sky. Off to my right, the cavern lit up as bright as day.

If the kunoi noticed me, they no longer paid attention. Rather, they were howling mad, galloping toward the light—light that I knew came from Rohka.

Just before I turned to run, I noticed that there were also kunoi standing underneath him, howling angrily.

Those kunoi must be guarding something over there, but what could it be? And then it hit me. *The dungeon!*

Running back toward the tunnel from which I entered, my

mind raced as I formulated a plan to come back and rescue Cora.

CHAPTER 39

Back in the barracks, I pulled out my scroll. As expected, the story of Daybe and the city of Arritu was still there. I reread the opening lines:

> *In those days, the king of Sebi summoned Daybe, the head of the royal treasury, saying to her, "Daybe, I have heard rumors that the Salt Reapers in the city of Arritu have been cheating on their taxes, misappropriating money that should rightly be given to the royal treasury. Take one of your best accountants, pose as merchants, and investigate these allegations."*

Now more than ever, I was convinced that the story was relevant to my situation. When I read the beginning of the story the first time, it made such little sense to me that I just perused through it. Now, knowing exactly where I was, I dug into the words with a new intensity.

> *"Prepare the penalties for the management of the Salt Reapers," said the king sadly. "As for Zan, tell him to give those reparations to the poor and invite him here to join the royal accountants. Make him feel welcome and never mention his fraud to him or anyone else."*
>
> *"Yes, my lord," Daybe replied. "One more thing. How could the owner know that we were coming? I did not tell anyone, and I cannot possibly believe*

that my deputy did either. I have worked with her a long time, and she is completely loyal to you. There is no way she could or would have alerted the owner. Is it possible that someone knew about this other than the three of us?"

"No," said the king. "Just the three of us knew. But do not worry, I am perfectly aware of who leaked the information."

"You are?" Daybe said, astonished. "Who was it?"

"Me."

The part about the king leaking information to the management of the Salt Reapers was the part that confounded me.

"Rohka, why would the king tell the owner that Daybe was coming? Didn't the king want to expose the owner's fraud?"

I thought some more as I stared at Rohka perched at the end of my mat.

"But Daybe didn't end up bringing the king any evidence in the end. Nothing that the king didn't already know anyway. So why was Daybe sent to Arritu? It couldn't have ultimately been about business fraud, could it? The only thing Daybe brought back was Zan's testimony, which didn't convince the king because the king was already convinced—

"—Wait a minute! Zan's testimony wasn't really what Daybe brought back from Arritu. It was Zan himself! That's why the king sent her. That's why the king leaked the information! He was looking for anyone who was willing to be rescued."

The realization swept over me. I was not in Cindropolis to discover fraud at Salt Works. I was in Cindropolis to rescue Cora.

Having abandoned Esah, Rabah, Domi, and Emma when I escaped from Lithown, I was determined not to do the same to Cora in the dungeon. I reached into my pocket for a Gibra portion, ready to eat it as a reward for escaping the kunoi in the cavern and for deciphering my scroll. As I held it in my hand, though, a question arose: *If the snakes empty their venom into the Great Tree, what does that mean for the Gibra that's produced from the tree's leaves?*

Not wanting to know the answer, I pushed it out of my mind. Instead, I took the Gibra and wandered down to Stig's room to see if he wanted to hang out for the evening. I thought about inviting him to help, but the more I considered it, the more I convinced myself that the only thing he would take seriously was goofing off—though in reality, I was too afraid of rejection to ask—so I dropped it from my mind completely.

It was just me. And Rohka.

* * *

The next morning, I woke up determined to rescue Cora. It was all I could think about, except for the anticipation and after-effects of my twice-daily dose of Gibra.

I made my way back to the secret corridor. Summoning my shield and helmet, I dressed for battle before entering. The shield and helmet filled me with confidence.

Rohka and I retraced my steps until we arrived once again in the vast opening underneath the center of Cindropolis. With the base of the Great Tree in front of me, I set my face toward the space Rohka had shown me before. Kunoi growls crept into my ears, but I'd devised a plan for dealing with them.

"Rohka, I need a distraction. Fly to the other side of the Great Tree and light up for the kunoi to see, will you?"

Rohka took off. "Sling," I said as I grabbed a rock from the ground at my feet. Loading it into my Shadom, I hurled the stone as far as I could in the general direction Rohka flew. Since it was my first time using a sling, the rock didn't go exactly where I wanted it to, but it was close enough. The rock clattered around as it fell. Rohka lit up a moment later and, almost immediately, fierce snarls filled the sky. Kunoi galloped toward Rohka. I ran in the opposite direction toward the dungeon. When I neared the entrance, the glow coming from inside made it immediately clear that not all the kunoi went in search of Rohka. Four remained to guard the entrance.

To my left, Rohka danced around as fire shot into the sky at him.

If Rohka can keep them busy for just a little longer . . .

I stationed myself behind an old stone wall amid the ruins near the dungeon entrance. Next to me was a large, man-made pile of rocks that looked like they marked a particular spot. Engraved on the rocks was a word, "Achor." As I read the word, the taste of Gibra filled my mouth, and I wondered how much Gibra Cora would give me if I rescued her.

Stay focused! I have a job to do.

"Bow," I whispered. Calling for an arrow, I pulled back the string and released.

The shot hit its mark. The kuno fell. I dropped back behind the wall while the enraged howls and frantic scramble of the other three kunoi filled the air above me.

Popping up, I took aim at a second kuno, but my arrow missed badly. Worse, it gave away my position. One of the three immediately raced off in the direction of the Great Tree. The two remaining kunoi rounded on me.

"Spear!"

I hurled the Shadom at the kuno on the left. My spear passed through a shower of fire blazing toward me. My shield blocked the flames, which were extinguished quickly because my spear had found its mark.

"Return!"

Meanwhile, the second kuno launched himself at me. It was all I could do to turn toward him and get my shield around as he smashed full force into me. Down we went in a pile. The impact knocked the wind out of me, and I gasped for breath as he quickly pinned my right arm to the ground. My other arm was trapped against my chest underneath the shield between us. The kuno slashed at my neck with his teeth. I parried with my helmet as best I could. He slashed again and again. I turned my neck right and left so my helmet could intercept his attacks. His breath was foul. Hot saliva fell from his drooling mouth onto me.

"Dagger," I yelled. The Shadom transformed. It popped out like it was an extension of my thumb. But my wrist was pinned, and I couldn't reach him with the dagger's blade.

If only it was protruding from the palm of my hand instead, I thought.

The Shadom obliged. Torqueing my wrist as hard as I could, I jabbed at him. The Shadom impaled his arm, and he recoiled with a howl. Now with greater range of movement, I jammed the dagger into his side.

"Sword!" I yelled. The dagger extended straight through his midsection.

I rolled him off me, stood to my feet, and noticed Rohka flying toward the dungeon entrance. After getting my bearings, I bounded out of the ruins after him. Behind me came a disturbing sound. More kunoi were coming, summoned, I was sure, by the kuno that had escaped me.

Sprinting down the path away from the Great Tree, I headed into the dungeon. It was dark and dank. The main path split into several downward sloping paths. Rohka headed down a path to my left, so I followed.

"Cora!" I cried out. "Cora, it's Rom. Where are you?"

Additional paths broke off from the one we were on. At the

fourth or fifth opening, we turned right. That path ran straight and then split into narrower ones.

The dungeon is huge. The kunoi will have a hard time finding me in here.

Finally, after branching off several more times, the path offered no more options for turning. Instead, every thirty or forty feet was a rounded cell, barred and locked. Each cell had someone asleep inside it.

I had spent enough time tending my grapevine during the past months to realize that the whole dungeon structure was set up like a grapevine. We entered at the base of the vine, proceeded down various branches, and then arrived at the newest growth at the end of the branches, where the paths were the narrowest. The cells were like buds, evenly spaced along the new growth.

Rohka stopped in front of one of the cells, and I saw Cora asleep inside.

"Hammer!" I whispered, though I needn't have bothered. Once I hit the lock, the loud boom echoed through the hallway. But Cora didn't wake, and the padlock didn't give way.

"Halberd!"

I slashed at the lock with my two-fisted axe. The Shadom rebounded off the unbroken lock without even scratching it.

An idea popped into my head.

"Key!"

The Shadom remade itself into the shape of a key. I jammed the key into the lock and tried to turn it. It didn't open.

Another idea came.

"Hammer," I called. I felt the Shadom flowing from my forearm, forcing more material into the key that was still shoved into the lock. With all the strength I could muster, I pressed my right hand hard against the lock, refusing to accept any recoil coming from the expanding Shadom. It was like a balloon inexorably inflating as it obeyed the command. The lock shuddered, shook, and then exploded with the force of the expanding Shadom. Opening the prison door, I ran to Cora who lay on a stone slab.

"Cora, Cora, wake up!" I shook her gently. Her hands were bound with cords, so I cut them free with my Shadom. Still, she didn't wake.

While I sat next to her on the stone slab, Rohka came and landed on her shoulder. Leaning over her ear, Rohka seemed to whisper something to her. Her eyelids fluttered and then she was fully awake.

"Get up? Where am I?"

"Cora, we have to get out of here. Follow me."

She stood to her feet, rubbing sleep from her eyes. Recognition dawned in her eyes. Grabbing her hand, I guided us into the corridor. Rohka flew off in the direction we came. I raced after him.

We hadn't taken more than a few steps when Cora called out, "Ow, Rom, you're hurting my hand. Let go."

She was right. I was squeezing her hand with all my strength. *What am I doing?*

I let her go, but my right hand swung around and slugged her in the chest, felling her. *Wow, that felt incredible.*

"Rom, what was that for?" Cora coughed out in a betrayed voice.

My foot began to lift off the ground as if to stomp on her. *Why do I so badly want to step on her?*

My mind tried to take control of my leg, but my racing heart soon overrode it. Down came my foot on her leg. Cora cried out in confusion and pain.

I reached down to try to help her up, but she screamed, "Don't touch me! Don't come near me!"

Far from shocking me, her rejection sent a surge of pleasure racing through my veins. All my nerves tingled. My leg swung back readying to kick her, and I heard my voice cry out, "Stop, stop!"

"You can't stop," came an icy reply from behind me. So, I kicked Cora with all my might.

The subsequent rush of ecstasy satisfied my cravings enough that I was able to wrench my body away from Cora to face the icy voice.

Standing in front of us was a towering woman, whiter than milk from head to toe. In her hand was a magnificent golden wand, sparkling and bejeweled. Her countenance was joyless and bitter. She wore an evil sneer, made more menacing by eyes that were black as coal.

I raised my shield and summoned my sword.

She raised her wand. My heart began to race again. My shield felt so heavy on my left arm that I could think of nothing but dropping it to the ground.

As my shield fell, a wave of pleasure enveloped my brain. I tasted Gibra in my mouth.

The woman waved her wand again. Suddenly, my head felt trapped inside my helmet. The walls of the helmet were closing in, ready to crush my brain.

I have to get this helmet off immediately!

Ripping my helmet from my head, I cast it away. As soon as it was gone, my vision began to blur.

Her arm moved again, and my left leg felt like a spider was crawling on it. The itching and tickling feeling was maddening.

Oh, the pleasure that would come if I drive my dagger through the spot that itches.

"Dagger," I called. I swung, longing to pierce my leg and release all that pleasure. But just on the verge of impact, the Shadom retracted, and I simply punched myself in the leg instead. Mixed with pain was pleasure.

"What's this?" said the woman. "No matter."

Again, the wand.

If I could just throw myself into the wall.

So I did. Again ecstasy.

But that time, the lingering pain outlasted the momentary pleasure. Since my leg hurt where I punched it, and my shoulder ached from the wall, the pain did its job and began to awaken my mind.

Don't do that again!

But my heart overrode my brain, and I threw myself against the wall. The second time felt even better and then even worse.

The wand waved again.

Evil thoughts fashioned themselves into words and burst out of my mouth, raining down insults on Cora. I heard her crying as I reviled her for being a worthless failure.

The woman laughed aloud. As she laughed, I heard my voice saying what my eyes and heart didn't believe.

"Cora," I said. "Do you see how stunning she is? If only you were as beautiful as this white queen, then maybe you'd be worth rescuing! Instead, you're ugly and useless. I don't even know why I came down here for you."

Cora cried more and more. Somewhere in my ear, in the faintest voice I heard, "Why are you doing this?"

But I was powerless to stop. I wanted to hurt Cora. I wanted to shower praise on the towering woman. I longed for the wand to move again, knowing the rush of ecstasy that would follow.

The woman raised her wand again, but this time there was no ecstasy. Suspicion crept into my brain.

"You want to be with Stig, don't you? You wish it was Stig who came here to rescue you, don't you? I've noticed the way you look at him! Well I don't want anything to do with you." But I did. The more I said I didn't, the more I did. Suspicion turned to rage, and rage quickly turned to panic.

Confusion reigned, but in the confusion a thought arose deep in my soul.

Rohka. Find Rohka. He can help.

I searched desperately until I found him fluttering behind the white woman's shoulder. With my blurred vision, I could just make him out.

The woman saw what I was looking at.

"You!" she cried out, turning on Rohka. "Don't you dare fly near him! Do you know how much Gibra is in his veins? He's mine to control!"

The wand waved once more. Blue dust billowed out of my pores, like smoke from a brush fire. In seconds a blue haze filled the space in front of me, isolating me from Rohka. He was gone.

The woman emerged from the blue haze as if she was one with the smoke. She raised her wand, jeering at me once more.

"Rohka can't save you, fool, even if he wanted to, which he doesn't. You're a venomous cesspool of pollution, and he can't come near you."

CHAPTER 40

The woman's wand swept downward, yet it wasn't her voice I heard, but Cora's. She wasn't crying anymore. Instead, her voice dripped like honey, rich and alluring. My brain began to tingle. Fine blue dust wafted up from her wrists like incense. The salty-sweet smell was intoxicating. I could think of nothing except her. Somehow it felt as if the attraction to her had been there all along. I was sure that whatever Cora asked me to do in that moment, I would do. All she had to do was say the word.

While I thought of Cora, I forgot about Rohka.

But he hadn't forgotten about me.

It was so soft at first that I didn't hear it start. But gradually, I heard a song growing in my ears. Cora's voice was still in my head, but Rohka's song was deeper and stronger. It reached further into me, past my head, through my heart, and down into my very soul. I strained to listen.

The song was sad and beautiful. At times I wanted to plug my ears and focus only on Cora's voice, but something deep inside of me longed with greater passion to hear the rest of Rohka's song. There were no words, but I began to cry. Shielding my eyes and turning away from the woman to hide my tears, I fell to my knees.

"Yes, yes!" I heard the woman say as Cora's alluring voice became louder. But the song was still within me. Slowly the music overwhelmed me, and my heart began beating along with the tune. My crying turned to weeping, and my weeping turned to sobbing. My chest felt like it was going to explode as sobs racked my body. With a great heave, I reached up and tore my tunic from top to bottom. I clutched at my chest.

But, to my surprise, instead of skin, I felt leather. I began groping around my torso, and my eyes searched through the blue haze to determine what my hands had discovered. Somehow, I was wearing a leather vest.

The vest was dirty and grungy, caked with old, dried blood. Looking more closely I saw something inscribed on the vest in the ancient language.

"Ginoskete," I sang softly in tune to the music.

The words reorganized themselves in my brain: A gift for Rom.

It dawned on me that this vest, which wasn't mine, was somehow mine. This sudden realization, which I knew to be true in a way that I could never describe, caused my soul to burn within me. It felt for a moment like I'd eaten one of my grapes, but this time the burning sensation spread throughout my entire body.

The fiery feeling felt purifying as it flowed toward my extremities. When it reached my fingertips, toes, and the top of my head, it reversed itself and flowed back toward my chest. The fiery sensations merged together at my heart and then flowed out into the vest. The vest turned the deep blue color of Gibra and then blood-stained brown again.

My heart was at peace. I rose from my knees and turned to face the woman. She waved her wand again.

Nothing happened.

"What's wrong?" she cried out in a startled voice.

Recognition dawned on her face.

"That vest. I know that vest. Where did you get it?"

"It's mine," I said, hardly believing that it could possibly be true. But it was.

Her voice turned to pure hatred. "Who do you think you are to wear that? You're a vile, filthy addict. You're a despoiled, disgraced, useless piece of trash. You're . . ."

I reached down and put on my helmet.

To Cora I said, "Don't listen to anything she says." But Cora didn't seem to be listening. Atop her head was a magnificent golden Corinthian helmet, adorned with carved feathers. Her eyes shone with gratitude and joy. She was focused not on the woman, but something beyond the blue haze, low to the ground.

Cora advanced defiantly toward the white woman as I grabbed my shield and sword to join her. The woman waved her wand again, and the blue haze that hid Rohka began to swirl around her like a whirlwind. From out of the whirlwind she cried, "Nehushtan!" Blue smoke shot down the corridor toward the exit, as if being sucked into a giant vortex in the distance. She was gone.

As Rohka reappeared, hovering above the ground, I saw what looked like a small puppy scramble toward Cora, leap into her arms, and disappear.

Rohka squawked.

"Cora, let's go. We've got to get out of here. Hurry."

Rohka flew up the passage, and we followed behind at full speed. Each corridor merged into a larger one until we finally burst into the main passageway. The entrance to the dungeon was ahead of us.

But we were too late. We both stopped dead in our tracks. Cora gasped. My heart rose into my throat.

It looked like the floor in front of the dungeon was moving toward us. But it wasn't the floor. It was snakes. Hundreds of them. Maybe thousands. White mining snakes. They streamed in the front entrance toward us, surging forward like the whitecap of a breaking ocean wave.

"Rohka, what do we do?"

He turned and flew back down the main corridor, past the branch that led to Cora's cell to another branch farther along. We ran as fast as we could after him.

Turning and turning, the hallways narrowed as we headed back into the heart of the dungeon, the snakes not far behind.

As we entered a branch with more prison pods, I saw light ahead of us. It came from a cat sitting on the ground. Light radiated from the cat's eyes illuminating the cell in front of it.

Rohka chirped, the cat meowed, and a woman stuck her head out of the cell.

"Hey crew," she called out. "Get out here!"

"Snakes!" I yelled as I ran toward her. "Hundreds of snakes are coming!"

Five well-armed warriors popped out of the cell, three men and two women. The first woman struck the wall with her fist with such force that chunks of rock fell off.

"Build a barrier," she cried as she continued to hammer the wall. Cora and I joined in, grabbing rocks and stacking them up.

"This won't work," one of the men said. "They'll just climb over."

"It'll narrow the space they can climb through and separate them," the woman countered.

We didn't make much progress before the snakes were upon us. They came at the barrier like a river of death. One of the men called out in the ancient language and flames shot from his hands toward them. The smell of burnt snake filled the air.

"I'll take the center," I called. "If we can kill enough of them, the dead bodies will create more of a barrier."

A woman appeared on my left side, sword in hand. She wore the boots of a warrior and greaves to protect her shins, I noted jealously.

"I've got the left," she said.

As the snakes breached the barrier, I slashed and hacked with my sword at the twisting pile in front of me. The problem was, sliced snakes still wiggle. It was impossible to tell if the heads I saw were still attached to a full body or not. So, I chopped at anything moving.

Cora and the others tried to smash any snakes that our first line of defense missed. The barrier became more and more impassable with every moment. But try as we might, it was impossible to stop the snakes from coming through.

Soon I heard Cora shout, "Rom, your leg!"

The sting of teeth sunk deep into my flesh. I kicked and smashed down with my shield, severing the snake's head from its body, but I could feel the venom running into my leg, burning as it went. A moment or two later, another bite arrived on my left arm. Then another on my shoulder. I flung off the snakes, but I stumbled backward feeling dizzy.

Someone rushed to take my place.

My head began to ache, and the bites burned like acid from the inside out. Whether it was real or imagined, I felt deadly poison crawling toward my heart.

Somewhere in the distance, I heard Cora yell my name.

My eyes closed as darkness drifted over me and something like a deep sleep settled down on me.

CHAPTER 41

I found myself standing at the side of a mighty river, which flowed among lush green hills. On the terraced sides of the hills and in the valleys between them were well-watered gardens and vineyards. Children ran and played. On one hill, food was being gathered for a great feast. On another, the sun shone down on the slopes with a warm brightness that I'd never seen before. On a third, hundreds of people participated in a great dance party. My eyes drank it all in.

Through the middle of it all flowed the river. The water sparkled clean and pure, and it smelled alive. A thirst began to grow in me. I knelt to drink. Cupping my hands, I drew the cool, crisp water to my mouth.

Suddenly, a fiery pain shot through my leg, arm, and shoulder. I cried out. Searching for the source of the pain, I remembered my snakebites. Each snakebite had become a festering sore.

"Your wounds are incurable," came a deep, rich voice behind me. I turned and saw a man standing before me whose face and arms shone like polished bronze. He wore a simple, dazzling white linen tunic, girded around the waist with a belt of silver.

"The snakes that bit you were drunk on the poison of the Great Tree. When they eat the grapes, their bodies manufacture venom. When the venom is injected into the Great Tree, it forms the poison that's at the heart of the Gibra you have ingested for so long. Have you not noticed that the Gibra is highly addictive? Did you not stop to ask why taking Gibra drove you to work ever harder at cultivating your grapevine? When you drank the Gibra, did it not strike you as a cheap substitute for the water of life you tasted in the past?"

Everything he said made perfect sense.

"Is this why the grapes from my grapevine burned when I ate them? Because they were poison?" I thought I was starting to understand. "But why did Stig's grapes taste so good and not affect me at all?"

"Stig's grapes were filled with the poison of Cindropolis, the poison of pride. When you ate them, they tasted natural to you because of all the Gibra in your system. As for your own grapes, who helped you with your grapevine? What did you use to make it grow?"

"Rohka helped me," I responded. "And I used the shield for light, the helmet for water, and the Shadom to loosen the earth." It dawned on me. "That's why my grapes stung when I ingested them, isn't it? Because they were pure . . ."

". . . and you were not," the man said.

"You're right" I confessed. Regret grew as I came alive to the truth.

But the man wasn't done.

"Have you not guessed why you were entrusted with that shield, helmet, breastplate, and weapon? Do you not understand what you are being summoned to do? You have correctly figured out that you are not in Cindropolis just to learn the mining craft, nor to expose fraud at Salt Works. You are there for the same reason that Daybe came to Arritu all those years ago. To rescue. It is a great honor to be given such a task, because Cora is deeply loved. But in the process, you have wounded yourself with incurable wounds, and you have wounded her too."

"But what could I do?" I protested. "The white woman is the one who made me try to hurt Cora. I didn't want to do it. And what were we supposed to do about the snakes? The woman summoned them, not me."

"And what did she use to control you and to summon them, if not the Gibra from your veins? Why do you think you turned on Cora so easily? Why do you think the snakes came after you when they broke through the group's defenses? And why do you think their bites did such damage to you? The queen bears the greatest blame, it is true, but your love of Gibra furnished her with all she needed to do her work."

When he said it, I knew it to be true. I felt ashamed and humiliated.

"I'm sorry," I said, my head bowed low. My eyes fell upon the bloodstained vest I wore. For the first time, I noticed that one of the bloodstains looked like a giant snake coiling around itself.

The man's voice pulled me out of my thoughts.

"That vest," he said. "is what finally protected you from the woman's wand. Wear it always underneath your shirt, so there is nothing between it and your heart."

"Where did this vest come from?"

"Look at that far-off mountain," the man said, pointing as he spoke. Because of the distance, it looked almost as if the river itself flowed out of the mountain. "Do you see anything?"

I strained my eyes. "I think I do," I said, not wanting to disappoint him.

"Why don't you put on your helmet and try again."

I opened my mouth to summon the helmet, but then noticed it was already in my left hand. Placing it on my head, I focused again on the faraway mountain, willing myself to see farther than before.

"I see a wooden pole standing erect. Something is lifted up on it."

With this, my vest squeezed tighter around my chest. Power flowed from it through my veins. I felt life filling my body.

"Your wounds have been healed," said the man.

I looked at my wounds, astonished. It was true. Where there once had been open sores, only closed scars remained.

"I thought you said they were incurable?"

"They have been healed, not cured."

"What's the difference?"

"To be cured would be to make it as if these wounds had never happened. Healing is a process of restoration whereby you attain a higher level of health because you have come safely through something to the other side. The longer these wounds remain closed, the more resistant they will become, but the danger is that healed wounds can still be reopened, and such wounds are especially susceptible to what injured you in the first place. But the healing you have experienced will make you stronger, wiser, more empathetic, and more full of life because you have come safely through."

I rubbed my fingers over the scar on my shoulder.

"In the days to come, you will understand these things better." He turned to leave.

"When will I understand?" I asked in exasperation. "Please, forgive me, but this is all so confusing. I don't know what I'm doing or where I'm going. I don't even understand where I am. I feel like I'm on a journey, but I don't know where it's headed. Do I even belong here? There's so much I don't understand. Everyone else seems to know their place and what they're doing, but I'm lost."

The questions and frustration that had built up over time came tumbling out. The man in bronze replied, not unkindly, but without any real empathy.

"Do you not know? Do you not understand? It is not my place to tell you. But look at the armor you are being given. Look at the weapon of incomparably great power that has been entrusted to you. Do you not understand about the goat and the White Power and the Iron Guardian and the kunoi—how your adversary enlisted them to derail your journey? Do you not know what your name means? And what it *could* mean? Do you not understand about Daybe and Peytos and those who came before you?

"You are on a quest, a journey, an odyssey. Yours is different from those of Peytos, Daybe, Ataymah, Avi, Emma, Rabah, Esah, Cora, and the rest, but it is also the same."

"But how will I know when the odyssey is done?"

"When you finish your assignment and arrive home."

"But how will I know when I'm home? Who can go on a journey if they don't know the destination?"

The man stared at me incredulously. "You are highly favored, but surely that is a declaration made from mercy and not merit.

"No one knows how a journey will end when they begin. Any end you envision will always be different when you arrive. You will be different, and it will be different. But this is not a story like those found in common scrolls and books. This is life. Who knows how life will turn out? Who understands what is around the next corner? But can you not see where home is?"

"That's home," I said, pointing across the river, "isn't it? That's where I want to go."

At this he smiled. "Yes, young one. You are learning. But it will look different than this when you arrive. Where you cross the river will matter. How you cross the river will too. What you have been through and what is yet to come will determine what you will experience on the other side of the river. This is only a vision. The joy, the laughter, the beauty, the life—these are real, but they are only envisioned here."

I thought I was beginning to understand. "But how will I know if I'm going on the journey the right way?"

"How did you get this far?"

"I don't know. I just started and then kept going," I guessed.

"You are detaining me longer than I'm allowed to stay. I have other assignments the king has given me to do. But if you figure out how you got to where you are now, you will know how to keep going, only this time more intentionally."

He turned to leave.

"Please," I begged, "just one more question. Please. I am still confused."

The man stopped mid-turn, cocked his head slightly as if listening, and then looked back at me.

"Just tell me what I am supposed to do next. Should I stay in Cindropolis or go somewhere else?"

For a spell the man was silent. Then he responded, "Ask Rohka."

"Rohka? Sure, he rescued me so many times, and I'd be lost without him, but he's a bird. I need someone who can talk. Someone who can answer my questions. Someone like you. Can you come with me on my journey? I need more guidance and clarity than Rohka can give."

The bronze man's bronze jaw dropped open; his eyes grew wide as saucers. The only word out of his mouth before he turned to leave was, "Mercy."

CHAPTER 42

When I awoke, I was no longer in the dungeon. My wounds were just as they had been in the vision, scarred but healed. I was lying on a padded, narrow bed.

The man from the dungeon who shot fire from his hands was there, and he introduced himself as Simon. He told me I was in the house of Sheen. Before I could ask what happened, he began peppering me with questions about how I broke into the dungeon. I tried to explain about the entrance near the mining fields, but since he'd never been to the mining fields, he ran off to find someone who had.

When Simon returned, Cora was with him, as well as the woman with the cat, though I didn't see the cat with her. She introduced herself as Susa. Cora, Susa, and Simon had taken turns caring for me, with Cora shouldering most of the responsibility—at her insistence.

It took me a while to put together all the pieces of the story. Susa and Simon were part of a rebellion of sorts. Likeminded individuals had banded together against the imprisonment of people in Cindropolis and were working to free as many as possible. They discovered an entrance to the dungeon on the other side of the Great Tree near the workers' barracks. Susa, Simon, and their teammates had gone into the dungeon to rescue a man named Danos and were in the process of extracting him when Cora and I showed up, pursued by the river of snakes. After I was bitten and passed out, the makeshift wall of rocks and dead reptiles slowed the mass of snakes down enough for the group to defeat them. Everyone but Cora and I had greaves and warrior's boots, which proved remarkably helpful. They were able to carry me out and bring me to Sheen, where I'd remained unconscious for many days.

Soon it was my turn to answer questions. Simon, Susa, and Cora all listened as I recounted my entrance into the dungeon and my fight with the kunoi. Tears ran down Cora's face. Seeing her cry made me realize the impact of the decision to rescue her. She wasn't just an assignment to be completed, but a person who was saved; someone of great value, worth risking a life for. Simon seemed oblivious to her reaction to my story, but Susa watched Cora's reactions closely. She stood near her, as if to protect her. Susa's blue eyes sparkled with compassion and moistened with empathy as Cora kept interrupting me to say thank you. Her eyes reminded me of Emma's.

After I finished, Simon said, "Cora, do you know where we could find that entrance?" Turning to me, Simon explained, "I invited Cora to go with us back into the dungeon. Since we killed a majority of the mining snakes, Salt Works is in shambles. Most of the workers have disappeared."

"Yes," Cora replied. "I think I can find Rom's entrance."

Simon looked at me, "You should come with us."

Susa rolled her eyes. "All business. I'm surprised you didn't ask him about his sword or bird."

"That's right!" Simon burst out. "I forgot."

But Cora interrupted before he could ask.

"Stig is one of the ones who disappeared."

"Then count me in," I said.

"You should rest," said Susa. "It's just an exploratory trip, not a rescue operation. We don't know who's down there, and we don't have keys to any of the cell locks."

"By the way, where did you find Cora's key?" Simon asked.

"It's time to go," Susa urged. "Let him rest."

Cora hung back.

"Look at this," she said as she pulled out a gleaming silver double-edged sword. "Susa got it for me. She said she'd teach me how to use it."

"It's pretty great," I commented, turning the sword over in my hand, feeling its heft and slashing imaginary enemies as I cut through the air.

"I also have these for you . . . just to say thank you." She placed four pieces of Gibra candy into my hand. "I mixed them myself."

I knew I needed to tell her that Gibra was dangerous, but no words came. The memory of the taste of Gibra clouded my thoughts, and I closed my hand around the candy, glad for the gift.

"Thanks," I said.

As Cora departed to join the others, I sat up in the bed, surprised at how weak I still felt. I hated the feeling of weakness. It dawned on me that I could take one of the Gibras to give me some energy. My heart started to beat faster at the idea. I lifted my shirt and noticed that I still had my vest on.

There won't be any real problems while I have this on, will there? If there is, I'll throw away the other three. Besides, I deserve to feel better.

As I got ready to eat one, Rohka flew into the room. I coughed a couple times and covertly popped it in my mouth. Rohka didn't seem to notice.

The Gibra tasted fantastic. I soon felt myself re-energized and thinking more clearly. But the Gibra still puzzled me.

Didn't the man in the vision say Gibra made me vulnerable to the queen? I bet it was the Gibra that I won from Spinning Crystals. Clearly, I cheated to win that Gibra, so it was tainted. If I shouldn't have taken that Gibra, Rohka would have stopped me.

As soon as the Gibra kicked in, I no longer wanted to sit in bed and rest in case I missed an exciting new development in the rescue mission. With Rohka on my shoulder, I set out to find my way from Sheen to Salt Works. As I walked, it dawned on me that if the Salt Works operation was shut down, I wouldn't get paid any more Gibra.

When I arrived, Cora seemed excited to see me. Unfortunately, they hadn't yet found Stig. They did discover that the cavern entrance I used was crawling with people trying to figure out what happened. Worse yet, the dungeon was completely inaccessible.

"What does all this mean?" I inquired.

"It means if your friend Stig is in there, you're won't be able to rescue him anytime soon," Simon replied. "We've been discussing the possibility of heading south to the nearby town of Banura. A salt runner named Rabah told us there have been reports of workers going missing from the Salt Works operation there. We figured there must be another dungeon with more people we could rescue."

"Rabah? From Lithown?"

One of the others present, whose name I didn't know, said, "Yes, he's from Lithown."

"Is he helping you?"

"Yes," Simon replied. "Why?"

"I know him, that's all. I had no idea he was connected with these rescue operations. Does he know someone captured in Banura?"

"No."

"Do any of you?"

"No."

"You're going to try to help free people you don't even know?"

"Yes." Simon looked at me the same way I looked at him: as if we were having the strangest conversation. "It's what we do. Cindropolis, Banura, or wherever, it doesn't matter. Our mission is to rescue people. You should come with us."

"Really?"

"Yes, please come," Cora implored.

"You're going?"

"Rom, it was horrible in that dungeon. If there are other people being held as prisoners, I want to help them. What else am I going to do? The Salt Works operation is a mess and those are the people who imprisoned me. I'd never go back to work there."

"Listen, Rom," said Simon. "Can't you see that this is where your journey is leading? You somehow broke into that dungeon on your own, defeated those kunoi, and rescued Cora. You have the potential to be a mighty warrior. You're not the first one to walk this path. Come with us and put that promise to good use. We can help you discover how to use your weapons and abilities for good, instead of wasting them."

I agreed to think about it, though in truth I had no intention of seriously considering it. First, I needed to find Stig.

* * *

I left Cora and the others to search for Stig on my own. At the mining fields, it was indeed chaotic. People were everywhere. The vineyard areas were still intact, but instead of mining, groups of people sat around eating grapes off the vines. There was almost a festive atmosphere, as if work had been the one thing restraining people from embracing chaos.

I made my way over to my plot of land. As opposed to other plots, the wall between my space and Cora's was broken down. My grapevine looked as if it had been pillaged by a wild animal. Grapes were squashed into the ground; leaves were shredded; branches were strewn everywhere. The ground looked like it was bleeding, stained with juice from the grapes. Parts of the trellis and accompanying branches had been burned and were still smoldering.

Why would someone attack my grapevine?

Without warning, pain ripped through my head. My knees buckled, and everything went black.

CHAPTER 43

Why *do I smell musty dogs?*

I opened my eyes, or so I thought, but everything was still black. I reached up to feel my face but couldn't move my hands. They were tied together behind my back.

A rough voice called out, "Did he just move?"

I went limp.

Someone kicked me, but I didn't scream.

"No, he's still out cold," said a second voice.

"Look, the queen told us to kill him. From what I heard, he snuck into the underground caverns and helped kill the snakes. You heard her vindictive rant about him being a worthless trouble-maker. We're far enough away from Cindropolis, why don't we just do it now?"

A familiar voice replied, "Do you see those travelers approaching ahead? We have to wait until they pass."

"Why doesn't the queen just kill him herself?" said the second voice.

"I don't know. Why don't you ask her when we get back?"

"They look like traveling merchants."

"Traders."

I tried to gently feel around my wrists to get a sense of what was binding them and how to get my Shadom to cut them.

The familiar voice—*Shafat, that's who it is!*—said, "Don't you think traders might be—"

"Hey, I saw his hands move!"

A kuno growled. A sharp claw jabbed into my back. It was all I

299

could do to keep my mouth shut, but my body went rigid.

"Knock him out again," the rough voice said.

I have to get out my . . .

PART 6: KARSA

CHAPTER 44

"**W**ake him up."

"I'm trying, sir. He's out pretty good, but I think he's starting to stir."

"Try sitting him up."

Where am I? What's going on?

I opened my eyes. Standing in front of me was a man dressed in leather armor. His face was serious, but not unkind. His dull brown eyes examined me carefully.

"What's your name, son?"

"Rom."

"Rom, my name is Jukes. Do you know where you are?"

"No."

"No, sir," came the reprimand from next to me.

"Go easy on him, Shep."

"Rom, you're in the city of Karsa. More specifically, you're in the Phoenix, the military outpost for the city of Karsa."

"Wait, Karsa? I've never heard of Karsa." My mind scrambled to make sense of it all. "Are we in the Valley of Salt?"

"No, son, the Valley of Salt is east of here quite some distance," said Jukes. "Do you—"

"But I can't be here," I exclaimed. "I need to be in the Valley of Salt. I have to find Stig. I'm Daybe. There's another Zan to rescue. Where's Shafat? Why did he bring me here? Where's Roh—"

I thought better of mentioning Rohka aloud.

"Calm down, son," said Jukes. "You were brought here by traders. We purchased you to work in the Phoenix."

"What? You purchased me? But I'm not for sale," I protested. "Am I a slave?"

"Yes," Shep answered immediately, jeering at me.

"Yes and no," said Jukes calmly. "You're more like an indentured servant. We paid the traders a certain amount of money for you. When you work off what we paid for you, you're free to go. Or, you're welcome to begin the process of incorporation into Karsa. I myself started as you are, but after I purchased my freedom, I began the process of incorporation. The work is fulfilling, the pay is good, and I committed to help Karsa win their battle against the Dardar.

"What if I don't want to stay?" I said defiantly. I began to summon my Shadom, but Shep's brawn and Jukes' leather armor and calm demeanor made them appear quite formidable, so I decided to continue conversing.

Shep answered, "You can try to escape, but nobody gets out of the Phoenix. When they stop you, you get assigned to sorting rubbish, or worse. I came here out of one of those assignments. Trust me, boy. Working for Jukes is a pretty good gig. You can't hardly ever earn enough to work your way outta those other places. It'll add years to your time."

"How long do I have to work here until I buy my freedom?"

"It usually takes four months to work off what was paid for you. The process of incorporation happens after roughly five years, depending on how well you do on your various assignments."

Four months? I might actually be stuck here for four months!

"Where do I sleep?"

"Right here. This is where you'll be staying."

And that was it. Discussion over. Jukes and Shep left, abandoning me to assess my surroundings and my situation. The room—my room, apparently—didn't look that much different than my room in Cindropolis: a mat for sleeping and a small wooden table for possessions. There were no windows, but the room was well lit. Small boxes hung on the wall emitting light. It took me a minute to figure out that when you wanted the light to go out, you placed a small cover over the light box.

My heart sank. It felt like Lithown all over again. *But this time I have my scroll!* Immediately, I unrolled it, hoping a new story would make sense of what was happening. Part of me was sure that it would still be the story of Daybe and Cindropolis because it didn't feel like my time in Cindropolis was over, but something new was on the scroll.

"Ginoskete," I said with slight trepidation. The words reshaped themselves in my mind, and I read aloud:

One day the king himself decided to take a tour of his kingdom. Everywhere he went, he saw his people enjoying the beautiful countryside. He heard reports of new areas being developed and people exploring the farthest reaches of his kingdom, which pleased him greatly.

The king's joy, however, was dampened when he came upon a group of people living together in a walled fortress, the self-proclaimed City of the Forge.

The fortress was shaped like a ziggurat, with four tiers of buildings, the highest in the center. The shortest tier stood some twenty feet off the ground, and the highest tier reached into the sky. Atop the walls of the fortress were battlements, and along the battlements were guards armed with all manner of projectile-launching machinery. The only entrances into the fortress were well-guarded ascending ramps running along the *faces of the square base.*

It was made of bricks that covered an iron frame and had been glazed the color of a dull maroon. Fields of crops surrounded the fortress. Littered throughout the fields were tools for irrigation, plowing, threshing, and harvesting.

Disguising himself as a peasant, the king decided to take a closer look. As he wandered through the fields, he overheard two farmers having a discussion.

"Did you hear the smiths are working on an exciting new invention?"

"No, what does it do?"

"It is rumored that they figured out how to harness the power of the sun to give movement to machines."

"Really? How will that work?"

"I don't know, but they say that Tubal is working on it."

"The man is a genius. There is nothing he cannot figure out. Wow! Imagine machines that move by themselves. What will they think of next?"

"I don't know, but every advancement solves another problem. Imagine working in the fields and not being tired. Imagine how much more work we could do. Imagine how many more crops we could plant and harvest. Imagine how much more money we could make!"

Continuing on, the king slipped unnoticed past the guards on the front ramp and entered the fortress itself. On the first level, he passed a man and woman arguing about money. Another woman boasted to her friend about how she had worked for ten straight days with minimal breaks for sleep. A group of people fantasized aloud about plans to build a fifth tier on the fortress with money that could easily be plundered from less technologically advanced people groups.

As the king ascended to the highest point in the fortress, he came to a room decorated like a shrine. Inside he found an ornately engraved message on the far wall:

To the wise maker of clothing, the first to invent;
To the great builder of cities, who showed us the
　way;
To the strong designer of tools, who opened the
　door;
To the creator of weapons, who gave us the key,
The poetry of pride.

Reading the words, the king said to himself, "They have indeed made some ingenious things, but they have created nothing. Is there any breath in these inventions? Can they give guidance? Nothing these people plan to do will be impossible for them, but they do not see the inherent danger."

As the king spoke, a finger of fire appeared and, digging deeply into the stone wall, wrote these words in blazing red:

Those who make them will be like them,
　As they trust in them,

Those who rely on what's been made,
    Love what cannot save.

As quickly as the words appeared, they ab-
sorbed into the stone as if being swallowed, hid-
den from the naked eye.

When I raised my eyes from the scroll, I noticed Rohka sitting at the end of my mat.

"So, it's Karsa, huh?" I said as I lay down to sleep.

* * *

The next morning there was a knock at the door. My mind awoke, hoping it was someone with Gibra. It was Shep. And he didn't have Gibra. He had what felt like the opposite of Gibra.

"Let's go, boy. Time for work."

Shep was red. Red curly hair. Red bushy beard. Red face. The red accentuated his wildness. Whereas Jukes looked like a soldier, Shep gave the impression of a barely tamed wild man. The more I watched him, the more I believed he'd worked in some pretty rough places.

"What are we going to do?"

"We test weapons. Blacksmiths make the weapons. We test 'em. Jukes says the Phoenix is stockpiling weapons, so we've got to get as many tested as possible."

"What are you stockpiling weapons for?"

"The War Council wants land just south of here. But reports say there are Dardar entrenched there."

"Dardar? What are Dardar?"

"You don't know what a Dardar is? Ha! People call them the 'Cursed of the Earth.' They're monsters, rising up out of the ground itself. They hurl all sorts of nasty things. Darn near impossible to destroy. Can't burn 'em. Can't stab 'em. Can't crush 'em. They usually leave well enough alone, but if they're holed up in the land south of here, Karsa can't have that land until they get rid of 'em. The Mastersmith is working on new weapons, and we're going to test 'em."

"Mastersmith? Is his name Tubal?"

"Tubal? No. Never heard of Tubal. His name's Pytho."

While we talked, Shep opened a door off the same hallway as my sleeping quarters, and we walked into a large staging area with weapons everywhere: swords, spears, bows, war hammers, slings, catapults, and many I didn't recognize. There were also piles and piles of dirt.

"Let's get to work. See that enormous box of war hammers? Take each one and hit it twenty times against that testing rock. Take out any that crack. When you're done, we'll heat 'em up to see if they crack."

"What are you going to do?"

"There are some new weapons to test in the next staging area."

"Can I help with that instead?"

"No. You're the slave. You get the slave job."

Testing the first few hammers was actually kind of fun as I tried to crack them on the testing rock. They were remarkably heavy compared to my Shadom. I understood where Shep got his muscular forearms. With each swing, a loud echo reverberated through the room.

But, fun soon gave way to the realization that testing was slow and tiring work. When none of the first few cracked, I proceeded to test the next ones less and less.

Who's going to know if I did it twenty times or not? Besides, my arms are getting tired. Boredom and my own sense of self-importance conspired to discover a better and quicker way to finish the seemingly useless task.

At one point, I took one hammer in each hand and alternated hitting them against the rock like a pair of drumsticks. Ten hits with each hammer still sounded like twenty, though I doubted Shep was listening that closely.

Still, it took a long time to test them. After I finished, I walked over to Shep's area to tell him I was done. He was standing at one end of a long archery range. At the other end were large piles of dirt, as tall as a person. He carefully filled sacks with two different colored powders.

"You finished? That was fast."

"I'm a good worker," I boasted.

"Let me show you how the furnace works."

"What are you working on here?"

"I've got to fill half of those containers with red powder and the other half with green."

"What for?"

"Just do what you're told."

The furnace was already quite hot as we added more coals. He showed me how to test the hammers in the fire. Then he left, and I began. A couple of them cracked.

This is dumb! We should have done this test first.

When I finished, Shep was already done for the day and getting ready to leave.

"Where are you going?" I asked.

"Out. I'm done 'til tomorrow."

"So, do I just stay down here?"

"Yep."

"But I'll go crazy."

"Stinks, don't it? Tell you what. If you do a good job over the next couple days, I'll ask Jukes if you can hang out upstairs when you're done for the day." Then he added, "Unless you can figure out how to get up there on your own."

In my exploration, I discovered that the corridor that held my sleeping quarters and the testing area was part of a giant square. By the artificial light, I saw the walls of the corridor were made of dressed stone and the surface of the floor was smoother and more even than anything I'd ever seen before. Some of the houses in Julat were more beautiful, but that corridor alone was far more impressive. There were doors along the corridor, but they were all locked.

There was no way out. I was imprisoned. But for some reason, instead of feeling trapped and claustrophobic, my heart was filled with anticipation. My time in Julat and Cindropolis had replaced the longing for freedom I felt in Lithown with a craving for success and renown. I might be at the bottom of the ladder, but Karsa felt like an important place.

CHAPTER 45

The next morning started off the same. Shep woke me up, and we headed off to test weapons.

When we arrived at the testing room, Jukes was waiting for us.

"There's a new breastplate design that needs to be tested. Rom, can you work on this? Shep, how are the projectiles coming?"

"They're all set up. I should start trials today."

"Good. Show Rom how to shoot thorns at the breastplates. After that, test them again with arrows and spears. Got it? Rom, Shep said you did a good job yesterday."

"Thanks."

The breastplates were made of tightly woven mesh with small pieces of metal interspersed liberally throughout the front and back. Shep helped me set them up on a stand.

"Here's the thorn launcher. All you do is hit this bladder with one of those hammers from yesterday."

He proceeded to do so, and a spray of small metal thorns shot out of the end, most of which embedded themselves in the breastplate.

"When you're done, check the back side of the breastplate and feel if any points are sticking through. Then reload the thorns and do it again until you've shot ten batches. After that, shoot arrows at it—you know how to shoot, don't you?"

"Yes."

"Good. Shoot ten arrows at it, from back there. From this closer line, throw this spear ten times, marking down how far the spearhead penetrated each time. Come find me after you're done, and I'll check your work."

Off he went, back to his red and green tubes.

The back of the breastplate didn't have any points from the iron thorns sticking through, so I refilled the thorn launcher and tried again. Nothing got through the breastplate. I refilled and fired a third time and prepared to repeat the process again.

Why don't I just use my own hammer instead of this heavy piece of junk?

Putting down the iron hammer, I summoned my Shadom. It was light as a feather compared to the iron hammer.

I swung the hammer with great force, smashing the inflated bladder. The thorn launcher shuddered under the violent blow. Metal thorns screamed out of the barrel. About eight thorns pierced the breastplate and stuck out the other side.

Taking the breastplate off the stand, I went to find Shep. He was at the firing range. When I arrived, I noticed two of the human-sized mounds of dirt had red tubes sticking out of them and two had green. Smoldering arrows were scattered all around them. While a few were impaled in the dirt, none were near any of the tubes. Shep was drawing back a bow loaded with a flaming arrow when he saw me approach. Loosing the arrow, it flew over the head of the middle dirt mound, clattered off the wall, and joined its errant brothers.

"Hey, you distracted me. What are you doing here?"

I showed him the breastplate.

"I'd say that's a catastrophic failure!" He sounded excited.

"Do you still want me to use the spear and the bow?"

"May as well. They'll want a full report. Otherwise we'll just get it back with slight changes and have to go again. If you ask me—and nobody does—they should stick with the metal plates we always used before."

"How's it going over here?" I asked.

"Something's the matter with this bow," Shep grumbled. "It doesn't shoot straight."

"Can I give it a try?"

"Fine. Why not."

The bow did feel awkward and heavy in my hand, and the string was difficult to pull back.

"Need a smaller bow?" Shep sniggered.

I let the arrow fly, but it wobbled and fluttered and barely lodged itself in the dirt pile next to the one I was aiming for.

"I'm not used to the bow yet." I protested. I tried again and then again. The improvement was meager.

"I'm going to get a different bow," Shep said.

After he left, I popped out my Shadom as a bow. As I pulled the string back, I tried dipping the arrow in the fire at my feet. It was impervious to the flames.

Placing the tip of my arrow back into the starter flame, I whispered, "Catch fire." The tip of my arrow caught fire, and I shot. It was close but not on target. I heard Shep coming back.

"Catch fire," I whispered as I dipped a new arrow in the flames. Taking aim, I released. Kabloom! There was a small explosion as it hit the red tube dead on. Dirt flew everywhere, leaving a sizable chunk missing from the pile.

Shep ran over. My Shadom quickly retracted.

"You hit it?" He glanced down at the old bow lying on the ground where we'd left it.

"Yeah," I said as nonchalantly as possible. "The red one."

He measured the size of the crater in the pile of dirt.

"Can you hit one of the green ones?"

"I'll try. Maybe I should use the smaller bow you brought."

That bow was a little more manageable. Although I missed three times in a row, each attempt was close. On the fourth, I nailed the green. The blast radius was not as wide as the red, but it was deeper.

It took two shots to hit the next one. I hit the last one in three.

"You're not a bad shot. Where'd you learn to shoot?"

"I've been in some fights before—a pretty big one, actually, at the Fortress of Liga in the Plains of Orech. Some kunoi attacked us."

Shep's face was implacable. I couldn't tell if any of what I said registered or not. So, we just went back to work. I repacked the dirt piles. Shep fit new tubes of powder onto shafts and jammed them into the dirt.

"What exactly are we testing here?"

"One warrior shoots these tubes into a Dardar and then another warrior hits the tube with a flaming arrow. We're supposed to test how well the powder explodes, but the whole idea is stupid. It's hard enough trying to hit these on stationary piles of dirt. What about when the Dardar are moving? But those fools don't ever listen to us. They just want us to do what we're told and keep our mouths shut, as if being a warrior or a smith makes one an expert on how things work. That's why they stuck us in the bottom of the building."

"Do the Dardar have hands?"

"Of course they have hands!"

"Won't they just pull the tube out before the flaming arrow gets there?"

The scorn was evident when Shep laughed. "You'd think so, wouldn't you?"

It took the rest of the day to finish testing the powders. When Jukes checked in, we showed him the results. I hadn't finished testing the breastplate, but since the thorns were still in it, he could show it to the blacksmith the next day.

When Jukes and Shep left, I overheard them debating whether I was on track to earn a chance to go upstairs with them in the future. Their dispassionate evaluation of my situation made me feel like one of their test subjects in the lab.

* * *

That night I sat in my room trying to figure out a way to make the exploding powder work. I may have been in Cindropolis to rescue Cora, but I'd also tasted success. Succeeding in growing a grapevine and learning to mine copper had lit a fire in me to earn praise by solving problems. I could almost taste Gibra in my mouth as I wondered what sort of praise would come my way when the blacksmiths saw my test results. How would they respond if I could solve the problem of the exploding powder? While pondering the problem, Rohka flew in.

"Hey, I'm glad to see you. Where have you been?"

That question never elicited a response, but I always asked it anyway, as if he owed me an explanation. He settled on my chest as I rested on the mat, so I chatted with him about the arrows. He appeared to listen politely. When I talked about the exploding powder, he flew to the top of one of the light fixtures. He bent his head and tapped on the side glass with his beak.

I was too tired to try to figure out why Rohka was acting strange, so I drifted off to sleep dreaming about arrows and exploding powder and trying to envision a Dardar.

* * *

The next morning, Krib, the blacksmith who designed the breastplate, came down. He was thin and on the taller side, with a clean appearance and a subtle hitch in his gait. He dressed in the same leather armor as Jukes, which made me assume they were equal in rank.

Confident he'd be excited that I identified a problem in the design, I was disappointed when all he muttered was, "Show me the test," after examining the breastplate.

317

"Rom, go set it up, and we'll run it for him," said Jukes.

"Um . . . don't we need a new breastplate?"

"Just take the thorns out of this one and run it again."

Some of the thorns were embedded so far into the breastplate they had become enmeshed in the weave, so it took a while to get them out. I yanked and pulled, all the while wondering how to repeat the results without using my Shadom. The longer I took, the more agitated Krib became.

"Just shoot it again with those last two still in it," he fumed.

I set up the breastplate, loaded the thorn launcher, and hit it with the iron hammer. As I expected, all the arrowheads bounced off or barely impacted the breastplate. Krib inspected it.

"What is this? It passed." He looked at Jukes, and Jukes looked at me. With a measured tone, Jukes inquired, "Rom, it appears to have passed. Am I missing something?"

I was ready to take the blame when Krib grumbled, "Stupid kid." Turning to Jukes he continued, "I think you should spend more time training these idiots and less time milling about. Can you sign off on the breastplate now? I'm going back upstairs. I've got important work to do for Karsa, unlike what goes on down here."

I felt my face get red. "I used a different hammer before," I bawled out. "That's why they went through."

"We don't need to waste any more time," Krib demanded. "Just sign the paper, Jukes."

"No, I want to see this," Jukes replied.

I reloaded the launcher. "I have to get the hammer." I made a show of fumbling through a pile of weapons and came out with my Shadom in the shape of a hammer.

"What's that?" Krib exclaimed. "It's red!"

"Stand back," I cautioned.

Fury raged inside me as I swung with all my might. A blink of an eye later, thorns hit the vest. Two went all the way through and popped out the other side.

Krib and Jukes went to inspect the breastplate. I put away the Shadom and followed them over to examine my handiwork.

Jukes let out a low whistle. Krib rounded on me. "Let me see that hammer."

"I put it away."

"What do you mean? Where? Go get it!"

"No."

"Jukes, make him retrieve that hammer."

Jukes calmly addressed me. "I would be glad to see the hammer as well, but I'll respect your right to your own stuff." Then, turning to Krib, he said, "In the end it doesn't matter what hammer he used, the breastplate failed the test."

"No thorns will be going that fast," Krib complained. "That's not a fair test."

"How fast do the Dardar fire their thorns?" Jukes asked.

"I don't know," Krib said less brashly, "but not that fast."

"Maybe you should figure it out. If it's slow, like the first trial, I'll sign off on the design. If they come faster, like the second, then you'll need to bring back an upgraded breastplate."

Krib stormed off.

"Next time, use our hammers," Jukes told me. "And tomorrow, when the Mastersmith comes, let's avoid making him mad on purpose."

* * *

That night in my room I boasted to Rohka about embarrassing Krib. When I talked about the Mastersmith coming the next day and the arrow project, Rohka again flew up to the light box. But this time, instead of tapping on glass, he pushed his little head against the side and flapped his wings as if he was trying to push the glass to the right.

"What are you doing, Rohka? Do those move? I don't think you're going to get that to budge. They make things pretty strong around here—except maybe breastplates!

Rohka ignored me, and I grew frustrated.

All we need is for that light box to come flying off the wall. It would probably ram into something and catch fire and . . . wait a second . . .

"Rohka, you're a genius!"

I went to sleep excited for the next day.

CHAPTER 46

The next day, Pytho the Mastersmith arrived to see his exploding weapons. He was a tall, thin, bald man with a brownish beard that projected off his face. Shep told me he was the youngest Mastersmith in Karsa's history. A group of older smiths had taken him under their wing when he first arrived at Karsa and taught him much about weaponry, or so the story went. Their guidance, combined with his natural brilliance, put him on the fast track to achieving the rank of Mastersmith.

A man named Binsur accompanied Pytho, and together they made quite a contrast. Binsur was overweight, though tall enough that he didn't look spherical. His round, beardless face gave him a boyish appearance, and a nicely coiffed mop sat atop his head.

Shep's eyes grew big when he saw Binsur, but Jukes was calm as ever as he made the introductions. Binsur was Chief of the Smiths and a member of the Karsa War Council. Jukes introduced me as an indentured servant, a good worker, and a good shot with the bow. Both men eyed me carefully, and then the test began.

Although I had practiced quite a bit, it was nerve-racking with Jukes, Binsur, and Pytho watching. I took up the bow, notched my arrow, dipped it into the fire, and took my shot. It missed the tube by the smallest of margins.

No one said anything, but my face felt flush, and I sensed tension building. I quickly took another arrow, lit it, steadied my nerves, and shot into the heart of the tube. The tube exploded as usual.

Pytho spoke first, his voice soft. "I noticed you didn't shoot the tube into the dirt first. Was there a reason for that?"

Jukes answered, "The tube is heavy, and we had trouble launching it. A stronger archer might not have as much trouble, but we did our best. Would you like us to give it a try now?"

"Yes."

Shep went down and removed the green tube from the next pile of dirt and brought it to me. His eyes met mine in a glance of trepidation. I struggled to keep the tube arrow steady enough in the bow and didn't compensate my angle of trajectory enough for the heavier weight. The tube crashed on the floor, skittering into the bottom of the dirt pile. Green powder spilled everywhere.

"Sorry. Let me try again."

"No, it's okay," Pytho replied. Then he turned to address Binsur as if the rest of us weren't there. "They're obviously not ready."

"But Pytho, we need this," Binsur objected. "We're supposed to launch an attack soon, and these weapons would make all the difference. What if you had a stronger archer firing the tubes with a heavier bow and a second, more accurate archer firing the arrows?"

"The problem is that there's no margin for error. Dirt extinguishes fire. If the arrow could continue burning after it hit, we'd have a better chance. But the Dardar will be moving. If they're dumb enough to leave the tube in, it'll still take a perfect shot."

"But it's better than nothing," Binsur protested. "The exploding powder itself is a marvelous invention. The War Council will be much more confident if we can tell them we have new technology coming. And the hope of new technology will assuage the warriors' anxiety and buoy their spirits."

Pytho and Binsur both realized their conversation had turned into a private one, so Binsur said politely, "Excuse us, friends. Thank you very much for your great work here. It's much appreciated."

As they started to leave, my heart began pounding in my chest as thoughts bombarded my brain. Words welled up inside me, and they burst forth before I could swallow them back down.

"Stop!" I yelled. "Can I say something?"

Binsur and Pytho stopped; Shep's eyes widened and registered total shock. Even Jukes looked slightly rattled.

"I've been thinking about the problem since we began testing. This may be dumb, but what if you could attach the fire to the tube so they're shot as one projectile?"

"Fire burning that close to the exploding powder before it's launched is far too dangerous," Binsur said in a patronizing voice. "But thank you for the suggestion."

He turned away dismissively, but something—whether the need to prove my usefulness to powerful people or my wounded pride—wouldn't let me give up so easily.

"What if the fire was contained in a box of some kind, like the light fixtures in my room?"

"But that isn't fire. The light fixtures use glowing stones that react to each other to produce light."

"But what if it was fire in the box?"

Binsur's civility disappeared, and his response was curt. "Thank you, but we have more important things to discuss and must be going."

Binsur moved to exit, but Pytho didn't follow. Instead he raised his hand and said, "Wait a second." He paused, thinking. "So how would you get the fire to leave the box and ignite the powder?" he asked me.

"I don't really know," I admitted, "I figured the fire would just crash into the powder when it hit the target."

Pytho's eyes sparkled. "Yes. If there were two tubes and the first one had the powder and the second one had the fire, then the first tube would hit and the second tube would ignite the powder upon impact. If we could indeed put fire in a box, it would prevent the powder from exploding before impact. That might work!"

By this point, Jukes spoke up, "But if one tube is too hard to shoot, how could you shoot two?"

Pytho waved his hand, "We just have to change the delivery method, that's all. We can't use bows and arrows, but there are other ways to launch projectiles."

Binsur spoke the words I thought. "Are you actually considering this? Do you think there's something here?"

"It's an idea. We can't know if it'll work unless we try. I need to consult the Book of Knowledge."

The Book of Knowledge?! That's what they talked about in Cindropolis!

"But how long will this take to make?" Binsur asked.

"It might take less time if I had more help," Pythos said. "Rom, was it? I'd like you to come and work on a model with me."

Everyone stared at me. My mouth dropped open. My brain buzzed as if I'd just swallowed Gibra. Their attention energized my excitement. My voice rose in pitch and the words burst out of my mouth.

"Sir, I'd like to earn my freedom. Since I was sold to Karsa, I'll work wherever you assign me. If I can help with this, it would be an honor."

Pytho smiled a slender smile. "Done, then. Jukes, help him find his way upstairs."

Binsur may have been the Chief, but the Mastersmith was calling the shots.

"What can I tell the War Council, Pytho? Is this something that might actually work?"

"Tell them to light a candle to Tubal," said Pytho, "If we can get this to work, I don't think we'll have much trouble from the Dardar."

As they left, Shep whistled. "Well, well, well. How do you like that? You move pretty fast," he said with equal parts surprise, respect, and jealousy.

"Get your things, Rom, and I'll take you upstairs," Jukes said dispassionately.

* * *

When I arrived back in my room, Rohka was there.

"Rohka, you're brilliant. Thank you! We're going upstairs to work on the arrow problem. Whatever they have for me upstairs, I certainly could use your help. I don't know the first thing about this stuff."

Rohka chirped once.

"Do you want to ride up there on my shoulder?"

Rohka flitted onto my shoulder and suddenly I felt joy. Mine or his or both, I didn't know. I tucked my scroll into my pocket and set off to accompany Jukes.

"Is that a bird on your shoulder?" Jukes asked when I caught up with him.

I took a deep breath and then answered.

"It is. He hangs out with me sometimes. I've had him as long as I can remember."

"Interesting," Jukes said thoughtfully.

"Are you mad that I'm leaving the testing area?"

"No, Rom. Your idea is a good one. If it'll help Karsa defeat the Dardar, then that's the most important task to be done. Maybe when it's done you can bring it down here, and we can test it together."

"Jukes, when the Mastersmith said, 'Light a candle to Tubal,' what did he mean?"

"Haven't you heard that before? It's nothing, just a figure of speech. I don't exactly know how it developed, but a long time ago if you wanted an invention to work, you asked for Tubal to come help you. I don't know if there was ever a real person with that name or not, but over time he's come to represent human ingenuity and technology."

Jukes stopped as we reached a nondescript section of the wall in the outer corridor. He pulled out a shiny metal object and tapped a pattern onto the stone wall. The metal object produced a singsong sound, and the wall slid back to reveal a hidden staircase.

As we walked up the stairs, we entered the heart of the Phoenix. The structure was massive and must have held hundreds—perhaps thousands—of people. Jukes and I were on the main floor. He explained that counting the basement where I'd stayed, the building was six stories tall. Above me I could see portions of the third, fourth, and fifth floors as we entered an atrium in the center of the building. The atrium measured roughly five to ten thousand square feet in area and extended from the main floor to the bottom of the sixth floor in height. Whatever was on the sixth floor was completely hidden from view.

As Jukes and I walked through the atrium, we passed a large rotunda. Carved into it were the words: The Kings and Queens of Karsa.

"What's that?"

"The rotunda houses sculptures of the great men and women of Karsa, Mastersmiths in particular. Perhaps a long time ago there were kings and queens in Karsa, but now the title honors the great men and women who make contributions through intelligence, creativity, and accomplishment. I have no doubt that if Pytho can get this exploding weapon to work, he'll earn his place."

All around us people moved busily from one place to another. Many were dressed in the garb of soldiers, but, like Jukes, it didn't look like they were outfitted for actual war.

After crossing the open space, we ascended a staircase to the third floor, which was a place of bustling activity. Weapons were being hammered, bows strung, and arrowheads forged and fitted to shafts. The whole area smelled of oil and fire, but without much smoke. We walked through the chaotic activity in the first area to a quieter area, cordoned off by a set of doors. Jukes wasn't cleared to pass through the doors, so we knocked and waited. Guards came to escort me in.

"Good luck, Rom."

CHAPTER 47

I entered the quiet area on the third floor of the Phoenix. The guards led me to Pytho's team space, where I was assigned a place to work and another location to sleep. Pytho wasn't there and no one stopped me, so I began to explore the area.

In the middle of the floor was a communal space and at the center was a table loaded with food. Other than a few grapes in Cindropolis, I hadn't eaten anything since Julat, and I missed the taste and texture of something edible. The food was brightly colored and looked artificial. One tray had round balls of an unusually bright red color, piled neatly in the shape of a pyramid. Next to them were blue squares with a glossy finish, the sight of which induced a mouth-watering craving. I wondered if the color came from having Gibra as one of the ingredients. My eyes hungrily scanned the rest of the table, feasting on the cornucopia of edible pleasures of every size and shape. There weren't any browns, grays, or dull blues; instead there were vivid purples, shiny oranges, and brilliant rainbow stripes. A man stood near the table chowing down on some purple-hued, pie-shaped delicacies.

"Are those any good?" I asked without being introduced.

"You've never had Tika before? They're amazing. Try one."

I popped one in my mouth and was immediately overcome with a rush of sweetness. The texture was crumbly once it broke apart, and I used my tongue to push the crumbles against the roof of my mouth to squeeze more of the unnatural fruity taste out of it.

"Wow, that's delicious."

"Karsa is known for their food technology," he said. "Have another." So, I did. And another. And another. I was gorging myself as fast as he was.

"I should warn you that in about an hour you'll start to feel a little sick."

"What? Are these poisonous?"

Laughing, he said, "No, no, no. They're not poisonous. In fact, when you start feeling sick, eat one of those brilliant white wafers down at the end. They don't taste as good, but they'll make you feel better."

Sure enough, an hour or so later as I continued to wait for Pytho, my stomach began to ache. I went over and popped one of little white wafers into my mouth. It tasted a little bitter and chalky, but it made my stomach feel somewhat better.

Not long after, however, a wave of exhaustion swept over me. My eyes became heavy. I wanted desperately to lie down, and if I couldn't, I thought I would die. I sat down for a moment, hoping my head would clear.

A woman nearby said, "Are you new here?"

"Yes" I responded feebly, my eyes starting to shut.

"Did you eat a Coima? One of the white wafers?" she asked, handing me a blue square. "Here, eat one of these. It will counter-act the Coima."

It took all my powers of concentration to stay awake long enough to get the blue square into my mouth. Then, surrendering to the overpowering urge to sleep, I closed my eyes and dreamed of eating a Gibra apple. Immediately, however, I was awake.

The woman who gave me the blue square watched me with an amused look.

"Thank you," I said.

"No problem," she replied. "But you should know that in a few hours you'll probably break out in a rash. When that happens, just eat one of these."

She pointed to one of the bright red, round balls. "They taste delicious, so if you want to eat some now you won't have to worry about the rash."

"What will happen if I eat those?"

"Most people say that nothing happens if you eat those, but they make me crazy with cravings for everything on this table. Sometimes if the cravings get too strong, I eat some of those green dots over there. We call them Baka. Just make sure you follow those up with some Tika."

She must have seen the bewilderment on my face because she added, "Every invention has unexpected consequences, but nothing that we can't invent a solution for. That's why we call this table 'Our Daily Happiness.'"

I decided I would try my luck with the rash.

*   *   *

Over the next few days, I learned my way around the third floor of the Phoenix. Pytho was quite the Mastersmith, because he was already working on my idea—a viable solution he called Boxed Fire. I didn't see him much, nor did I get to work on the Boxed Fire idea. Instead, I was given the task of working with the group that was designing a new launcher. Pytho designed something like a giant crossbow that was to be loaded with round tubes. The tubes were like the ones Shep and I worked with in the basement but longer and with a greater circumference. In the crossbow, each tube rested on a channel and was propelled forward by a band made up of multiple bowstrings attached together.

I was assigned grunt labor jobs. No one seemed to know or care that Pytho had invited me to help or that part of the new invention was my idea. Truth be told, I wasn't sure I had much to contribute to the creation of the launcher. The smiths talked about materials and ideas I didn't understand, but it was fascinating. I was proud to be part of it. The people around me were generally civil, some even friendly, but there was a strange sense of competition in the air.

Most people seemed oblivious that Rohka was perched on my shoulder. I hypothesized that only certain people could see him, though I hadn't yet worked out why.

So, it caught my attention when a man named Sebastis noticed Rohka the first time we met. Sebastis was pretty far down the pecking order of smiths. He reminded me a little of Stig and Esah because he was easy to be around, quick to laugh, and didn't appear to be in competition with anyone. His job was rounding up wood for the launcher supports. Sebastis always insisted on taking breaks during the day. Occasionally, other smiths joined him, but many were openly disdainful of Sebastis and his work breaks, as if he was lazy, and they were too vital to the project to take breaks.

One day, Sebastis and I were sitting at the Our Daily Happiness table stuffing ourselves with snacks. By that point I had discovered an order for eating the various snacks that, when timed right, would allow me to gorge myself as much as I could. The trick was to take various counteracting foods at particular intervals until I ended with a Coima before going to sleep. At that moment, it was time for Tika, the purple pie-shaped creation. I loved eating them.

"Where's Pytho? I never see him around," I asked Sebastis with my mouth full of crumbly goodness.

"Pytho can't be bothered with these more mundane things. Haven't you heard? He's one of the greatest smiths Karsa has ever had." There was a twinkle in Sebastis' eyes as he spoke.

"But where does he go?"

"Sometimes he's off at Karsa Major for War Council meetings or other things. Sometimes he's here explaining his design or checking on its progress. But he also has access to the sixth floor, and some think he spends time up there."

"What's on the sixth floor?"

"It's said that it houses the great power of the Phoenix. That's why it's called the House of Power."

"What's the great power of the Phoenix?"

"I have no idea. But some say it's the room that gives Pytho his brilliant ideas. They even claim that when he comes down from that room, his face has a slight shimmer to it."

"What do you mean 'shimmer?'" I asked, recalling the momentary shimmers glistening on the faces of various people I had come across in Sebi, especially Peris.

"I don't know. I've never seen it. But when he came up with the exploding powder idea, the first people he explained it to said it was as if there was light shining off his face when he talked."

"Really? How do you get to the sixth floor?"

"You can't. As far as I know, the only one around here who's allowed up there is Pytho. Although maybe Binsur is too. Almost everyone on this floor longs to get in there. That's why people work so hard. They think if they can come up with a great idea, they'll gain access to the House of Power."

"Don't you want access?"

Sebastis laughed. "No, not really. I mean, yes in theory, but I'm never going to get there, so why bother thinking about it? A person can only receive what's given to them."

As I prepared to object, the floor started to shake. The table began to vibrate. Food started spilling off the table onto the floor.

I shot a glance at Sebastis. Shock and bewilderment had replaced his normally laid-back demeanor. He clutched the table, wide-eyed and white-knuckled. The rumbling and shaking increased. Crashes and screams filled the air around us. The wall in front of me began to rise. The floor beneath me started to slant downward. Within moments, the table started slipping downhill toward the back wall, threatening to crush me when it hit.

"Get on the table!" Sebastis yelled. I scrambled to get atop the table, clawing at anything solid to grasp hold of. Plates of food slid toward me, pummeling me as they fell. I'd just managed to pull myself up onto the table when the back legs broke and folded under it. The slope of the floor increased, and the table accelerated toward the wall. The broken back legs compounded the angle of the table's slant, and I started to slide down it, back into danger of being crushed.

"Dagger," I shouted. I drove my Shadom into the table above my head. Pulling myself up, I held on. The table sped toward the fast-accumulating pile of rubble behind me.

The table rammed the rubble with a deafening crash. My momentum yanked me backward, but the Shadom held fast as I gripped it with all my might. Fortunately, the table was heavy, or else the momentum would have pulled it over on top of me. Bodies and furniture followed hard after the table. Something slammed into the table's left front leg, and it buckled. The tabletop dipped, causing me to roll left.

At some point, the floor stopped rising, but it remained at a steep angle. It took only a few seconds for gravity to pull the furnishings down the floor, creating a massive heap against the back wall. In the moment's respite from the landslide, I tried to get my bearings. People around me screamed and cried for help, but one cry rose above the rest.

"Dardar!"

CHAPTER 48

Disentangling myself from the rubble, I scrambled up the sloping floor to the atrium in the center of the building. The whole building had been lifted off its foundation from the east. All of the furnishings east of the atrium on the third, fourth, and fifth floors had fallen through the opening in the center of the building, like sand through a tilted hourglass. The rotunda on the still-level ground floor had been swallowed up by the avalanche of rubble from higher floors, and the resulting mountain of wreckage was over twenty feet high. I didn't see anything that might be a Dardar.

The remaining furniture, tools, and supplies that hadn't fallen through the atrium had pooled against the westernmost wall of the Phoenix. It was from this heap of rubble that I'd escaped. Others were struggling to emerge from the landslide on the third floor as well. I ran back to help. Sebastis was assisting a woman whose leg was caught in the pile. She was crying in agony.

Suddenly, a voice boomed throughout the whole building: "All Karsians, hurry to the east side to repel the Dardar! Leave the wounded. We must fight the enemy first."

Sebastis pointed to me. "Go. I'll stay here and help to free the others. We can't abandon these people to die! All those fools care about is protecting their plunder. Go. I'll send some more to join you as I get them free."

I ran back uphill toward the opening. Hardly any from our floor responded to the call to fight, presumably because they were injured, dazed, or still trapped.

The massive mountain of rubble reaching up from the ground

floor was like a ladder. As I climbed down the pile, I saw the Dardar. I froze at the sight of the enormous beasts.

They were great hulking chunks of dirt in human form. It was as if the earth was alive. Growing out of their bodies were roots and plants. Each stood around six feet tall and almost as wide. They looked as if they weighed thousands of pounds. Though they had heads, there were no mouths or ears or noses, only eyes and the eyes looked like stones, black and hard. Their rough necks turned as they surveyed the scene. Ten, or maybe more, were already in the building. More were entering from under the raised wall on the east side.

As I watched, it became clear how the east wall had been raised. Three Dardar walked straight into three columns of dirt which supported the elevated wall. The whole building moaned as their massive bodies were absorbed into the dirt piles, jacking up the wall and tipping the building even further.

"Bow!" I cried.

I fired at the closest Dardar. The red arrow jabbed into his dirt-flesh but he didn't notice he'd been shot. Instead, he raised his hulking hand to engage the Karsian soldier nearest him. A torrent of thorns streamed out from his dirt hand, shooting out like the blast of water from a fire hose. The soldier's shield deflected some of the thorns, but many penetrated the mesh breastplate he was wearing—the same type of breastplate I'd tested. He soon slumped to the ground.

I need to get beneath the open sky, so I can get my shield and helmet.

I watched for a moment, plotting my route. The Dardar were slow. Clearly, they were well equipped for defending or taking ground, but not for chasing victims. In fact, they didn't appear to be concerned with the soldiers attacking them. Rather, they were intent on destroying the building and everything in it. One Dardar headed for the stairs to the third floor; another pummeled furniture in the rubble pile.

Clambering down the pile, I ran along an open lane toward the raised east side. I raced past two or three Dardar who paid me no attention. But one Dardar, who just entered the building, thought I was racing to attack him. I swerved to avoid him as he lowered his arm at me.

"War hammer!" I yelled.

Thorns shot out of his hand. I felt the blood-stained leather breastplate under my tunic stiffen around my chest. The thorns hit and rattled off. My adrenalin surged, and I leapt into the air. A roar of intensity forced its way past my lips as I swung my war hammer with all the strength I could muster.

The hammer sank into the Dardar's arm, just below the shoulder, with a heavy thud. It lodged deep into his arm but didn't fully cut it off. The Dardar showed no signs of pain, even though half his arm was sheared off. He swung his other hand toward me, his fist in the shape of a rock. I jerked my hammer free, grabbed its handle with both hands, and swung as hard as possible at the oncoming fist. They met like a bat connecting squarely with a ball, and his hand exploded. Dirt flew everywhere, showering down on me. Whirling into a backswing, I extended my arms and smashed my hammer into his face. The Dardar's whole head shifted back a few inches from its position on his neck. I continued to pummel his head and arms. His heavy stump of a right arm landed a blow on my back that buckled my knees, but I continued the onslaught, blow after pounding blow, until I separated his head fully from his neck. He collapsed to the ground, a lifeless pile of dirt.

Fighting the Dardar was exhausting yet exhilarating—to lose myself in mindless fury; to channel pent up aggression, anger, and adrenalin without restraint was enlivening. Panting hard, I forced myself to run again toward the east-side opening.

Waiting for me outside, the Phoenix was a terrifying vision. Hundreds of Dardar were slowly advancing toward the opening. Some were still far away, but others were quite close. Some merged into the columns, raising the building even further; others headed into the Phoenix itself.

"Copaqeren. Thureos."

Down came my shield and helmet.

A manned catapult at the top of the Phoenix was hurling boulders at the advancing Dardar. But there were too many.

We need to get the opening closed and set the building back down on the ground.

I ran back into the Phoenix. More soldiers were entering the fight, but many had fallen prostrate—not dead, but asleep from poison in the thorns. I tried to wake one of the men, but he was unresponsive.

Racing across the room, I came upon another soldier deflecting thorns with a shield and solid metal breastplate. But the Dardar he was fighting shot vines around his leg and pulled him to the ground.

"Sword!" I yelled, and I slashed at the vines. I cut him free, but the thorns on the vine had pierced his leg, and he was drifting off to sleep. The Dardar moved toward me. As he lifted his leg, I smashed into him with my shield and helmet, pushing with all my might. It was like pushing a giant boulder, yet my timing was good. His balance was off just slightly, and I managed to knock him backward. He toppled over, and I went with him.

"Dagger!" I called as I tried to stab the Shadom deep into his neck to sever his head. But it didn't work; my dagger barely impacted the surface. The Dardar began crawling back to his feet, so I ran off toward the rubble pile.

I spied a group of workers standing near the pile, looking unsure of what to do.

"Go and get shovels and pickaxes," I shouted. "We've got to get the dirt posts out from under the east wall. Hundreds more are coming!"

Other Karsians were climbing down the pile of rubble. Some were wounded; some were only partially dressed for battle. It was a ragtag group.

"We have to get the opening closed! Is there any of Pytho's exploding powder on the third floor? Find it and bring it down along with anything you can dig with—shovels, metal stakes, or anything else."

A woman yelled back, "Who are you to order us around? We don't work for you!" Many others, however, scrambled to obey.

"Look," I pleaded. "I'm just trying to help. We have to work together or this whole place will be destroyed."

A man climbed down the pile toward me. "I'm Orn," he said. "I'm the Assistant Manager of Earthworks Equipment. I can get a whole bunch of tools."

"That would be awesome. Hurry!"

"Okay, but maybe I should help you give the orders—we could be sort of a leadership team."

"Fine. Get as many shovels and pickaxes as you can and have people bring them over to the east wall."

Surveying the fray again, I called out to all the nearby soldiers to come and fight.

"We're going to need help over by the east wall. Please, can you leave these Dardar and come help us? We need a defensive perimeter by the east wall."

A soldier replied, "What are you talking about?"

"Listen, the east wall is propped up by earthen columns. Outside that wall, there are hundreds of Dardar coming. If we don't close the opening, we'll be completely overrun."

"How are we going to get rid of those columns?"

"Workers with shovels and pickaxes. But they're going to need protection."

"All right. Let's give it a try. I'm Hon by the way."

"Rom."

"Let's get to work."

Hon began barking out instructions to the troops who were available. They made their way to the east wall. Meanwhile, workers arrived with shovels and pickaxes.

"Let's go after that first column on left." I instructed, pointing them in the right direction.

"Hon," I started.

"I'm on it."

Hon formed a perimeter around the first column as Dardar continued to rumble in, attacking the soldiers who got in their way.

More people with shovels in hand joined the work, but it was extremely tough going, like digging through solid clay.

I began to ask around, "Are you from the third floor? Did anyone find the powder?"

No one knew what I was talking about.

I ran back to the opening and climbed up the pile, shouting to the levels above me, "Does anybody have Pytho's exploding powder? We need as much of it as possible. And we need more workers and soldiers."

"Rom," Sebastis yelled. "The powder's over here. Some tubes are broken, but there are some usable ones left. I need help carrying them all."

"Great job, Sebastis! Can you bring me a couple?"

He brought me two. "I'll go get some more."

I hustled down the pile with the two cannisters. Along the way, I called any soldiers I saw—even if they were fighting Dardar—to come help us at the eastern wall. Most ignored me, until I mentioned that Hon was leading the charge.

Together we raced toward the action. While the workers were making some progress on the first column, the soldiers guarding them were faring poorly. Almost half the Karsian soldiers had been knocked out in the fight. The reinforcements that came with me were a welcome sight.

I ran to the middle column and jammed the two tubes into it. *Now I just need some way to light them.*

Running back to the group, I cried out, "I need fire! Does anyone know where I can get fire to light an arrow? Does anyone have anything I can light a fire with?"

One woman dropped her shovel and ran over to me. She looked around tentatively at the other workers.

"Where do you need the fire?" she whispered.

"I need to light an arrow to ignite those tubes."

She hesitated as she studied my face, and then, looking around to see that no one was watching, she spoke a word under her breath. Between her cupped hands a flame appeared. Before I could get out my bow and arrow, she said something else and the fire formed into a ball. With her eyes shining brightly, she reared back and hurled the fireball toward the second column.

The shot was dead on. The first tube exploded, igniting the other. Dirt flew every direction. Gasps went up from workers and soldiers. The building shook as the middle column weakened.

I raced back to the pile to find Sebastis and get more tubes of powder. Sebastis was just coming down with another three.

Taking the three tubes, I returned to the eastern wall. More soldiers advanced to strengthen Hon's forces as more and more Dardar engaged them. The battle was intense, but the Karsians were holding up.

I jammed the three tubes into the middle column and went to find the woman with the fire. She was hard at work digging out the first column. As her shoulders heaved up and down, I noticed a small lizard, like a chameleon or a gecko, nestled into the nape of her neck, mostly hidden by her shirt.

"Is that a lizard on your shoulder?" I inquired as I got her attention. She blushed slightly.

"Is that a bird on your shoulder?" she replied. She locked eyes with me for a moment before her expression softened, and her face became awash with radiant warmth.

"Friend," I said quickly. "I need you to ignite those three tubes."

The explosion rocked the building. When the dust settled, I urged workers with shovels to go over to the middle column to excavate the loosened soil. The eastern wall shuddered as its support weakened.

Sebastis and a few other workers approached with more explosives, but a Dardar attacked them. One man went down as an array of thorns flew at them. All his explosives crashed to the ground. Vines shot out from the Dardar toward Sebastis as I hurried to help.

"Ischuro!"

I blew a wave of force in the direction of the Dardar. It hit his arm and knocked off his aim slightly, but some vines still enveloped Sebastis. I charged. Lowering my head, I rammed into the Dardar. The horns of my helmet drove deep into the midsection of his back.

"War hammer!"

I slashed at his right leg with a vicious blow and it buckled ever so slightly. He swung a massive dirt arm at me. My shield deflected it, but the force was jarring, like a load of bricks had fallen on me. Regaining my balance, I struck again at his weakened leg. This time I knocked it out from under him and he toppled over.

"Take those tubes and jam them into the final column over there," I instructed the two workers who were still conscious. Sebastis and the other worker were out.

"Battleaxe!"

I chopped at the prostrate Dardar's head, as if chopping a tree. Thorns and vines flew everywhere, but by the third or fourth blow I severed his head. Scooping up the rest of the explosives, I rushed to catch up to the two workers. Together we crammed all the tubes we carried into the third column. The explosion was deafening. The whole Phoenix shook as the column was completely destroyed. The weakened first and second columns couldn't hold the full weight of the wall anymore, so the east wall slowly lowered down, compacting the remaining two columns and bringing the whole building closer to level. The gap between the wall and the ground closed to about two or three feet, too small for any Dardar to fit under.

A cheer went up from the workers. But Hon and some of his soldiers were still outside the wall. And within moments, we felt the Dardar assault the eastern wall anew.

CHAPTER 49

W hat now?"

Everyone was looking at me. It was immensely satisfying to think that people were waiting for me to tell them what to do. But I didn't know what to do next.

"I'll take it from here," said a deep voice oozing with authority. A man appeared dressed in handsome, well-crafted, silver armor with an elegant green cape flowing behind him. He exuded power. All eyes locked on him.

For a brief moment, I saw a shimmer of light sweep across his face. It looked exactly like what I'd seen on Peris' face. As soon as the man spoke, I found myself inexplicably drawn to him and his words, just as I'd been with Peris.

"I'm Captain Naymeer. I was sent from Karsa Major as soon as word reached us that you were under attack. Who can tell me what's going on?"

Again, all eyes turned to me. I opened my mouth, but Orn spoke first.

"Captain Naymeer, I'm Orn, Assistant Manager of Earthworks Equipment for the Phoenix. My men here have worked tirelessly to get the eastern side of the building back down after the Dardar raised it. There is also a small, embattled group of soldiers trying to hold off the hundreds of Dardar outside. We need to keep them out."

"Thank you, Orn," came the reply. "And thank you to all of you for working so hard. Continue to dig out the remaining dirt under the wall. Do you have any more of that exploding powder?"

"Umm . . . I'd have to check, sir," Orn stuttered.

"Good. Get checking and report to me as soon as possible. Everyone else, get to work."

I grabbed Orn's arm as he started to head off. It was clear he was hoping to escape talking to me. The guilt on his face was obvious.

"Rom . . . I . . . I should have told Naymeer that—"

"Orn," I interrupted, "I don't know if there's any powder left on the third floor, but if there is, try searching for it on the northwest side. That's where Sebastis found it."

"Th-thank you," he stammered, his eyes wide with surprise. He ran off in the direction of the rubble pile.

Captain Naymeer was addressing the troops who accompanied him, and each headed off in a different direction.

"Come with me," Naymeer said in my direction.

"Me?" I asked. My heartbeat quickened.

"Yes. Come with me."

We walked back toward the middle of the Phoenix.

"Is your name Rom, son?"

"Yes sir," I replied. "How did you know?"

"Rom, you have the look of a warrior." Another shimmer flashed across his countenance. Though I tried to restrain it, a gleeful smile spread across my face. I fought to restore a look of seriousness.

"I've dispatched men to take care of the Dardar inside the Phoenix," he continued. "Now we must address the Dardar army outside, or they'll simply raise the wall again."

Naymeer walked quickly and with purpose. I almost had to run to keep up. When we reached the northern end of the Phoenix, he opened a door and strode outside.

The sunlight, dim as it was, felt good. It had been a long time since I had been outside. As we hurried around toward the eastern wall, the noise of battle filled the air. Turning the corner, I saw a great host of Dardar, most of whom had reached the wall. Hon and his forces were overrun and all of them lay prostrate around the battlefield.

Naymeer's reinforcements were attacking the northern flank of the Dardar. There were only about thirty or forty Karsian soldiers, but they distracted the Dardar enough to keep them busy.

"Sir, shall I go and join the fight?"

"No, Rom. Wait here a moment."

"Don't we need every soldier possible? We're seriously outnumbered."

"Numbers don't matter when you have technological superiority."

Naymeer pulled a small horn from his belt and blew a series of signals. His men started to fall back. The Dardar ignored the retreating men and resumed their attack on the eastern wall. Some of the Dardar threw themselves into the ground near the opening and more rammed into them, merging their bodies together to form new columns that pushed the wall up again.

Naymeer blew his horn again and yelled, "Release the bulls."

From a cluster of trees nearby came two soldiers sprinting toward the mass of Dardar, their blue capes flapping in the wind behind them. After the soldiers came the sound of thunder. The earth began to shake. Twenty or so bulls roared out of the trees, fixated on the waving blue capes. Into the heart of the Dardar went the men, with the bulls close behind.

The soldiers abandoned their blue capes in the crowd of Dardar and fled to the southeast. The bulls smashed, threw, and trampled the Dardar, throwing them into chaos. Streams of thorns flew at the bulls, covering them like quills on a porcupine, which only enraged them more. But, despite their rage, a few bulls soon started to slow.

Watching the battle unfold from the safety of a well-guarded command post, Naymeer looked at me.

"Is that a bird on your shoulder?" he asked with a frown.

Rohka was indeed perched in his usual spot. "Yes, sir. Is that a problem?"

I was surprised that Naymeer could see him.

"Birds like that belong in cages. This is a battle. Get rid of him."

For the briefest of moments, I felt a desire to please Naymeer, but the thought of being in battle without Rohka, even if I wasn't participating, felt beyond foolish.

"Captain Naymeer, I feel much better with him here. If you want him to leave, I'll be leaving with him. But I think you'd be better off allowing us to go into battle and see what we can do."

I couldn't quite judge the expression on his face. It was either disdain or begrudging respect, or maybe just annoyance. All he said was, "Just wait. You may get another chance to fight."

More bulls began to tire. Many of the Dardar were vanquished, but some remained.

"Prepare the model. Let's see if Pytho has earned his title of Mastersmith."

Three soldiers brought out of a more advanced version Pytho's launching system than the one we had been working on. This other model was shaped like a giant crossbow, resting on three supports, the shortest of which was in the back so that the projectile pointed upward slightly. The projectile was one long tube, the diameter of a small tree. The soldiers wound back the band on the crossbow with a winch.

One of the people manning the model opened the back section of the tube and nervously lit a fire in it. Closing the tube, he couldn't get away from the projectile fast enough. Two others used mallets to simultaneously knock away the restraining pegs holding the band in place. The machine fired.

The projectile followed a low-arcing trajectory into the crowd of Dardar. It embedded itself into the back of one of the Dardar, knocking him to the ground. Yet there was no explosion. The Dardar slowly began to rise, but the projectile was so heavy it threw off his balance, and he stumbled repeatedly. When he finally got to his feet, he staggered around, unintentionally smashing into other Dardar.

Naymeer laughed.

"Tell Pytho that he has indeed invented a new weapon, but not the one he thought. Maybe he needs another visit to the House of Power."

Finally, the tube broke and powder spilled onto the ground.

"Hit it with fire arrows!" came the command.

Almost immediately, three or four arrows rained down fire. The first explosion was the pile of powder on the ground; the second explosion was the projectile. The sound was loud. Either Pytho had managed to increase the potency of the powder, or perhaps there was just more of it. All the Dardar nearby were either severely damaged or incapacitated.

"Fire another projectile," yelled Naymeer.

A second one was loaded, lit, and fired. This time, it didn't hit any Dardar but skidded to a halt in the middle of one of their groups. It lay there for a few moments.

Before anyone could shoot it with an arrow, the projectile exploded on its own, taking out three or four of the nearest Dardar.

"There's one left, sir."

"Fire it."

The final projectile impaled a Dardar in his chest. No explosion. The Dardar hammered at it with his rocky fists until the tube broke and powder ran everywhere.

"Light him up!"

Three or four fire arrows came from Naymeer's soldiers, and the explosion decapitated two Dardar.

"Go clean up the mess."

Twenty to thirty Dardar remained. Naymeer's men were armed with harpoons. Working in groups of four or five, Naymeer's men used harpoons to bring the Dardar down. When a Dardar fell, a soldier quickly decapitated it with a large bladed device.

It wasn't long until the battle was over.

CHAPTER 50

Inside the Phoenix, rubble and destruction were everywhere. People were saying it would take months—perhaps even years—to recover.

Worst of all was the devastation to the population of the Phoenix. Though there were less casualties than expected, countless men and women had been incapacitated by the Dardar and needed to be transported to Karsa Major for care. I was told it could take a few months for them to return to consciousness.

After several hours of addressing the most pressing needs, Naymeer had the few remaining Karsians gather near the giant rubble pile for something of a celebration. He commended his soldiers for a job well done and promised rewards for those who had distinguished themselves. In particular, he mentioned Hon. Though Hon had fallen into the sleep of the Dardar, he'd be honored when he recovered.

Naymeer then addressed the rest of us.

"Men and women of the Phoenix. As I've talked with some of you over the past few hours, I've come to understand just how unprepared the Phoenix was for this onslaught. We were so busy planning how to attack our enemy that we didn't bother to consider that we might be attacked. Our self-confidence was misplaced, and we'll do better next time—I'll make sure of it."

Another of those momentary flickers of light brightened his stern face as he continued.

"Though the devastation is overwhelming, if it weren't for your actions, all would have been lost. Karsian soldiers are trained for warfare, but it was your bravery, courage, and ingenuity that saved the Phoenix today."

He continued. "Where is Orn, the equipment specialist?"

"Here, sir."

"Orn, what should be done for the person whom Karsa wants to honor for quick thinking under duress, courage against a fearsome enemy, and unrelenting hard work in the face of grave danger?"

"Captain Naymeer, sir," Orn replied, stepping forward, his voice brimming with confidence, "such a person should be promoted."

"Indeed," said Naymeer. "A promotion would be appropriate for you. I'll see to it. Well done. And what if someone deserves greater honor than a promotion?"

Orn's eyes sparkled greedily. "I'd grant him entry into the House of Power."

"Entry into the House of Power is a great and rare honor, bestowed upon only a few," Naymeer replied. "But in this case, you're correct that it would be a fitting reward . . ." He paused, while all eyes focused on Orn, who couldn't stop beaming.

". . . for one who has shown unexpected leadership. Rom, please step forward."

It took a moment for Naymeer's words to register. I was only convinced when I saw embarrassment flood Orn's face.

"Rom, I've come to understand that though you're only an indentured servant and have been at Karsa just a short time, somehow you've managed to help Pytho with his exploding powder, defeat Dardar on your own, and engineer the plan to lower the east wall.

"You are headed for great things, and a fitting reward for your work and investment is a trip to the House of Power.

"Rom, I don't know what state the sixth floor is in, but I doubt anything could damage what's in the House of Power. Give me some time to make sure it's ready, and then I'll see that you gain entry."

* * *

Captain Naymeer was true to his word. It turns out "captain" was a bit of a misnomer. He was the commander of all the forces of Karsa, serving under the authority of the War Council. Upon him had been conferred, among other things, the right to grant access to the House of Power. He had spent a great deal of time in it himself, though he gave me no hint as to what I might expect to find.

In the few days it took to ready the room, I experienced a range of emotions and reactions to my reward. I basked in the attention, felt known and valued, and received encouragement and affirmation from many. But others were antagonistic, spiteful, and gossiped openly that I was unworthy.

I was glad when the room was finally ready. The anticipation was almost more than I could handle.

With Rohka perched in his usual spot on my shoulder, I met Naymeer near the rotunda. He was smartly dressed, with an ornate purple cloak falling off his shoulders. He led the way to the sixth floor.

"Are you ready, Rom?"

"Yes, sir."

"Are you excited?"

"Yes, sir."

"Are you nervous?"

"A little."

"I imagine you'll take that bird with you into the room?"

He sounded resigned, but perhaps I sensed a touch of pity in his voice as well, as if Rohka was a security blanket that I hadn't yet learned to live without.

"Yes, sir, I am."

"Where did you find him?"

I thought back to the very beginning of what I could remember. "It's more that he found me. We've been together for a long time, but I'm still discovering new things about him."

"Does he have a name?"

"It's Rohka."

"Rohka, huh?" Naymeer said, pondering it.

"You don't like him, do you?" I boldly ventured, glancing down at Rohka. He was looking intently at Naymeer.

"He makes me uncomfortable, but I can't explain why. He reminds me of something, but I can't quite remember what. Something from a life long ago—before Karsa, before I became the captain. It's almost like . . ."

But he never finished his sentence.

"Well, here we are," he said. "This is the stairway to the sixth floor. I won't accompany you up the stairs, nor will I be here when you get back. You can find your own way. This door will lock behind you when you leave. You're allowed to stay in the House of Power as long as you like."

And then he added, "Congratulations, Rom. This is the start of something big for you. No one who comes out of the House of Power can ever be a servant in Karsa again. You've won your freedom. More than that, what you'll find in the House of Power is truly more magnificent than anything you've yet seen in Karsa or anywhere else, I would dare to venture."

Naymeer unlocked the door and left. My palms were sweaty, my heart was beating fast, and my mind raced, trying to grapple with all I had endured to reach that point. I stood in front of the door for a moment, took a deep breath, turned the handle, and entered.

PART 7: THE HOUSE OF POWER

CHAPTER 51

At the top of the staircase stood a small, oval-shaped room. Mirrors lined the wall on the far side, making the large, round, polished table that dominated the room seem even larger. Many chairs surrounded the table, but among the common chairs, one chair stood out. It was like a throne, made of dark, ornately carved wood that was trimmed with gold. In front of it on the table were two ancient iron boxes. Walking over to the table, I noticed an engraved placard situated in front of the throne. I pulled out the chair, sat down, and read it:

Are there any leaders among you? Let them show themselves in the choice they make in this place, for in return they will receive the power to decide.

Two gifts are available to you, each of great power, but you may only choose one.

You are not the first to be offered these gifts. Leaders who have come before you have chosen one or the other to great profit, for in order to lead, one must make good decisions. These gifts have been handed down from generation to generation. They are of the ancient world, being neither technology nor magic but from the root of both.

Your instinct will be to find a way to choose both gifts. You cannot. While one box is opened, the other will remain locked until the first gift is returned to its place. This doesn't mean you can't possess both gifts at some point in your life, only that you may not get them both here.

Try one and return it to its box. Then try the other. Then choose.

On the left is the Face of Humanity. On the right is the Book of Knowledge.

The mention of the Book of Knowledge sent a shiver of excitement through my body. I'd heard of it several times—Shafat offered it as motivation in Cindropolis, Noch said it would make all the difference in being successful in life, and Pytho apparently used it to help him invent his masterpieces. I knew I wanted the book but thought only a fool wouldn't at least see what else was being offered.

A key stuck out of the box containing the Face of Humanity. I turned it, and the top opened. Gazing into the box, I caught sight of an object shimmering with translucent light. Reaching in, I felt

something warm and soft, like a steamed towel. Picking it up, it was light as the wind. I examined what I held. Though it was near- ly invisible, I saw it was a mask. There were openings for the eyes, nose, mouth, and ears.

By this time Rohka had hopped off my shoulder and onto the table. He stood perched equidistance between the two boxes and stared intently at me.

"What do you think, Rohka? I guess I'm supposed to try it on."

I slipped the mask over my face. It fit perfectly. In fact, I barely even felt it on my skin. I looked into the mirrors across from me. The mask was invisible.

If I chose this one, Naymeer would never even know it if he saw me, I thought.

Suddenly a voice spoke clearly in my head, "You should tell Naymeer what a great leader he is. That's what will make him like you. It'll make up for the fact that he dislikes Rohka."

Are these my thoughts? I wondered.

"Think of what Naymeer could do for you. You should tell him you want to work for him. He'll like that."

At that moment, I saw something in my reflection. During my inner dialogue, my face shimmered ever so briefly in the light of the room.

I know that shimmer! I saw it on Naymeer's face and Peris' face. I even saw it once on Ataymah's face.

"You should go back to Julat," said the voice in my head. "Atay- mah will love to hear what a successful young man you've become. So will Avi and Emma. Tell them that they're responsible for help- ing you achieve what you've achieved."

"So that's how Peris convinced us to go on the adventure in Liga!" I blurted out. "He knew just what we wanted to hear. That's how Ataymah sensed the Julatians didn't like his plan in the for- tress. That's how Naymeer knew to tell me I had the makings of a warrior. It's the Face of Humanity."

The words tumbled out of my mouth as fast as the thoughts entered my mind.

I dug my fingernails in behind my ears, clawing at my skin. At first all I felt were my own ears, but then I gripped something and felt the mask peel off. Into my hands it fell.

I stared in wonder at the shimmering mass of power I was holding.

"Rohka, imagine what I could do if I knew what people were thinking or what they wanted to hear! I could get them to do important things they might not do otherwise! I could easily make decisions they'd want to follow!"

My heart longed for the mask. It longed to know more of what others desired, but the allure of the Book of Knowledge was strong. So, I placed the mask back into its iron box and reluctantly closed the heavy lid. The key from that box also opened the one on the right. Not surprisingly, I found a book inside. It was paper-thin and light as a feather. Rather than looking ancient, it appeared brand new. I opened to the first page and began reading.

"The key to being a great leader is making great decisions. The key to making great decisions is knowledge. And the key to knowledge is abundant information. A well-informed decision is a smart decision. So, what's the most important decision you need to make right now?"

Probably whether I should stay in Karsa or not.

I glanced back at the book. Information about Karsa appeared under the question I'd just read. I continued to read. It contained some of the history of Karsa, a discussion about the separation of Karsa into Karsa Major and Karsa Minor, and the kinds of people who lived in Karsa.

On the next page there was more on Karsa. I skimmed the information and turned the page again. Still more information.

I skimmed the page, trying to absorb some of what I read. But the more I read, the more there seemed to be. There was information about the Phoenix and the kind of work that went on in the Phoenix. The book talked about the smiths of Karsa, the history of invention, and some of the names of the people in the rotunda.

This is amazing! There's an almost limitless supply of information here. No wonder Pytho is such a great inventor. No wonder the people at the Salt Works have become so good at mining for copper.

Immediately, at the top of one of the pages was the heading, "Mining for Copper." I read the information with interest. Apparently, snakes weren't the only animal that could mine for copper. And grapes were not the only food that could be used to train them to mine for copper. I read with great interest the various theories on mining and the strengths and weaknesses of each. It was almost dizzying.

"Rohka, this is unbelievable. If I had this Book of Knowledge, I could do anything. I wouldn't need people like Avi or Emma or Ataymah around to explain stuff to me. I could just read this."

My mind longed for the Book of Knowledge, just as my heart was still craving the Face of Humanity.

How do I even make this decision?

The irony of needing help to decide between two things that were supposed to help me make decisions finally dawned on me. I laughed at my foolishness.

Taking the Book of Knowledge in my hand, I said aloud, "Which is the wiser choice, to choose the Book of Knowledge or the Face of Humanity?"

But when I looked at the pages of the book, they were blank. I rephrased my question: "Tell me about the Book of Knowledge and the Face of Humanity."

There in front of me appeared pages and pages of information about both, but the more I read, the more confused I became.

"But which one is better for me?" I inquired in frustration.

The pages of the book went blank again.

Discouraged, I placed the book back into its iron box and refitted the Face of Humanity onto my head.

Words echoed in my heart.

"Naymeer and Ataymah will be disappointed if you don't choose the Face of Humanity." I started to feel anxious.

"Pytho and Noch will be disappointed if you don't choose the Book of Knowledge." I felt more anxious.

And what about Sebastis, Hon, Stig, Cora, Gaius, Emma, Avi, Domi, Esah, and Rabah? What about the people of Karsa, Cindropolis, Julat, and . . .

My mind was drawn all the way back to Lithown. I tore off the Face of Humanity and laid it down on the table.

"No matter what I did in Lithown, I couldn't please those people. What good would the Face of Humanity be in such a place, unless I was willing to become a different person?

"As for the Book of Knowledge, I've seen one of these before, haven't I? Only it was called *The Law of Lithown*, and it belonged to the Elder."

Thoughts of Lithown stirred my heart for the scroll that the Elder had tried to steal and that Avi, Emma, and others had worked so hard to help me get back. I got out my scroll and unrolled it on the table.

The scroll still contained the story of the king visiting the great technological City of the Forge. Rereading the story highlighted the strong similarities between Karsa and the City of the Forge. My attention was piqued when I read that the king traveled to the highest room in the city and saw these words:

To the wise maker of clothing, the first to invent;
To the great builder of cities, who showed us the way;

> *To the strong designer of tools, who opened the*
> *door;*
> *To the creator of weapons, who gave us the key,*
> *The poetry of pride.*

My eyes lingered on the words the king himself wrote using fire on the wall,

> **Those who make them will be like them,**
> **As they trust in them,**
> **Those who rely on what's been made,**
> **Love what cannot save.**

I knew better than to look for those exact words etched in the House of Power, but as I reread my scroll, I was sure they were there in spirit. The king was opposed to the spirit of the City of the Forge, which meant he'd certainly be opposed to some of what was going on in Karsa.

I thought more about the Face of Humanity. *Who designed this? What smith was able to make such a thing that can tell you what others want to hear? With such a tool I could advance to the heights of Karsa. But what would happen to me if I began to wear it?*

I turned my attention to the Book of Knowledge. *What kind of smith would invent a book that supplies an almost infinite amount of information? On the surface its power is obvious: to have at one's fingertips so much information . . . but information is not wisdom.*

My mind turned to the vision of the bronze man, the mighty river, and the joy of home I'd seen in the tunnels of Cindropolis. The bronze man told me that I was on a journey, an odyssey. My adventures were meant to take me somewhere and turn me into someone. So, I wondered which of the gifts would help me cross the river. And then I thought of the gifts I'd already been given and how I got them.

For the first time on my journey, things were starting to make sense. My mind began to burrow deeper.

This room isn't really the House of Power, is it? Naymeer thinks it is, and the people of Karsa think so too. I bet many of the people of Lithown, Cindropolis, and Julat would think so too, though I wonder what Avi, Emma, or Ataymah would make of this place. But there's no real power here. This is the City of the Forge. The Face of Humanity and the Book of Knowledge are connected to the poetry of pride.

My mind was opening up, drinking in understanding. The fog was lifting, and I was seeing more and more clearly.

There's a warning on my scroll. A warning about this place, who I am to become, and where I am to go in this world. But it's not just a warning. There's an invitation too. I'm not just being warned about what not to do . . . I'm also being told what to do. But what?

I was almost there. I felt the answer coming.

And then came the clarifying thought. As it popped into my head, it immediately organized all my other thoughts, like a puzzle piece that finally allows you to see the big picture.

The king was opposed to the poetry of pride, but I've received gifts of grace: the scroll, my armor, and the Shadom. Where did they come from?

There was only one answer that made any sense. I wondered why I hadn't seen it before.

Rohka.

Rohka was there in the beginning. He led me to the scroll. He gave me the helmet, shield, breastplate, and Shadom. *If I'm ever going to get home, if I'm ever going to get to that place in the vision, Rohka is the one who will get me there. Isn't that what the bronze man told me to do when I wanted to know what to do next? He told me to ask Rohka.*

Finally, it made sense. This was the choice. *Whatever I trust to help me make the decision about the next stage in my odyssey will de-*

termine who I will become.

I looked at Rohka. His eyes had never left me.

"Rohka, what am I supposed to do next?"

Silence.

"Rohka, I'm not leaving here until you tell me what to do next."

Silence.

"Rohka, whatever you tell me to do, I'll do. Just say it."

Still silence.

I picked the Face of Humanity up off the table, put it back into its box, closed the lid, took out the key, and set it at his feet.

"Rohka, you're the gift I choose in the House of Power. I don't want the Face of Humanity or the Book of Knowledge. Everything good I have came from you. Even my suffering in Lithown, the darkness of doubt in the underground caves, the failures in the Cavern of Contest, the wounds in the dungeons of Cindropolis, and my time here have turned out for my good because of you. I don't know how it all worked, but I do know that it's connected to you. Tell me what to do next."

Rohka stared at me.

"Please, Rohka. This is hard for me. I might be crazy, but all these thoughts can't be in vain. If I choose the Face of Humanity or the Book of Knowledge, then I'm choosing pride. I'm choosing me. But I know now that I didn't get myself to this point, and I can't find my own way to whatever is next. I need help. I want help. Please. You have to tell me before I go crazy."

I felt tears forming in my eyes.

"Please."

Then, deep in my soul, in a still, small voice too loud and clear to be audible, I heard these words,

"Rom, you've chosen well. Come with me. I'll show you the way."

ACKNOWLEDGMENTS

Writing the *Scroll of Remembrance* has unfolded a little like Rom's story. It began with God waking me up to this assignment and faithfully leading me on the journey of writing this book. There were multiple opportunities to give way to doubt, fear, idolatry, and especially pride along the way. Despite temptations and failures in the face of spiritual opposition, God has been my compassionate and faithful Guide, leading me and this project every step of the way.

One of the major blessings God provided along the way was people to help this unusual assignment become a reality. Lisa, George, Grace, Abigail and James—my family—have walked with me, graciously reading manuscripts, asking questions, providing insights, cheering me on, making sacrifices and praying for me. Lisa's God-given wisdom and gifts for editing were a special blessing from God. I am so grateful.

Alyssa Karhan provided Spirit-filled editorial help and direction. Rob Teigen listened to the Lord's leading and by faith made the publishing of this story a reality. What a blessing! Emily Franklund's artistic abilities are a true gift to the book. James Armstrong did an excellent job of copy-editing and laying out the text.

Writing this book has been part of a bigger journey that includes the privilege of serving at Calvary Church. The church and its people have molded and shaped me, loved me, and allowed me to serve God using my spiritual gifts. Jesus is present in real and tangible ways at Calvary Church and that has made all the difference.

In Luke 17 Jesus reminds us that although everyone receives blessings from God, not everyone comes back to say thank you. I am writing this to give thanks. He also reminds us that after we have done everything, our heartfelt response should be, "I am an unworthy servant. I have only done what I was given to do."

PRONUNCIATION GUIDE

Frequently Appearing Character and Place Names

Lithown (lih-THOHN)
Rom (RAHM)
Rabah (RAH-bah)
Esah (EE-sah)
Domi (DOH-mee)
Timela (tih-MEHL-ah)
Sebi (seh-BEE)
Avi (AH-vee)
Plute (PLOOT)
Peytos (PAY-tohs)
Rohka (ROH-kah)
Julat (joo-LOT)
Ataymah (ah-TAY-mah)
Daybe (DAY-bee)
Cindropolis (sin-DRAH-poh-lis)
Shafat (shah-FAHT)
Karsa (KAHR-sah)
Jukes (JOOKS)
Tubal (TOO-ball)
Pytho (PIE-thoh)
Naymeer (NAY-meer)

Less Frequently Appearing Character and Place Names

Mot (MAHT)
Hudati (WHO-dah-tee)
Dolia (DOH-lee-ah)
Hazar (HAY-zahr)
Minal (mee-NAHL)

Jaykah (JAY-kah)
Ina (EE-nah)
Kauma (COW-mah)
Akouso (ah-KOO-soh)
Gaon (gay-AHN)
Haron (hair-AHN)
Shinar (SHY-nahr)
Tikto (TICK-toe)
Gaboah (GA-boh-ah)
Lukas (LOO-kiss)
Yatza (YAH-tzah)
Peris (PEH-rihs, i.e. Paris)
Orech (OH-rehk)
Liga (LEE-gah)
Mori (MOH-ree)
Gaius (GUY-uhs)
Noch (NAHK)
Arritu (AIR-ih-too)
Zan (ZAHN)
Mikra (MY-kruh)
Jethera (JETH-era)
Stina (STEE-nah)
Rhea (REE-ah)
Kala (KAH-lah)
Achor (AY-kohr)
Danos (DAH-nohs)
Banura (BAA-noo-rah)
Binsur (bihn-SOOR)
Sebastis (say-BAH-stis)
Orn (OHRN)
Hon (HAHN)

Made in the USA
Monee, IL
13 July 2022

99578071R00207